D0331193

THE

INSOMNIACS

ALSO BY MARIT WEISENBERG

Select
Select Few

THE
INSOMNIACS

Marit Weisenberg

FLATIRON
BOOKS
NEW YORK

This is a work of fiction. All of the characters, organizations, and events portrayed in this novel are either products of the author's imagination or are used fictitiously.

THE INSOMNIACS. Copyright © 2020 by Marit Weisenberg. All rights reserved. Printed in the United States of America. For information, address Flatiron Books, 120 Broadway, New York, NY 10271.

www.flatironbooks.com

Designed by Devan Norman

Library of Congress Cataloging-in-Publication Data

Names: Weisenberg, Marit, author.
Title: The insomniacs / Marit Weisenberg.
Description: First edition. | New York : Flatiron Books, 2020.
Identifiers: LCCN 2020017250 | ISBN 9781250257352 (hardcover) |
    ISBN 9781250257369 (ebook)
Subjects: CYAC: Insomnia—Fiction. | Diving—Fiction. |
    Memory—Fiction. | Neighborhoods—Fiction. |
    High schools—Fiction. | Schools—Fiction.
Classification: LCC PZ7.1.W4347 In 2020 | DDC [Fic]—dc23
LC record available at https://lccn.loc.gov/2020017250

Our books may be purchased in bulk for promotional, educational, or business use. Please contact your local bookseller or the Macmillan Corporate and Premium Sales Department at 1-800-221-7945, extension 5442, or by email at MacmillanSpecialMarkets@macmillan.com.

First Edition: 2020

10 9 8 7 6 5 4 3 2 1

FOR KATHLEEN AND DAVID WEISENBERG

THE
INSOMNIACS

CHAPTER ONE

2:48 A.M.

Maybe I could still make sleep happen.

Since the accident, where there should have been a memory, there was nothing. My whole life, I'd been able to fully recall each competitive dive; it was part of my process and I knew I couldn't dive without it. But now there was just a blank space where a dive used to be.

I tried not to panic. I had four weeks to heal from the concussion and remember what exactly happened in the time between when my feet left the board and my body hit the water. Once I had that memory back, I'd be able to climb the ladder and know that I wouldn't fail in front of a crowd again, I wouldn't disappoint my coach, and I wouldn't break my neck. The memory would be there if I could just sleep.

What I could do was imagine my favorite part of every dive before my last—slicing into the water, thousands of sparkling bubbles shooting out all around me. Then that moment under-water alone, deep and looking up at the light.

I could also imagine my surface break followed by an auto-matic glance to Mike, my coach I adored, on the deck. Usually, a big nod of approval meant solid execution with notes to follow. A headshake meant the opposite. He was always right there. We always connected before and after.

Something had thrown me before the last dive. My neigh-bor's presence was the only thing different about that day. Van, so out of place at the pool, his hand on my teammate's lower back. When he tilted his head to kiss Caroline, our eyes met. Af-ter that, all I remembered was Coach Mike poolside, watching, ready for me to go, then . . . blank, black. Then faces floating toward me through clouds of pink water.

My eyes snapped open.

Lying flat on my back, I stared at the ceiling, listening to the drip of the leaking faucet in my half-broken bathroom. Other than that, it was so quiet, just ambient noise from devices and appliances plugged into outlets. For a second, I was sure there was another presence in the house.

The clock now said 4:33 A.M. Whatever I'd been doing—actively not sleeping, growing more and more anxious as daylight neared—I'd been doing it for hours.

I was going to call it. This was night three with no sleep.

CHAPTER TWO

Actress and singer Brooke Carter married longtime boyfriend, hip-hop producer L. Roth, in a lavish ceremony in Lake Como, Italy, over Easter weekend. The couple's two daughters, ages three and seven, were flower girls at the two hundred–person event. The family will continue to live in Los Angeles and New York City.

Accompanying the news item was a photo, taken at London Heathrow Airport. My dad wore sunglasses, his black hair buzzed short, the tattoo he'd gotten back in his competitive diving days snaking up his neck from his collar. Brooke was a head taller than him. She also wore large sunglasses and her black hair cascaded down her back. Their little girls looked like dolls. Dressed in fur coats, they were two puffballs. Each parent held a daughter by the hand.

In the waning spring daylight, I swiveled my ugly, plastic desk chair to face the windows as I absorbed the news and looked out at the cul-de-sac as maybe my dad used to see it. Three abandoned boys' bikes littered the Andersons' front lawn. Twelve-year-old

Mary Seitzman practiced her ballet on the sidewalk, pirouetting in front of the Kaplans' bay window before wiping her brow. The Loves' new puppy attacked the arc of water shooting out from a sprinkler. The action appeared right outside my windows like my own personal movie projected on a screen. I allowed myself the barest glance to check if Van's car was in his driveway.

"Ingrid?"

My mom put her shoulder to the warped bedroom door and opened it with a burst. I twisted to look at her but a bolt of pain lit through my head to my stomach. I leaned against the armrest to keep the burning light at the edges.

"Babe, you okay?"

My coach's voice rang in my head: *Depending on your mental strength, you can bear any pain.*

I blinked hard and the world sharpened into view again. Slices of my girlish bedroom, decorated long ago in hues of yellow, became visible behind my mom. On the wall were framed illustrations of my initials "I" and "R" and a poem written in Hebrew, which I didn't understand. I wondered if Brooke had converted for my dad like my mom had.

"Hey." I tried to sound nonchalant. I focused my eyes on my beautiful Swedish mom, who had once been an actress herself. She was dressed in green scrubs, her worn-out blond hair in a high bun and her face more heavily lined with each passing month. I felt disloyal even noticing. She surveyed me from where she stood at the foot of my double bed, floral duvet half off and sheets intentionally tangled to give her the impression that I'd rested.

"Come look," I said, nodding to the computer screen. She joined me at my desk and read, the stiff sleeve of her scrubs grazing my bare arm.

"I hope it works out for him this time." She kissed the top

of my head. Without my permission, she closed the laptop.
The puffy Totoro sticker I'd stuck on the top laughed up at me.
"How'd you find out?" she asked. She wasn't surprised. I wondered how she'd heard. From his business manager or my aunt
in Kansas City who tried to stay in touch as an apology for her
younger brother?

"Izzie." My best friend had emailed me the link, most likely
understanding that I probably hadn't heard the news.

"Did you tell him? About the concussion?" I asked.

"No." She parted her lips as if to say more but then changed
her mind and folded her arms, holding herself tight.

I nodded. "What about the hospital bills?"

"I got it. That's not for you to worry about. Just get better."

I thought about my father every time something broke. I'd
been thinking about him today—maybe because I was broken—
and then coincidentally the email came in from Izzie. I wondered if my mom was in some way legally obligated to inform
him about my concussion. Even if she was, I doubted she would
tell him. When it came to my father, she wouldn't admit to any
weakness.

In the imaginary game of life, she didn't want my father to
think he had completely won with his jet-setter life and young
girlfriend—now wife, apparently—who he'd left us for seven years
ago. On the rare occasion that he checked in on me, my mother
was careful with how she presented our lives. She'd gone back to
school for a nursing degree and "loved" it. I was a straight-A student and, most important, a nationally ranked diver like he had
once been. I'd taken the slight introduction he'd given me to the
sport and made it my own. Without any of his help.

To say my mom had a lot of pride was an understatement.
In the divorce, she had said she didn't want anything from him.
She was given the house and child support, which mostly went

right out the window to pay for diving. I sensed my mom didn't like talking about the days when he lived here, so I was careful to avoid bringing up any memories that included him. Between barely speaking of him and years passing between visits, he'd become like a phantom in my mind. His ghost lurked in all the decrepit details of our once beautiful, modern box of a home, now breaking apart one piece at a time. My mom bled money between taxes and upkeep. I'd wait to tell her about my broken toilet so she wouldn't stress about a plumber.

"You look pale. I can find someone to cover my shift." My mom smoothed her hand over the back of my hair, so dark and different from hers. I tried not to flinch as she passed over the staples.

"No, I'm feeling fine. I'll sleep the whole time you're gone." *Please let that be true.*

"Good. Rest. That's exactly what the neurologist said your brain needs. But even if you're fast asleep, I'm sorry you're alone at night. Especially with what's been going on."

My phone vibrated with a text. *Everyone misses you and sends their love.*

"Is that Mike?" my mom asked. I nodded. She gave a small groan and then laughed. "Oh my god, I'm already gearing up for the fight he and I are going to have over when you can dive again."

"Ha! I'm sure."

"Promise me you'll go slow, okay?" she said. "The accident was only four days ago. You can try school tomorrow but the doctor said no diving for the rest of the month. If it were a mild concussion, that would be one thing . . ." There was real concern in her eyes. It was nice to see since she was usually from the school of pushing through. She and Coach Mike had that in common.

"Mom, I know. And Mike was at the hospital. He gets it." I was getting impatient with my mom while, at the same time, so relieved to hear from Coach Mike after a few days of silence. I was used to seeing him on an almost daily basis. To me, Mike and his wife, Laura, were like a second family. Now I was suddenly isolated and cut off from the action. It made me realize that my entire life and most of my relationships were built around diving. Overnight, my world had shrunk.

My mom's voice turned gentle. "He was amazing at the hospital. He said everything I would want a coach to say to my child." My throat thickened at the memory of Mike telling me there was nothing to be ashamed of.

"But no matter what Mike says down the road, I can't let you go back to practice before you're ready. Like the neurologist said, it's a problem that athletes feel pressured to play through head injuries. Mike wouldn't be human if he wasn't a little worried about his program. You're the reason he's recruiting the best junior divers. And he just got all that funding for the expansion." Her eyes were soft when they met mine, and then she returned her attention to making my bed tightly, folding the top of the duvet back and leveling it neatly with one palm.

She had no idea the stress her words brought—that Mike's reputation, the entire diving program's reputation, hinged on mine.

From across the street, we heard Mr. Pierce snap at his wife, *"Renee!"* The bite of his tone carried through my window, cracked open two inches for air.

"He's from a family of Olympic divers," I said. "He knows a different side of it than the doctor. He knows taking a break is a bad thing." My headache was worsening and the room was stuffy, the air conditioner no longer doing a great job of cooling the upstairs. It kicked on with a strained hum.

"Sometimes our bodies just force us to take a break. In hindsight, you probably should have rested when you had that sinus infection instead of practicing through."

"That's not why I messed up the dive. It was just an off day." That sounded ridiculously flippant even to my own ears. My mom knew I was too hard on myself to ever be that casual about messing up on such a grand scale. I just couldn't take her questioning me when I was already questioning everything I thought I knew about myself.

"Then it was the first off day you've ever had." My mom watched me closely. "What do you think happened?" she asked.

I knew she'd been waiting for the right moment. I tried to imagine telling her what might have caused my accident. Maybe this was why Coach Mike discouraged romantic relationships. Or romantic feelings, in my case. It was a distraction. If I was distracted and got lost in a dive, that could result in breaking my neck, becoming paralyzed, or, in a few rare cases, death.

In the light of day, I was embarrassed even thinking about the crazy surge of jealousy I'd felt when I first saw Van at the dive meet, there to support his girlfriend. Still, it shouldn't have mattered if Van was there. Diving was the one thing I could do, where I was safe and could control everything. I was always able to shut out the outside world.

Instead I said, "I don't know! Maybe it was the blueberry muffin I ate for breakfast. Maybe I slept on one side and my balance was off." I swallowed down the truth. It was time to put away my ridiculous childhood crush on Van.

"It's okay to be scared."

No, it wasn't. Not in diving. I couldn't continue if I was scared.

My mom looked down at her black Dansko clogs, then back up to my face. She searched my features as if adjusting to a new version of me compared to the fearless one she thought she knew.

"I *swear* to you, I'm fine! And I know I don't need a full month to recover. I'll be able to dive before that." I knew I was going to need to do my best job to convince her in the coming days. I couldn't stay idle for a month.

"No way." Of course she would put my health first, but she had to be concerned. My previously assumed full scholarship to college was now in question. "Enjoy the free time. You never have any," she said more gently.

She was right. I didn't have any free time beside the ten minutes I crawled in my bed to nap between school and practice, and then again late at night. After a bruising workout, I would finally get home from practice and finish my homework and then thoughts of Van would flood my mind. Now I had nothing but time and nothing to focus on except things I didn't want to think about.

My mom moved to my window and gazed out on our cul-de-sac comprised of ten houses in a widened horseshoe, bordered by a dense swath of greenbelt—acres of protected city land made up of woods, sheer limestone cliffs, trails, and a creek bed that ran along its curved spine. The setting sun cast a specific glow that, to me, meant spring in Austin.

"It's like the movie *Rear Window*. Wow. I forget that you can see everything on the street from your room. The Kaplans' house, the Loves'. Did you know you can see right into Van's bedroom?"

Oh, I knew.

There was a long pause. Then, "If you're feeling so well, can you do me a favor? Can you go across the street and thank Van?"

My eyebrows shot up. "No."

"Stop acting like you don't know Van."

"Mom."

She sighed. "Look, sometimes you remind me of your father. You have that same laser focus. That's why you have all of this." She gestured to the trophies gathering dust on Ikea shelves. "But don't turn your back on people, okay?" *Like he does*, I silently filled in the blank. I was surprised by her voluntary mention of my dad. "You don't want to come off as indifferent or cold," my mom chastised lightly.

My exact problem was that I was anything but indifferent and cold. Was she really going to make me face the person I'd let utterly fuck up my headspace?

As if she could read my mind, my mom said, "I know you're not cold. I just see you shut off when you start to care about something outside of diving. Like you don't think you can have both."

That was similar to her theory about my father: that he loved me so much, he couldn't bear to look back. He couldn't manage the complications of an old life and proceed with a new one. Laser focus.

"Van was at the meet because he was watching his girlfriend dive. It wasn't a big deal for him to have his mom call you. He was right there." I pulled at a hair tie on my wrist.

"I don't know what happened between the two of you. You were so loyal to those boys. To all of your friends." I watched her consider the kids on the street and I knew what she was thinking. She worried that she'd somehow failed and I'd missed out on being a normal kid who went to tons of parties and had sleepovers. And when she worried, I felt like I'd failed her. All I wanted was to make her life easier.

Sure enough, the next thing she said was, "It's just that diving is a really lonely sport." She paused. "But I understand why you chose it." There was a weighted silence between us at her oblique reference to this last connection I had to my dad. "I guess what I'm saying is, there's other stuff you might want to experience that won't come around again. Isn't prom soon?"

I ignored that. "Mom, all *you* do is work and sleep." She worked in Labor and Delivery on a 7 P.M. to 7 A.M. shift so she could have breakfast with me, sleep while I was at school, and then spend a few hours with me, usually at diving, before going to work.

"I know. It's something we both need to get better at. Being more open. It's like I've suddenly realized you're really leaving next year. We've lived on this street your whole life. There are a lot of nice people who live here. Maybe we should try to make it to the block party this summer."

I joined my mom at the window. We watched two of the boys I'd grown up with, Max and Wilson, pull up to Max's parents' three-car garage in a beat-up silver Audi, stereo booming Post Malone. Along with Van, wherever they were, that's where the party was. At school and on this block.

It was the beginning of daylight savings, and activity out on the street had just been reinvigorated. Every year, for a short period of maybe four weeks, spring fever arrived on the cul-de-sac before the Texas heat crept in. The neighborhood would mingle outdoors until the inevitable bugs and triple-digit temperatures drove everyone inside or to the privacy of backyard swimming pools for the rest of spring, summer, and most of fall.

"Remember when we used to go out there every night? The adults would be having a drink and laughing and we'd ride our bikes, screaming our heads off?" I ran my thumb down a seam of the floral print wallpaper that had loosened from the wall.

I thought my mom would change the subject but her lips curved up slightly in a half smile. Up close, I loved her faded freckles. "Those were good days," she said, referring to the time before we'd retreated. "That was a long time ago. I can't believe you four are almost all grown up."

Me, Van, Wilson, and Max hadn't been "you four" for years now. One more school year and I could leave and start fresh. Once our proximity to the aquatics center and Coach Mike didn't matter, my mom could finally sell this albatross of a house and go back to a semblance of the life she'd had before my dad dropped us in this cul-de-sac. She was waiting on me. And I was so close to not being a burden.

"Sorry about these, by the way," my mom said. The paper shades from Home Depot had lost their stick and fallen to the ground. "Maybe next weekend we can get new ones." I liked how she used "maybe" since she was stretched too thin to keep up with promises. She kicked aside the paper shade that lay on the ground.

"Mom, don't. I'll tape it up tonight."

"Call the police if you hear anything, okay?"

I nodded and we both leaned forward to look at the limestone ranch house next door. Two years ago, a quiet family, the Smiths, had bought the house. Just like us, they had one daughter and kept almost entirely to themselves. All I knew was the dad was some kind of doctor, yet he never seemed to leave the house. I'd only glimpsed the young girl with her two perfect French braids out on the street a handful of times, riding my old bike—really Van's old bike—that my mom must have given to them. I'd said hello a couple of times but she never said hello back. I'd decided she wanted to be left alone. But she always watched me, looking lonely as hell.

About six months ago, the family vanished, leaving all their possessions behind. No one knew where they were or if they were coming back. The house just sat vacant.

This made the rest of the cul-de-sac anxious. My mom said it seemed like everyone was projecting all of their fears onto the house, into the void. She'd heard speculation of foul play, witness protection, involvement in a cult. Maybe it was that no one liked the feeling of not knowing, of not understanding the emptiness inside.

And then the break-ins began. Maybe that was the real reason I hadn't slept in four days; I was anxious because I was all alone next door to a house that had been robbed as recently as two weeks ago.

"He's home," my mom said. She must have also noted Van's 4Runner in the driveway. "Go, Ingrid. I thanked them but I'd like you to say thank you, too."

"You hate that the Moores helped us."

"I hate that I wasn't there when you had your accident but I am so grateful that Lisa hunted me down after Van called her. Come on, Ingrid. Go talk to him."

I could feel myself growing desperate as she backed me into a corner. *Please don't make me do this.* "It's just that it's not necessary. I don't want to make a big deal about it or he'll think we're weird." He already thought that, I was sure. Single mom publicly humiliated by her renowned then-husband, daughter with an old-lady name, ugliest house on the block, big, fat accident the first time he ever showed at a diving meet—the kind that makes you want to throw up after seeing it.

"We are not weird." My stoic, Nordic mother narrowed her eyes at me. "I am going to watch you from this window and make sure you go. Then I have to leave."

I was already nervous to face the long night ahead, alone. It was like the accident had changed me and broken the switch I had so easily flipped when I was ready to sleep. I couldn't remember all of what had happened on the board and it haunted me during the night. Pieces of memory seemed just out of reach.

"Mom?" From the slight note of whining in my voice, she knew I was about to tell her something important. For a second, I wanted to talk to her about the stage fright. How scared I'd suddenly felt up on the board and how swiftly the mental block came out of nowhere. Until that moment, I'd never thought it could happen to me; that the self-consciousness and fear were right there, lying in wait.

"Yeah?" She said it warily and leaned back on her heels, worried about the time this might take before her shift. The shadows were growing longer and I remembered my childhood dread of night, the thick woods of the greenbelt transforming into a palpable presence outside our locked doors.

"Nothing. I'm good."

It was fine. There was no reason to be scared. Since I knew what had caused my mental block, I could banish it on my own. I'd face Van and then make myself forget him. I'd get through this forced break and then I'd climb the ladder again. Everything would go back to normal. And, tonight, I was so tired, I was sure I would sleep like a baby.

CHAPTER THREE

It wasn't that I'd wanted to stop going over to Van's house. It was that I'd imploded inside when I saw the boys the morning my dad left. They were waiting for me on the street as usual and witnessed the end of it all.

I remembered them in a row, stunned as my dad stalked to the waiting black Town Car, blatantly ignoring my cries. When the car pulled out, it ran over the tire of my bike that I'd left in the driveway the night before. The sedan kept going, my mangled tire popping out from under it like a demented jack-in-the-box.

Max looked at me, then at my mom and, in a moment I would never forget, he cracked up.

It was the reaction of a kid. I knew that now. But it still haunted me. The humiliation of my strong mother, crying. The sound of my friend's laughter at her tears.

The world of a nine-year-old is free and open—or at least I'd felt that way on our cul-de-sac—and then, bam, I saw everything as a landscape of divisions like tiles in a mosaic. It actually wasn't so different from that moment on the diving board. Everything went still for a second; I felt naked, and then there was a fracture.

Later that day, I discovered Van's old bike on my doorstep. A note written in Van's handwriting was taped to the handlebars and read, *You can have this.*

As soon as I saw the present, I quietly wheeled it to a dark corner of my garage and never touched it. For some reason, I couldn't. For years, whenever I glimpsed Van's bike in the corner, I thought of it as the pity bike. Eventually, I forgot about it until, one day, I saw the little girl from next door on it, flying past.

Now I was embarrassed that I never thanked Van, or gave the bike back, or played with the boys again. At first they'd avoided me—probably out of awkwardness—but then they'd knocked on my door a few times to see if I could play. I didn't answer and they finally quit trying. They seamlessly tightened without me and no one beside my mom questioned why I was no longer a part of things.

Now, seven years later, I stood on the sidewalk in front of Van Tagawa's beautiful home. I heard the distinctive rattle of my mom's aged, kelly-green BMW station wagon behind me as she pulled out of our garage, headed to work, her eyes surely on me as she drove past. I spun to catch a glimpse of her but I was too late. Instead I saw our house across the street, painted white though the color had taken on a dingy, gray cast. The thatch of weeds in front made it stand out from every other house on the block, except for the now-vacant one next door.

I eyed the greenbelt in the encroaching darkness, the cedar elm forest black against the lighter sky. Who had been breaking in so close to my house? From what my mother had heard, the electronics had been stripped out. Everyone speculated that a homeless person had come up from the greenbelt and then spread the word about a place to sleep. I didn't even want to know about the night foot traffic that had always passed through our block from the trailhead that led into the wilderness. Everyone had paid for beautiful views but knew to secure their doors when the sun went down.

In the near dark, an outdoor lighting scheme thoughtfully highlighted the spare, native plants and clustering oaks at Van's. I was just across the street from my house but it was like escaping to a different world—a Disneyland. In addition to being beautiful, Van's was the fun house, the one where all the kids had always hung out.

Everything about Van and his home was, in my opinion, perfect. The house was a large two-story made of silvery Texas limestone with a bronzed metal roof. Olive trees flanked the path to the front door, lush emerald squares of evenly cut grass to either side. The sounds of Van's three younger brothers playing soccer carried from the backyard.

With my mom out of sight, I considered immediately going home, but when I glanced around, of course someone was watching me. Someone was always watching someone on Scarlett View. Max was a distance away but we made eye contact as he walked across the street, presumably to find Wilson after being separated for only a matter of minutes. It occurred to me that it had been weeks since I last saw Van hanging out with his two best friends.

I paused on Van's front step and glanced behind me again. Max was now at Wilson's door but still observing me. For a long moment, Max steadily held my eyes, not betraying if he was surprised that I was standing on Van's property for the first time since I was nine.

Max's fiery red hair stood out in the dusk. He also had intense freckles to match, which had faded only marginally over time. Maybe from years of being teased about his freckles, Max always struck first, his sense of humor cutting. Yet, when we were only seven, Max was the one who had carried me on his back for more than a mile when we all got lost in the woods and I twisted my ankle slipping in the creek. Just last week, there was a moment when my car strained to start in the driveway and, in my rearview mirror, I saw Max begin to jog across the street to offer his help.

Max's parental supervision was almost zero even though his hippie parents had retired early after selling their fruit-leather business for millions. Wilson's parents, on the other hand, watched their only child's every move. Wilson's mother was originally from India and a successful restauranteur. Wilson was named after his other mom—Leigh Wilson, a Texan—carrying on her Southern family's surname.

Just then, Wilson came out of his house. He joined Max on the doorstep and plopped down on the bench gracing the wide porch, sprawling his legs out in front of him, folding his fingers over his middle. Wilson was tall and lanky with longish, silky black curls and doe eyes that made him look eternally innocent. I still couldn't reconcile this seventeen-year-old Wilson my friends thought was so sexy with the little kid I'd splashed with in the creek wearing nothing but my Hello Kitty underwear.

Now both boys' eyes were on me.

I realized I was staring back at them. I remembered where I was standing and I was about to quickly knock, when Van's mom whipped the front door wide open, surprising us both.

"Ingrid." She put a hand on her heart.

"Hi, Mrs. Moore."

She relaxed and smiled. "I don't think you've ever called me Mrs. Moore. Always Lisa. I was just getting the mail. How are you feeling?" She touched my shoulder very gently, like she was worried I might break.

"Oh, fine." I said it like it wasn't a big deal. As if I didn't have staples in my head.

"I'm glad you're good. Concussions are terrible." She sucked in her breath. That bystander *yikes*.

I made myself look into her expectant cornflower-blue eyes. I missed her. Everyone loved Lisa. A former preschool teacher, she was the parent who had played with us, stretched out on her stomach on the living room floor. One time, early on a Saturday morning, Lisa had painted my nails while we waited for Van to wake up. Before Mary Seitzman moved onto our cul-de-sac, I was the only girl and I loved being doted on. Back then, I took it for granted.

"I just wanted to say thanks for tracking my mom down at work after the accident. My coach probably had her number buried in paperwork but it would have taken a while to find it."

"Of course! We all look out for each other," Lisa said. It didn't feel fake coming from Lisa but we hadn't been part of her circle for a long time.

"Thanks again." It would appease my mom if I said thank you to Lisa. I was about to say goodbye and head home to rest my head and stare at the ceiling, when one of the twins—Anthony, I guessed—knocked into Lisa and she caught herself on the door-frame. In a whirlwind, Gus, the other twin, came in a close second, and shouted over his brother who was actively telling on him. Lisa was immediately thrown into a whirl of chaos and negotiations. I cleared my throat, which jarred my head and made me acutely aware of the circumference of my skull.

"Bye. Thanks so much, Lisa," I croaked. I was concerned about the tendrils of cold that had begun to spread through my limbs, always a precursor to throwing up.

Lisa barely looked up but opened the front door even wider and gestured for me to come in quickly before their bull terrier escaped. "No, Stella!" To my horror, Lisa grabbed my arm, pulled me into the rectangular entryway and slammed the door shut just as Stella's muscular, gray body heaved into it, then slipped on the carpet. Her paws were muddy and Lisa grabbed

Stella's collar to pull her into the large, bright kitchen just to my left. Van's brothers ran behind and in front of their mother, almost tripping her.

Van's stepdad sat at the white marble kitchen island, his back to me, laptop out and loaded with stock market data, phone in hand. His large frame was bearlike. Kevin didn't look up at the fighting or help Lisa as she struggled with Stella near the kitchen fireplace. But then he twisted slowly on the barstool and gave me a little smile.

"Van's in his room," he said.

"Oh, I've got to go," I said quickly, and brushed my unkempt, sickbed hair from my face.

"Nah, go on up," he coaxed. He seemed to laugh at some private joke as he turned back to his screen.

The picture frames on the entryway table caught my eye. They all showed the Moore family, blond—with the stark exception of Van—and smiling on different expensive vacations. All the way in the back, I saw a token picture of Van's dad. In the photo, he appeared much younger than any parent I knew today, but he had been pretty young when he died. He looked so similar to Van with the same high cheekbones and direct, amber eyes.

Van had been five when he moved onto our street with his mom and her new husband. Lisa had been very open about being widowed and remarrying and I remembered every detail of what the neighbors had repeated to one another when the Moore-Tagawas first arrived—Van's Japanese-American dad had died less than a year before, he had been a medical resident, and he'd been killed changing his tire on the side of the road. Lisa didn't mention the last part; someone discovered it in a Google search.

Before Van's arrival, Wilson and Max and I had been our own tight circle. We'd let other kids play with us but no one became a lasting member of the group. When Van confidently wandered over to where we were setting up our orange cones that read KIDS AT PLAY, that all changed.

Almost immediately, we became a foursome but we divided into two teams—Wilson and Max, me and Van. If Max and Wilson were like my brothers, Van was my best friend. I remembered feeling like I recognized him instantly, that we already knew each other somehow. I'd never felt that way before. Or since.

Van's stepdad was still watching me, expectant.

"Okay," I heard myself say. Why in the world had I just agreed to go up to Van's room?

I recognized the adrenaline rush and the urge to challenge myself. It was my response to fear. My coach had pointed it out: consistent, consistent, explode. In one week, I could learn three new dives. He said it was the quality that made me continuously level up. Now I had that same feeling. I craved and hated the sensation: exciting and horrible.

I took the narrow staircase, freshly painted on a regular basis to cover the boys' greasy handprints. At the top of the stairs, the house more closely resembled what I remembered from years and years ago. The artwork was the same and so was the long runner that ran the length of the landing and was always bunched from kids tearing through the house.

Van's room was two doors down to the right and I could hear the sounds of Lyrics Born's "Callin' Out"—a song I knew because Van had played it nonstop this past month and it carried through his open window. Pretty soon it would be so much hotter and Van would shut his windows and it would be another year before I knew what he was listening to. He had great taste, in my opinion, except for the hits he played that were produced by my dad. I always wondered if he knew they were his. Then I'd think, *Of course he does.*

The bedroom door was partially open. I touched the handle and my heart began to pound.

"Van?" I said softly. Too softly, apparently.

My eyes caught on the Zildjian poster on the wall straight ahead. It was identical to the one my dad had given me when I was little: the drum kit and the giant cymbal. It had been flattened but white creases marred the print, and it occurred to me that it might be the exact poster that had hung on my wall before I'd crumpled it up and jammed it in the trash. I was wrapping my mind around that when, from the corner of my eye, there was a flurry of movement.

Van shot up quickly from his bed and stood next to it. Then I got all the confirmation I ever wanted or needed that they were, in fact, dating, when Caroline Kelly sat up much more slowly behind him. She looked down at the front of her shirt as though making sure it was buttoned all the way.

I unfroze. "Sorry." I quickly turned and left the room. He was nothing to me. This didn't matter. There was no reason to want to be sick.

"Ingrid."

I looked back at Van, who'd followed me into the hallway. My cheeks were flaming. He was barefoot and wore jeans and a band T-shirt. He looked completely unflustered. His eyes dropped to my chest for a millisecond and I instinctively pulled the old T-shirt I'd been wearing for two days away from my body.

We both paused, not saying a word. I hadn't heard him say my name since eighth grade.

He was waiting for me to speak, to explain why the hell I'd walked into his bedroom. Van Tagawa's inner sanctum. Which Van was he? The one I'd played Legos with? The one who had accidentally/not accidentally held my hand in eighth grade? Or the one who was six-two, gorgeous, and a king of our school?

I found my voice. "I came by to say thanks—for helping find my mom last week. And for trying to get on the deck." Oh god, why had I mentioned that? It wasn't like I'd seen it. I'd just heard many reports from the other girls on the team about his arguing to get down to the restricted swim deck post-accident.

Van gave me the smile I'd watched other girls receive over the past few years. "I can't believe those assholes wouldn't let me down there."

Oh. It was actually true.

My eyes rested on his for a long, quiet moment.

Caroline swung out of the bedroom to join us. Side by side, it was insane what a striking couple they made. My mom once said Caroline looked exactly like a young Cybill Shepherd in *The Last Picture Show* and pulled up an image. She was correct down to their shared honey-blond hair and slightly, perfectly upturned nose. My mom had called Caroline heartbreakingly beautiful.

"Hey! You walking out?" Caroline asked me. Not waiting for my answer, she added, "I gotta go."

"I'll walk you home," Van offered.

"No, no. I got it. I want to talk to Ingrid."

Van was about to say something to me when Caroline reached up and grasped his face in both of her hands, commanding his undivided attention. Then she very slowly kissed him. I realized I was staring.

I started for the stairs, my face beet-red again. Then I heard Caroline fall in line behind me.

Thankfully, the downstairs had emptied of the Moore clan. Stella, now abandoned, licked the kitchen floor. I realized what was behind Van's stepdad's smile. He'd known I'd walk in on Van and Caroline. He was teasing Van, who probably thought he was getting away with having his girlfriend upstairs. Nice. Kevin had always loved to rib Van. It seemed to be his way of subtly and not-so-subtly reminding Van that he was boss.

Caroline and I let ourselves out and walked single file down the pathway to the sidewalk. It wasn't yet twilight, but dim light shone from the cul-de-sac's two streetlamps. I wanted to hit the rewind button a million times over.

Caroline halted on the sidewalk and faced me. "How are you doing?"

She moved closer and boldly reached out to touch the back of my head, somehow instinctively knowing exactly where my staples were, her fingers on the matted ridge. I was tall and willowy like my mom and she was short and petite. I felt gawky next to her.

"I'm good. I'll be back sooner than a month, I'm sure," I lied. I hoped I sounded calm. Caroline dropped her hand. I took a half step back.

"God, I hope so." She made this sound like a remote possibility, like I had a long haul in front of me. "I hate practice without you." When a senior like her said that to a junior like me, it was hard not to feel special. Caroline stretched long like a cat, her graceful arms extended up and out, unafraid to take up space, chin tilted to the sky. She was so California-beautiful it wasn't even funny. She was also nice, so it was impossible to hate her.

Why him? She could have had anyone she wanted.

"You don't mind, do you?" she asked, and pointed loosely in the direction of Van's room.

"Why would I mind?" I asked. Izzie had once said that I was hard to read. I hoped she was right.

"Oh, I don't know. That was a dumb thing to say! It's not like you want a boyfriend anyway."

Caroline must have felt me stiffen. "What I mean is you don't have the time. That's what it takes if you want to go to Nationals. I remember with gymnastics," she said, wistful. Back in San Diego, Caroline had been a gymnastics superstar. She was one of the very few people I knew who understood what was asked of you if you wanted to perform at a higher level.

A lone police car swept onto the cul-de-sac on its sporadic patrol since the break-ins, its lights temporarily illuminating us as it looped the street.

"I didn't know you and Van lived *so* close to each other. He's the boy next door," Caroline said.

"The boy across the street." I acted like it was a joke, not a big deal at all.

Just before spring break, a teammate had asked me who the best male soccer player was at our school and I'd named Van. I hadn't known Caroline, the only other diver who went to my high school, was seated right behind me. That was all I had said but it was as though I had flagged Van and put him on Caroline's radar, because the next thing I knew, I heard the rumors about them at school and then I saw him in the stands at the meet, just moments before I messed up.

"He said you're named after Ingrid Bergman."

My accident had given them a reason to talk about me. Why would he tell her that? Why would he remember?

At my lack of response, Caroline supplied, "I saw *Casablanca* once with my mom." Then, "See you at school?"

I wanted to get away from her and I wanted her to stay because she made me feel safe in the dark. Bad things didn't happen to someone like Caroline.

"See you tomorrow," I said.

Caroline began her walk home, strolling leisurely down the center of my street while I crossed to my house. But Caroline had one more thing to say.

"Don't worry!" she called over one slim shoulder. "It's just a little injury. I had one in gymnastics before I moved to Texas."

She'd once told me it was her injury that forced her to quit.

CHAPTER FOUR

SUNDAY, APRIL 3

For hours already, I'd tried to sleep. Full of optimism that tonight would be the night, I tucked myself in at 9:30 P.M., my body cocooned into the comforting divot in the middle of the bed. But now the start of school was only six hours away. I had to rise in five to shower and get ready. My heart began to pound from the worry and anxiety of not falling asleep.

I tried not to think about Van. Or the pain. Or about the medication I couldn't take because I wasn't supposed to mask the headaches in this first phase of the concussion. The house popped, then settled. Maybe if the lights were on downstairs I could rest more easily. Any prowlers next door would think twice about breaking and entering or walking through my backyard. I kicked off my top sheet and sat very still for a moment to see how the headache would land when I was upright. Every pain was stronger. My mom always said everything seemed worse in the middle of the night.

When I had wrapped my mind around the full extent of the

pain, I made my move downstairs. I started with checking the locks on the windows. My dad had loved windows, maybe left over from his LA canyon-living days. He'd designed this house from Los Angeles, where he'd been living with my mother at the time. In her version of the story, he wouldn't let her interfere with the planning at all. Even though she had great taste herself, she happily relinquished the job to him because she didn't give a shit about the details. He had been insane about each and every one.

My father fell in love with Austin when he came to work on an album. He convinced my mother that it was a great place to raise their kids, away from the pressures of LA. According to my mom, my dad would say he was building my pregnant mom a nest; a beautiful house in an area where they had few friends and she was far away from the action of her career.

In her early teens, my mom, an only child, had relocated to Santa Barbara from Sweden for my grandfather's job in oil and gas. When her parents returned to Stockholm a few years later, she stayed behind for college. She'd told me Southern California had felt like the promised land and she never wanted to leave, she was so in love with the Pacific Ocean, the palms, the warmth.

As a young actress living in LA, she'd met my father through the same clique of fashionable friends—a collection of other artists, most of whom went on to become known. But back then, they had all been getting their start.

As my mother told it, she was the first to have a big breakthrough; she was cast as one of the leads in a TV show, an elaborate sci-fi fantasy. The only problem—it was a multiyear commitment to film in Ireland. Newly engaged, my mother turned it down. She assumed there would be other offers. And then I was born. The series went on to have an award-winning seven seasons. Sometimes, when my mom would stare out the kitchen windows at the large, untamed backyard and scrabbled wall of greenbelt, I imagined her thinking, *How the hell did I end up in Central Texas?*

I switched on the lights and dimmed them in the sparse living room occupied by two white leather sofas we never sat in. If my dad loved windows, he didn't like window shades, which was weird because he was the most private guy. But then, my father hadn't lived here much given that he kept getting called back to LA for work, commuting home to see us on weekends. I backed out of the living room swiftly, before anyone could spy me through the windows. My head briefly swam.

Down a short hall, I made my way to the quiet kitchen, graced with appliances that were once top-of-the-line trendy but showed their age now. They also no longer worked very well. The floorboard under the dishwasher was pliable and moldy from an unexpected leak. White walls, white subway tile, white marble counters, large windows, no shades, and unused round table with plastic space-age-looking swivel chairs, padded with orange seat cushions. My mom had scrubbed the kitchen clean before she'd left for work even though neither of us cooked. We existed mainly on bars and frozen entrées from Trader Joe's.

Continuing through the downstairs, I opened the door to my mother's room—the master suite—and bent at the side of her low, Danish modern platform bed to switch on a lamp. Clothes had been thrown on the end of the bed—a navy-blue bra, a pair of sweats—half the bed unslept in. The same paperback copy of *The Girl on the Train* had sat on her bedside table for months. The room smelled like her lavender shampoo and I wanted to call her, a pang in my stomach at wishing she was here. If I called, what was she supposed to say, though? Being afraid was my problem. I never, ever called her at work and I knew she barely had time to look at her phone during her shift.

There were a few more rooms to check downstairs but I decided to bypass the ones with the closed doors: the two guest rooms with their own bathrooms. We kept the doors shut to save on heating and cooling. I didn't know if my mom ever went in to clean or if she ignored those rooms—one my dad's old studio and the other a bedroom for nonexistent guests. The last time I'd entered, the unused rooms were beginning to take on the musty smell of an unoccupied house—ready to deteriorate as soon as you stopped living in it.

Midway up the staircase, I looked below and surveyed my work. I held the stair rail as a precaution. I had a flash of a scenario where my life easily spiraled out of control: a fall that led to a worse injury, which led to sitting out longer from diving, which led to never going back. For a second, I saw just how easy it would be to disappear.

Upstairs, the house didn't feel as huge. There was my large bedroom, my Jack and Jill bathroom connecting to another bedroom for an additional child who'd never arrived. The upstairs was more intimate, with a cozy den over the garage where my mom and I watched TV and ate together on the nights we found ourselves home at the same time. It completed the five-bedroom, four-bathroom, large, empty house filled with the two of us, just keeping our heads above water and pretending that was anything but the case.

Now that lights were on in almost every room, the house surely glowed from the outside. Back in my room, I stood at the window and lifted the taped shade very gently, just a few inches out. If my room was dark, no one could see in. But I could see out.

Van's stepdad, Kevin, smoked a cigarette outside in their front yard, a sign that the old battle between Lisa and Kevin waged on. Other than Kevin, the street was quiet; balls and bikes put away, doors locked, everyone sleeping peacefully. The portable basketball hoop in the Loves' driveway loomed like a dinosaur over two matching Lexus SUVs. The greenbelt made a beautiful halo, arcing against the line of homes. Kevin stubbed out his cigarette and walked back inside.

From my large street-facing window, there were three houses I could see well: the Moore-Tagawas', the Loves', and the Kaplans'. From the smaller window on my right, I had a side view of the Smiths', or what I now thought of as the abandoned house, partially obscured by a cluster of live oaks. When all the strings had finally broken on my Roman shades, my mom hadn't bothered with a temporary paper shade for that window. The side of the house was much more private. But for all I knew, the family that had lived there could have been as attuned to my habits as I was to Van's.

It had become part of my bedtime routine to check if Van's bedroom light was on. Then, I'd think about him—what he'd worn that day, if he'd glanced my way in class—for about five whole seconds before I fell asleep. It was the one dumb thing I did. Everything else in my life had a purpose.

I turned to my beat-up leather backpack that lay on my desk, folders and books perfectly organized, homework complete even though the teachers had said I could turn everything in late. As I sifted through some of the work, I realized I didn't remember doing it. It was like a monster had taken over my body. That's exactly what it felt like in those moments over the past few days when I'd swayed on my feet because I was so incredibly tired. I could see why sleep deprivation was used as torture.

Seated at my desk, I swiveled back and forth, back and forth, avoiding my bed and the stress I was beginning to associate with it. The doctor had said to take naps, to set a fixed bedtime schedule because, most of all, I needed rest to heal. I stared up at the peeling stars I'd once stuck to my ceiling and wondered what to do next.

A movement, a flash of light in my peripheral vision caught my attention. I turned my head slowly. Then I froze.

Through the tree branches, I caught a glimpse of a light on in the house next door.

I blinked.

Then it was gone.

I second-guessed myself. My eyes were so sandy and dry from not sleeping, scraping against my lids. But there had been a light on in that window. I wasn't hallucinating. I hadn't been awake that long.

Very carefully I rose to my feet. I flipped on my small desk lamp. I wanted to get a closer look from the window.

As I made my way across the room, I trailed my hand on the wall to steady myself and inadvertently caught the flimsy paper shade I had hastily taped up when I'd returned from Van's. Now it fell to the ground and, like the big reveal in a magic show, Van's window appeared.

My eyesight adjusted.

Van stood framed in his bedroom window, every light turned on in his room. He was staring out, a shoulder leaning against the window frame, his arms loosely crossed.

It took me a second to realize I was just as visible in my room, backlit by lamplight.

I leapt out of the way.

I squinted to see what he was watching. What was it? I allowed myself to sway into view, and then I realized what Van was looking at.

He was looking directly at me.

CHAPTER FIVE

Rain poured from the eaves in sheets. I kept my gaze trained on the fogged-up windows that looked out on the crowded school common while Izzie, her body twisted in her desk chair to face me, used both thumbs to quickly blend concealer beneath my eyes. Even with the door open between periods, the classroom air was humid and close with the smells of BO, hair, and snacks from the previous class.

"Don't move."

"Hurry," I said to Izzie.

Behind me, I heard the sounds of students filing into the classroom. This was my last class of my first day back at school since the accident. The entire day, I'd been self-conscious that people had heard about it and were whispering about me. I knew I looked like shit. Izzie was trying to help with the dark half circles that ringed my eyes. She couldn't do anything about the fact that because of the staples, I hadn't been able to wash my hair for days.

I was feeling less human every moment. At my appointment on Friday, the neurologist said to return to school gradually. My mom and I had agreed that my first day would be a half day, but I wanted everything to go back to normal as soon as possible. Or, at the very least, to appear normal. So I'd stayed for the entire school day. I didn't want to give in to the headache that seemed to worsen and settle over one eye as the day went on. I would have killed for about three ibuprofen.

Iz leaned back to observe her work. "Much better. You don't look as tired. Here, use this, too. I promise, I don't have herpes."

I took the gloss from her, smeared it on, and handed it back.

Izzie, a true theater girl, squeezed the tube, flipped back her long, black hair and slowly dragged it across her mouth, beckoning people to look at her. The opposite of me. I hated nothing more than drawing attention. Except in diving. But that felt like a separate world. Spectators seemed to fade.

More eyes had been on me since we'd returned from winter break. I was suddenly as tall as my mom, close to five-nine. I'd noticed them noticing my very late growth spurt—probably training so hard had delayed it—and, maybe it had to do with suddenly having what Izzie referred to as a "great rack." I now had boobs. Something I had doubted would ever happen. I liked it but I wasn't used to it. I was finding it harder to recede into the background.

In ninth grade, I'd been lucky enough to find Izzie Aaron—or she'd found me, extroverting my introvert. For some reason, she'd decided we were going to be the best of friends. Izzie was also part of a group of five other girls, all of them extremely into theater and dance. I hung out with them but I was on the fringe since I was away so often, either at practice or traveling to a meet. When I was with the group at lunch or on texts, most of the time I was in catch-up mode, trying to piece together what I had missed.

"Why don't you keep the lip gloss for tonight? Just reapply before your awards thing and, voilà! The rest of your makeup is already done."

Although I felt like death, I was looking forward to seeing Coach Mike at his awards dinner tonight. It might make everything feel normal.

"Why are you all dressed up, by the way?" Izzie asked as she zipped her small silver mesh makeup bag.

"I'm not! I'm just not wearing a hoodie for once." I wore a short-sleeve button-down and my best pair of jeans. I'd carefully put my hair in a bun in an attempt to cover up the staples.

"You should dress like this every day. You look beautiful."

"Stop."

"Why can't you take a compliment?"

"You sound exactly like your mom right now."

Izzie glanced up at the new arrivals. "He just walked in," she said, her voice breathy.

It was crazy but I already knew. I always knew the exact moment Van walked into English class. How the hell could I be so attuned to someone that I could *feel* them? I didn't look up. Instead I focused on the array of backpacks being thrown on the ground in dirty puddles left by wet shoes.

"Are you going to say anything to him?" Izzie asked. I watched her eyes and knew they were following Van. I'd told Iz about the previous night's events. But only that. She had no idea how I felt about Van.

"I don't know. Don't worry about it."

"But you think he saw the light, too, right?"

"Honestly, I could be making the whole thing up."

"Or there's a meth lab right next door to you and neither of you bothered to call the police."

"What if it had been nothing? I'm recovering from a concussion. I was freaking myself out. If I'd called the police, the whole street would know, and there's a good chance I would have been the girl who cried wolf."

"So? It would have been an honest mistake. No one would ever think you called the police lightly. And who cares what people think?"

Well, apparently, I would rather be murdered than look foolish in front of Van. I was sure he already thought I was crazy after I'd barged into his bedroom last night. Only to later be caught staring into his bedroom window.

After we'd locked eyes, I'd spun around, snapped off my light, and sat on the edge of my bed until dawn, wondering if I should do something, if Van was going to do something. I didn't have his cell phone number, so I couldn't contact him except through his social media. I'd grabbed my laptop but then bleary-eyed, I'd quickly lost any sense of urgency as I went down a rabbit hole looking at photos of Van, his band, so many long-legged girls, so many friends. He'd been careful to avoid posts of him and his friends partying. In addition to the rumors, it was easy to tell from the company he, Max, and Wilson kept that they had been partying hard this year.

When I'd looked up from the computer, the sun had risen.

"Just ask him." Izzie made it sound easy.

"Maybe after class."

Izzie was looking at Van and I was still looking at Izzie. "God, he just kind of sums up the word 'hot.'"

"I know."

Izzie turned all her attention on me, suddenly interested. "You think he's cute?" *Great.*

"Of course he is. Just look at him," I said, and nonchalantly turned my head to see for myself.

Today Van sat in his usual spot—all the way across the room

next to the wall of rectangular windowpanes. His legs stretched out in front of him, he was wearing a long-sleeve T-shirt that made his shoulders look broad, jeans with a hole at one knee, and Converse. I watched him aggressively scrub the top of his head with both hands as if he wasn't used to the fact that his hair had recently been cut short.

He was tall with black hair and deep brown eyes that lit up like no one else's when he was happy. They could also go stone-cold when he was mad. Until he smiled, Van always looked tough and serious. Oh, and then there were his beautiful, pouty lips.

Lisa used to complain to my mom that Van was so laid-back, too laid-back, late for everything, a slow eater, and that still seemed to apply. He had a relaxed quality, like nothing was important enough to get worked up about. Maybe when you lose a parent at age five, you learn that lesson early.

"And now he's with Caroline Kelly. Wow," Izzie was saying. "He's so hot, a senior is dating him."

I almost wanted to take credit for setting them up.

"I've seen him looking at you," Izzie suddenly said.

Don't feed into it, Izzie. I need him to go away. "He's probably looking at you," I said.

"No, he's looking at you, the Ice Princess." It was a joke between us after we'd learned that some boys from the chess club had nicknames for everyone in our friend group. Mine had turned out to be Ice Princess. Nice. Izzie's was the Baker's Wife, her role in the high school production of *Into the Woods*.

"Well," Izzie continued, "no matter what, he's out of our league with his dating-the-hottest-senior-in-school-as-a-junior thing. As if he needed to do more after being in the most popular clique and fronting the best band in school."

For some reason, that felt like a pinprick when she said it. But it was true. Compared to Caroline, I was invisible.

"Oh my god! I didn't tell you!"

"What?" I asked. Izzie seemed like she was about to fly through the roof.

"John Michael asked Anna if you had a date to the prom!"

"No," I said, shaking my head emphatically. He was my lab partner in AP Chemistry, and he was nice, but no.

"He's going to ask you," Izzie whispered in a teasing tone as our teacher, Mr. Brandt, closed the classroom door in anticipation of the bell.

I kept telling our friends over and over again that I had a diving meet out of town that conflicted with prom. But it was like they knew I was lying. I wasn't lying, but I wasn't being totally honest. It was just a practice and I could make it in time to prom if I wanted to.

And honestly, I didn't know what was wrong with me. John Michael would probably be our valedictorian, he played soccer with Van, and he looked a little bit like Clark Kent—super handsome, but sort of stiff and vanilla. When the topic of John Michael and prom had come up before the accident, one of our friends had sounded slightly snide when she asked if I was holding out for a better offer. Absolutely no. Of course not.

"Come on! Or ask him! Then you can go with us. Leave your meet early."

From our animated conversation, a few people had glanced over. Including Van. Right then, the bell rang and class began, drawing everyone's attention to Mr. Brandt at the front of the room.

As usual, I sat through class looking-but-not-looking at Van Tagawa. Somehow, in three years at our massive high school, we hadn't had a class together until this year. I'd had the thought that once I saw more of him, my crush would finally go away. Nope. It only deepened.

Of course I'd seen him in the halls but years had gone by

since our last meaningful interaction, and we'd ignored each other since. Actually, I doubted Van was actively ignoring me. It was more that I didn't cross his mind at this point. Beginning freshman year, there were so many new faces in his life. Van, Max, and Wilson stuck together at our new school, but the rest of the old middle-school friends were supplanted with new ones.

Over the past few years, I'd replayed our falling-out over and over again in my head. In eighth grade, Van and I had been randomly assigned to be partners for a history project. Since my dad had left, I didn't interact much with the boys, and the project with Van was our first contact in so long. Despite my shyness, we'd ended up laughing as we built our version of a Texas mission. I remembered feeling light and happy, completely in a partner bubble with him. He teased me that I wouldn't stop adjusting the roof when what we'd done was perfect in his opinion. I folded my hands in my lap to show him I was done. But then, I took a closer look at our work and I couldn't help myself. When I went to fine-tune a detail one last time, Van anticipated it.

Without even looking at me, he snatched my hand before it rose above the table. I remembered staring straight ahead and grinning as I lowered my hand to my lap. But Van didn't let go. In one quick movement, he flipped our hands over and interlaced his fingers with mine.

We both stilled. It could have been one minute or twenty. I'm not sure how long it lasted but we held hands for the rest of class, underneath the table, our hands resting against my denim-clad leg.

I remembered that all-consuming, intense awareness of Van. I couldn't breathe. It was addictive. My fourteen-year-old self knew it didn't get any better.

Then, to my total horror, Max leaned his chair back on two legs and exclaimed incredulously, "Are you *holding hands*?"

We'd dropped them like we were on fire.

I never told anyone. Maybe because I didn't want Van to do it first, I'd pretended it had never happened and that he didn't exist. Maybe because I'd thought it would make Max and Wilson's incessant teasing end sooner. Maybe because what I'd felt for Van was too much, an avalanche of big emotions. Of course, now I completely regretted how I'd acted.

The next morning after the "incident," Van smiled at me when I walked into the classroom. I ignored him. He'd ignored me back ever since. Until last night.

Now, three years later, I watched the face of the wall clock in my high school classroom and debated whether to try to talk to him. The second hand made one full sweep. Ten minutes left of class. I concentrated on our teacher who paced at the front.

I needed everything in my life to stabilize as soon as possible. It was in my best interest to go back to our default mode of non-communication. But, at the same time, I wanted to compare notes on last night. It would be so easy to catch him at the end of this class. I could also let it go.

There were seven minutes left of class, then two.

When the bell sounded, I had to keep myself from covering my ears. The ringing was definitely louder than usual. But no one around me seemed to notice.

Izzie chatted nonstop while I was underwater, moving in slow motion. I rubbed my cheek on my shoulder and surreptitiously raised my eyes to see if Van had already walked out. Across the room, he was shoving everything into his black backpack. Once he was packed up, he began to yank hard at the zipper.

Exhaling, I bent to tie the lace of my white tennis shoe, buying myself time. In hyper-focus, I noticed a smudge of gray dirt on the toe. *Come on. Just leave it. Let it go.*

"Hey, I gotta go," Izzie said impatiently as she waited for me. Izzie's next class was across campus.

"I'll call you later," I said.

Izzie raised her eyebrows as understanding dawned on her that maybe I was going to approach Van.

"Call me. Immediately." When she passed, she brushed my shoulder purposely.

The classroom kept emptying. There were only five people left, including Van. My last period of the day was free so I could linger. Even Mr. Brandt walked out, cell phone pinned to his ear.

Then, unbelievably, it was just the two of us left. Van headed toward the exit, his eyes on the ground. My heartbeat went into overdrive.

I started down my aisle toward him and, right when Van raised his head and looked over at me, a voice called out from the doorway.

"Good, you're still here!"

John Michael stood at the door. He grasped the doorjamb on either side, his body bowing into the classroom, effectively blocking the exit.

"Hey," I said, distracted. John Michael released his hold and stepped into the room. He was clad in a polo shirt, his broad chest narrowing down to a slim waist.

"Excuse me," Van said as he tried to squeeze past John Michael, who still blocked the path to the door.

"Hey, Van," John Michael said, moving aside.

"Johnny Mikes." Van nodded at him in passing. I almost smiled when I took note of the WARNING: HEAVY tag Van had obviously taken off a suitcase and strung onto his backpack.

"Did you take my folder by any chance?" John Michael asked me.

"What? Oh, let me check," I responded, opening my backpack. My mind followed Van through the door. I had the sudden urge to punch John Michael. But sure enough, I'd absentmind-edly taken the folder from chemistry.

As I handed it back, I heard Van call out, "Max!"

Over John Michael's shoulder, I saw Max and Wilson stop walking. The small group gathered just feet away from us.

"Where were you guys last night?" Van asked.

I tried to keep listening as John Michael continued to talk to me as he replaced the folder in his backpack.

"Home," Max said.

"Home," Wilson echoed.

"Nice tattoos," Van said, gesturing to Wilson's upper arm. I saw a flicker of vulnerability in his eyes.

Wilson's hand flew to it, like he wanted to cover it from Van's sight. I saw that Max had the exact same tattoo—something they had clearly done without Van. Both boys stood there, neither of them knowing what to say to their friend.

Seba, the boys' overnight new best friend, materialized. "What up, assholes?"

Wilson ignored Seba. He remained intent on Van, as if he knew he was about to lose Van's attention and wanted him to stay. "You coming over later?" The last carried the hint of a challenge, like he was just waiting for his friend to say no.

After a pause, Van said, "I'm meeting up with Caroline. Then band stuff." Van reluctantly turned his back on them, leaving his best friends behind.

"Tell your girlfriend hi from me," Seba called after him.

Van held up a middle finger, then disappeared into the sea of students.

Wilson muttered a curse word under his breath as he watched Van go, like the interaction hadn't gone the way he'd wanted. Max stared at the ground. Why wouldn't he look at Van? Wilson noticed me standing there and for a millisecond, his eyes swept over me.

"Ingrid!"

"What?" I focused on John Michael. He was looking at me strangely. I lifted a hand and touched the back of my head, as if to make sure I wasn't coming apart.

"You coming?"

"Oh, yeah. Yes." I adjusted my backpack but it slipped, flipped upside down, and spilled out about a million pens, loose change, and of course a tampon right at Max and Wilson's feet. Instantly, they both bent low and helped me gather up the mess. I had to hand it to Max that he picked up the tampon, along with a handful of pens, and put it back in the zippered pocket without a word.

I stooped next to Wilson to help and I was surprised when he caught my hand, placed a collection of coins in my palm, and then curled his hand over mine to close it. He continued to hold my hand for a beat.

John Michael suddenly butted in and picked up my backpack in a way that felt proprietary and annoying.

"I got it!" Wilson snapped. He rose and snatched the backpack from John Michael. Wilson gently handed it over to me.

"How are you?" he asked. His doe eyes were intent on mine.

"I'm good." What in the world was going on? Why was he suddenly talking to me and being so weirdly chivalrous? Then I remembered the accident. He was just being nice.

"Thanks," I said to Wilson and gave Max a quick smile as I followed John Michael's lead into the crowded hallway.

"Of course," I heard one of them say behind me.

I made my way through the swarms of students, replaying the scene I had just witnessed. I couldn't imagine a world in which those boys weren't friends.

CHAPTER SIX

Coach Mike had made me laugh earlier when he'd texted: *You coming tonight? This place is not the same without you. It finally happened! One of the pip-squeaks pooped in the pool. And there went practice.*

Now I hovered in the doorway of the garage. It was time to leave for the awards dinner but I paused. Why was my mind suddenly screaming, *Don't go?* I knew I was being selfish. This was an occasion honoring the person who had been there for me more than anyone beside my own mother. I teetered out to the car in heels higher than anything I was used to wearing.

I had on a little black dress I'd once bought when I briefly and foolishly thought I was going to LA for a weekend to visit my dad. I was a little appalled at how short the dress was now that I'd grown a few inches and the wrap-style showed a lot of cleavage. But I owned nothing appropriate for Coach Mike's awards dinner and I couldn't show up in my uniform of jeans and a hoodie.

The cul-de-sac was quiet for 5 P.M. Mr. Kitchen, a cranky

retiree, tore down the street on his bike in full, tight racing regalia but all the usual little kids were nowhere to be seen. It was verging on uncomfortably bright and hot at ninety degrees.

As I drove by Mr. Kitchen in my old white Mazda, I thought I saw his face contort and then he shouted at the car. When I looked in the mirror, his back was to me and he was biking in the opposite direction. Had he been yelling at me? Maybe he thought I was driving too fast.

I turned the corner, accelerating, just as a deer came bounding from the thick brush. It darted for the other side of the street, just feet from my car. I slammed the brakes, preparing for impact, and watched it miraculously soar over my hood as my body was whipped back and forth.

For a moment, I sat in the idling car, the smell of burnt rubber coming through the vents, panting from both the scare and the shooting pain in my head. Another car approached from behind and honked. I blinked hard and then continued to drive. I was completely losing it—one actual accident and one near-disastrous accident in just a matter of days.

When I arrived at the hotel hosting the awards dinner, my nerves were already shot. Before I got out of the car, I reminded myself to act like I was fine. I needed the team to treat me the same way they always had.

I slowly walked to the designated hotel ballroom, steeling myself, building my wall. I owed this to Mike. He'd once shown up for me by coming to a dreaded Father's Day breakfast in fifth grade. I'd been sweating it and complaining to him lightly that my teacher wanted my father's number so she could get him on the phone for me during the breakfast. Mike had fixed the problem by being my guest. I'd felt like a traitor, but when all the kids were drawn to Mike, I remembered wishing he was my real family.

When I entered the enormous room that was a sea of round

tables and floral centerpieces, I was immediately surrounded by fellow divers. Kisses and hugs flew. I was aware of their lean bodies and unworried faces. I could have been an old teammate who'd retired and come back to say hi.

"You look so hot," Alix, one of my better friends on the team, commented. I waved it away.

"No, seriously," Annie, our other friend, said. "Come sit with us. Mike said he wanted you up front when you arrived. You're late, by the way." I noticed all of their dinner plates being cleared away. I hadn't realized how late I was. It was the little details that were falling from my grasp. I honestly couldn't remember what time the invitation had said and I couldn't recall even checking it. Somehow, I had gotten myself here.

"How are you feeling?" Alix asked. "I've been waiting for you to text me back."

"It's all good. I'm fine," I lied. "I scared my mom more than anything else."

Walking into the ballroom was like being thrust from one bubble directly into another. I squeezed in between the girls and politely greeted Annie and Alix's parents, who sat across the round table and stared at me for a moment longer than I would have liked. I was sure it looked weird that I came without a parent. My mother felt bad about not being able to make it but she couldn't find anyone to trade shifts with her. The awards dinner was a glorified fundraiser for the aquatics center and a nice night for the team. Usually the swimmers got all the attention—translation: money—so it was a big deal that Mike was being recognized. It was also the unveiling of the plans for Mike's new diving facility. Obviously, it belonged to the aquatics center, but it was being built because of Mike.

"Look at him," Alix whispered, gesturing with her chin to a table up front where our coach sat with his young wife, Laura.

I guessed that Mike was around thirty-four now, though he looked younger. Sun-kissed, wearing a dark sport jacket and tie, Mike looked like someone who had grown up poolside at a country club and was totally at ease in a crowd of wealthy donors. But I knew he preferred to be surrounded by kids. He loved coaching and it showed.

Coach Mike was intense when we were diving but when we weren't, he was fun and funny. The little kids clung to his legs and he had silly nicknames for each of them: Charlie Tuna, Squirrel, Jack-a-Mole. With the older kids, he was firm when he needed to be but he also joked and made practice fun. When girls—Alix, for one—relentlessly flirted with him, he either ignored it or sent them off to go do burpees.

But what made him great? Coach Mike instinctively knew what would inspire us individually and how to draw out our best performance. We were always so proud he was our coach—of how young, smart, and cool he was—especially compared to the militant coach who barked at his swimmers at the next pool over.

"He looks so gorgeous, all fancy in his dress clothes. Like a hotter Roger Federer," Alix said.

"It's like Aquatics finally realized he can make them some money," Annie said. Then she suddenly grabbed my arm. "Laura's pregnant."

"I'm so excited for them!" I said enthusiastically, trying not to give away that I'd known for months.

"Laura told us a few minutes ago! And you'll see her. It's obvious. Mike's having a baby," Alix said, singsong.

"Shhhh." Alix's mom held a finger to her lips and pointed to a giant screen as a slideshow presentation began.

Over a medley of pop music that gave way to a more nostalgic song, I watched Mike's career play out in photos. The first slide showed Mike at the high school where he'd first coached.

A much younger Mike stood next to two rows of thrilled kids who excitedly brandished their impressive array of medals for the camera.

My eyes had left Mike in the photo and I was studying these kids who'd been his first team. The slide changed. *Go back.* I thought I recognized someone. I half stood and actually murmured, "wait," out loud. Our table snapped their heads to look at me. Alix gently pushed me down.

"Are you okay?" she whispered.

"Yeah." I pretended something was caught under my chair and scooted closer to the table.

Oh my god, I was becoming unhinged and forgetting myself in public. A trickle of sweat dashed the length of my neck. I drew a long breath and tried to concentrate on the photos now showing Mike when he first came to Texas, ten years before, to take the head coach position at the diving club.

Then I was front and center in 90 percent of the slides. If Mike was the star, I was his star pupil. Me with my trophies, me at regional, state, and national competitions with Mike standing right beside me. It was made clear that coaching a nationally competitive diver was a big deal for Mike.

Accompanied by a chorus of awwws and good-natured laughter, I saw a photo of myself as a little girl, standing next to Mike, tiny but looking up at him with an expression of total determination and focus.

That had been right after my parents divorced—within the year. Mike took over my coaching but more than that, he'd told me he would make me a champion.

It was like we had made a pact to save each other. He had blown it once again at Olympic trials and was retiring, giving up on his gold medal dreams and putting all his energy into a coaching career. I could tell my mom wasn't going to go out of her way to find me a coach since I was just at the beginning—mainly I'd been fooling around at the pool with my dad. I was on the verge of losing something I loved. Another thing I loved. When I dove, it was the last place I could still hear my dad's voice.

By the time this photo had been taken, I had already thrown everything behind Mike.

I shook my head to clear it. In my mind, I hadn't realized how little I had been when my dad left. For the first time, I felt a little empathy for that young girl in the American flag bathing suit.

More photos played out and I watched myself grow to ten, eleven, twelve, and my face get thinner and longer and my body lengthen and get more definition. Then the awkward years: thirteen, fourteen. At fifteen, I started to resemble myself. Mike still looked like a swim Adonis but he didn't look fresh-faced anymore.

Everyone was clapping, and Annie put her arm around me and her head on my shoulder. "Your mom should have seen that," she said.

Even I felt the weight of what Coach Mike and I had accomplished together and built bit by bit over the years. My dad once said, "You can go the distance and I'm the one who will get you there." Unprompted, Mike had said those exact words to me when he met me, almost verbatim. And then he'd repeated them again and again over the past several years.

I clapped along and kept my face pleased but neutral while heads craned between me and Mike when the overhead lights gradually brightened. Heat radiated off the back of my neck from being the center of attention. I focused on my folded hands resting on the red tablecloth strewn with used napkins and a butter dish nestled in a bed of melting ice.

When he was presented with Coach of the Year by the Aquatics Association, Mike dragged his chair back and took his place standing behind a small podium, our team logo projected on the screen behind him.

My mind drifted while Mike thanked many people, including his wife, who herself had been a diver at the University of Florida. Mike spoke about finding his calling as a coach. About his divers: "I wouldn't be up here if I didn't have amazing athletes." Then he said my name.

"Ingrid is *the* athlete. She has nerves of steel in competition. Focused, flawless. The one who comes along once in a coach's career if you're lucky. She has taught me how to coach just as much as I've taught her how to dive. I never stop learning from her. You are special, Ingrid, and I never want you to forget that. I don't say it enough, but I am very, very proud of you." He looked at me pointedly.

My face was bright red but I nodded and smiled. What he said meant everything. I hoped he still meant it.

"What a shitshow," Annie said.

"What?" I snapped my head to look at her.

"I said, what a great show," she said, looking at me curiously.

Mike made a closing remark I missed and then suddenly, the entire ballroom rose for a standing ovation.

I turned my head to scratch my bare shoulder with my chin. From the corner of my eye, I caught sight of a familiar cascade of tawny hair. I lifted my eyes. Immediately, I lowered them and turned face forward again.

"Oh my god, she missed the whole thing," Alix leaned over to say to Annie and me.

"Oh," Annie said with understanding. Then, "Well, if he was my date, I'd be showing up late, too."

"Do you think Mike saw her come in late?"

"No, but he doesn't care. She does whatever she wants and he knows he's not going to change her. If she were going to USC on a diving scholarship, it would be a different story. But she's not serious. She's just another former gymnast they recruited and she's almost out of here anyway."

I involuntarily looked back at Caroline. She was wearing a white lace baby-doll dress and black cat-eye makeup and looked like a French movie star. I accidentally met Van's eyes. He seemed to take note of my dress and I resisted the urge to run a hand through my hair. I quickly turned away.

"What's his name again?"

"Van. Right, Ingrid? Doesn't he go to your school?"

I heard myself say, "Yeah. He's a junior."

"I'm surprised she even has a boyfriend. She's so ready to move on from high school," Annie said. "She tells me that every day."

"He's a junior."

Annie gave me a look. "You just said that." Had I?

Alix blatantly stared over my shoulder. "But look at him. He's tall, dark, and handsome, but he's not cookie cutter. You know?"

"He has really nice eyes," I said.

Both girls looked at me.

I scooted the heavy banquet chair back from the table. "I'm going to congratulate Mike."

"Yeah. He's going to want to introduce you around. Fundraising."

I gave them both a hug and then picked my way through the ballroom, smiling politely at people, seeing myself through Van's eyes as I made progress toward Mike who was still only feet from the podium, the screen blank behind him, caterers swiftly clearing dessert plates.

Mike was chitchatting with the dad who ran our booster group and a silver-haired gentleman wearing a University of Texas longhorn tie. For the flash of an instant, I saw the younger Mike with his man-bun, telling my mom he planned to be there when I signed my letter of intent to the university with the best diving program in the US. That had been so many years ago.

I hesitated, deciding to melt back into the crowd, when Mike saw me and excused himself from the small group. I hadn't seen him since the hospital and now it felt like finding my best friend among a crush of strangers.

"Where do you think you're going?" Coach Mike said, smiling. He had a glow from just being in front of the large audience. He gave me our usual big, arcing high five. He seemed relieved to see me, too.

"I didn't want to interrupt. Hey, congratulations," I said.

"I wouldn't be here without you. You know that, right?" he said.

I smiled and shook my head, brushing it off, but it felt good to hear. Especially one-on-one and not just for the benefit of an audience.

Someone asked if they could take our photo together. Mike put an arm around my shoulder and, for two people who were rarely expressive with one another, we posed awkwardly for five seconds, then broke apart.

"I would have hit my head sooner if I knew you were going to start being so nice to me," I said.

"Don't even joke," Mike said. "I'm still recovering from my heart attack." Then, more seriously, "I'm so sorry this happened."

"Stop apologizing. It's my fault, not yours!" *I'm sorry* had been Mike's mantra when we got to the hospital, as though if he said it enough times, it would hit the rewind button. It was the only time I'd seen him rattled in all the years I'd known him.

I wished I hadn't brought up the accident and ruined the moment with Mike. Especially on his big night. Beads of sweat formed at my hairline, like I'd summoned my symptoms with mention of the accident. To change the subject, I was about to tease him about his fashion in the old photos when Mike put a hand on my shoulder. He made sure I met his eyes before he said, "Everything's going to go back to how it was."

The way he said it, his tone, gave me pause. Mike sounded like he wanted it to be true, not that he believed it. His eyes were serious and maybe even a little unsure, like he was reassuring us both. As my mom had said, and as he had just showed in his presentation, we were tied together. My success was his success.

"Of course. Everything's going to work out," I said. "I'm fine."

"Mike!" A meaty hand clasped his shoulder. While Mike was occupied with greetings, I called out, "I'll talk to you tomorrow," and beelined for the exit, my mind churning with an even deeper understanding of my responsibility to Mike.

"Ingrid!" I ran smack into Laura, Mike's wife. "How are you?" Laura smiled, showing off the small, sexy gap between her front teeth. I loved her natural beauty mark just above her top lip.

"I'm great. Thank you for the sweet get-well card. I just got it today. I'm sorry I didn't call you back," I said.

Laura wrapped me up in her arms. I was surprised to see how far along she was already. It seemed like only recently that Laura and Mike had me over to their apartment for dinner and told me the news. Over Laura's sun-streaked brown head, I caught sight of Caroline gazing off into a corner of the room with a thousand-yard stare. She was already bored.

"It's so good to see you," Laura murmured. "Wow. Look at you." She held my hands away from my body and checked me out. "How can you be even taller than when I last saw you? And I'm obviously fatter!" Laura dropped my hands and cradled her arm beneath her belly encased in a stretchy purple dress and laughed.

It was true—they used to invite me over regularly on Friday nights but it had been a few months. I'd finally been free to accept Izzie's invitation to Shabbat dinner at her house instead. I'd hoped it wasn't because Laura and Mike were embarrassed; they'd fought in front of me the last time I'd been over. Mike had missed Laura's doctor's appointment that day. Even to me, it was clear he was in denial that his life was about to change.

"I'm so excited for you guys," I said, genuinely. "Did you find out if it's a boy or a girl?"

"Mike didn't tell you? Girl."

"That is awesome. Mike will be the best dad."

"He will be. Tough, but a good dad."

"Mike will be the best dad."

Laura gave me a concerned look. Had I just said that again? The fogginess seemed to worsen at night and the noise of the crowd wasn't helping.

"He will be for sure!" I laughed, trying to cover but sounding a little manic. I dried my clammy palms on the skirt of my dress.

I glimpsed Van scanning the crowd.

Suddenly, I needed to leave. I had to get out of that ballroom, immediately. "Laura, will you tell Mike I had to run?"

"Of course! But are you sure you have to leave?"

I pretended I couldn't hear her. I gave Laura's hand a squeeze, backed away, and made it through the ballroom doors.

When I got in my car, in the dark corner of the surface lot next to a trio of scrawny trees, I made sure my doors were locked. I made sure no one could see me. Then I replayed my conversation with Coach Mike. I didn't see how I could tell him about my stage fright unless I had to. Then I thought of my surprise at seeing Van tonight. Compared to my fear of disappointing Mike, why would the sight of Van and Caroline, of all things, make me feel like I was about to hyperventilate?

I pounded the steering wheel one time. Hard. For a long while, I sat quietly in my car and mindlessly watched the leafless trees shiver in the wind.

CHAPTER SEVEN

After my embarrassing, erratic departure from the awards dinner, I paced my bedroom. I listened to trance music and reminded myself over and over again, *I'm still the same. Nothing has changed.* I hoped I would eventually wear myself out and stagger to bed.

It wasn't working. I was wired and the full moon seemed obnoxiously bright. It flooded my bedroom through the curtain-less window.

Frustrated, I yanked out my earbuds. I sagged against the window frame and stared out into the night.

I was preoccupied, observing a slice of the neighbors' backyard through the window but not really seeing it. I listened to the soothing sound of crickets. I was thinking how I loved that sound when, uncannily, something in my eye line stirred. I straightened.

First, I heard a fragment of a scream. Then, there was movement close to the house. Through the trees, I thought I saw a petite back and streaming hair. It was a girl frantically sprinting away from the house toward the greenbelt. And then she disappeared from sight.

*

Where were the police? I'd waited for thirty minutes, unmoving under the covers with my phone tucked close to my body. First, I'd called 911. Then I'd repeatedly called my mom. It rang and rang.

Finally, there was a pounding on the front door that traveled through the floorboards.

I scissor-kicked the sheets off the bed, freeing myself from my hiding place. At the street-facing window, I glanced down to the walkway where two police officers lingered impatiently at my front door.

One officer was male, blond with thinning hair on the crown that I could see from my vantage point. He walked back a few feet and then looked up at the second story to determine whether someone was inside. Backing away from the window, I snatched my sweatshirt off the desk chair. The clock said 4:36 A.M. There was temporary relief that it was morning.

A carpet tack punctured my bare foot as I ran down the stairs. My head pulsed. Between the exertion and the cortisol coursing through my veins, I'd undone any healthy convalescing.

"Who is it?" I called.

"APD. Austin Police Department."

"Can I see badges?" Wasn't that what I was supposed to do? I was so alarmed and alert, I wasn't sure I was thinking clearly.

Two outstretched arms held up some sort of identification that appeared blurry through the smoked glass slats in the front door. Good enough. For the flash of a second, I was pissed at my mom that she wasn't home.

I opened the door about a foot wide. The female officer was much younger than the male officer and had black hair drawn tight into a miniscule ponytail.

"We received a call about a possible prowler?"

"I'm the one who called. A girl came running from the house next door. I heard her scream. You probably already know about what's been going on over there—"

"Okay. Do you have a parent present?"

"No. My mom's at work. Did you already look next door?"

"Father home?"

Pause. "No."

"So, you're here by yourself?"

Should I be giving out this information?

My silence must have been enough for them to assume I was alone. Completely.

I launched in. "Did you go over there?" I pointed next door.

The police officers glanced at each other and didn't answer my question. With rising disbelief, I noted their unhurried stances. They weren't buying into my emergency.

"We'd like to ask you a few questions about what you think you may have seen next door."

"Okay." I shifted to my other leg and leaned on the door. When it moved, I almost lost my balance. Mike always said I had incredible "kinesthetic awareness"—that I always knew where my body was in space. Without sleep, my coordination was going.

The woman stepped forward to steady me when I swayed with the door.

They seemed to eye me for a second and then understand we'd be doing the interview in front of the house. I looked past them. There were two police cars parked on the cul-de-sac and I noticed the other officers walking down the lit path of the Moores' house. Lights were on in about five houses, indicating that the cops were interviewing everyone, knocking on doors before daylight.

"Around three thirty a.m., you said there was activity outside your home?"

"Yes, I was upstairs in my bedroom, listening to music, and then I heard something. So I walked over to the window. I heard a scream and then I saw someone—someone with long hair, run from the house next door." I pointed to my left. "I'm pretty sure the person was female. And then she disappeared."

"Can you describe her?"

"No. Just that she was female. I only had a glimpse of someone running and that she had long hair."

"Hair color?"

"Brown. Maybe? I'm not sure. It was hard to tell, even with the full moon."

One of the other officers walked up. There was a side conference. When the cops interviewing me returned, I said, "Also, the night before last I saw a light in the window of the house. A lamp seemed to switch on, then off. But I wasn't sure if I was seeing things."

"Why would you be seeing things?"

"I've had a head injury." When I said it, I realized I'd just undone my credibility.

"What time would you say that was? When you saw a light go on."

"After midnight, for sure. I can't quite remember." I'd never heard my voice waver before. "Can you tell me what the neighbors said?"

"No one heard or saw anything," the female police officer said.

"They must have heard the scream," I pressed.

As though he was frustrated with the girl crying wolf, the male cop began pointing at my closest neighbors' houses. "This person is on vacation, according to their next-door neighbors who are caring for their lawn. That neighbor fell asleep with the television on. That neighbor got home from a red-eye and was asleep."

"You know the house is vacant and has been broken into recently, right?"

They nodded. "There's a patrol car making the rounds every night." The male cop swatted at a mosquito. In the porch light, I saw it fly into the house.

"Can we get your name?"

Was this really it? Was it my age? They carried an air that this was a fool's errand.

I gave them all my information. They gave me a card and told me to call them if I saw anything else. On the way to their patrol cars, I heard them discussing breakfast.

How was it that none of the neighbors could corroborate my story? Had I been wrong to call 911? The whole street would think so. For a second, I doubted myself.

But I'd seen her. And heard her. I swore I had.

＊

Now it was 5:00 A.M.

I stood in the hallway between the front door and kitchen, then slid down the wall to the concrete floor. A glossy brown cockroach slipped through a slim crack under the baseboard near my hand.

I tried to remember the last time I felt happy and safe. Before the accident, it hadn't even occurred to me that I wasn't either.

A memory suddenly came up from years and years ago. Fourth of July, after seeing the fireworks, being tucked into bed by my dad. "My sweet girl," he'd murmured. I'd watched his back as he left the door open an inch, my eyes halfway closed even before he'd left the room. The memory seemed to surface from out of nowhere.

The gentle knocking interrupted my thoughts. It was so soon after the police had left that I assumed it was one of them returning with a question. I pushed myself up off the cold floor and straightened my boxer shorts that had done a half-turn when I slid against the wall. Through the opaque glass, I saw one figure.

"Who is it?" I asked automatically.

"It's Van."

*

His voice was soft, as though he was worried he would wake up everyone in my house.

I opened the door wide. Van wore a navy-blue hoodie unzipped, a worn T-shirt that looked soft, and a pair of bright blue athletic shorts. Nothing he would ever wear to school. I was getting a glimpse of his private life. Seeing me in pajamas, he was getting one as well.

"I didn't mean to—I just saw the cops leave," he said, and jerked his thumb over his shoulder in the direction of the street.

I realized I was staring at him and I hadn't said a word.

"It's five a.m., I know. I told my mom I'd check to see if you guys were okay." I peered around Van and caught sight of Lisa in their doorway across the street. She took a step back into the foyer and closed the front door, leaving me and Van to ourselves.

So Lisa had sent him. "We're fine," I said brusquely. *You can go home.*

"Okay," Van said slowly, but he lingered. Fireflies dotted the landscape behind him. With the cops there were mosquitoes. With Van, there were fireflies.

"I'm the one who called the police," I blurted.

"That's what my mom said."

"You didn't hear anything?" I asked.

"I had headphones on."

So he'd been awake, too.

Van suddenly lunged forward to swat at a mosquito near my cheek. When he came so close, my vision blurred and he temporarily appeared in double.

Van stepped back again, straightened, and hooked his thumbs in his pockets. He shrugged a shoulder to brush something away from his own cheek. I waited for him to make his excuses and say good night.

"Your mom's car is gone." Van tipped his head toward our driveway.

"She works the night shift."

"You're by yourself every night?" Van asked huskily. It was inadvertent that it sounded suggestive and he coughed, embarrassed.

"Yep." Our exchange was growing increasingly awkward. He didn't strike me as someone who would ever be awkward.

Van looked over his shoulder warily. His house was dark again. "Do you mind if I come in for a sec?"

"Of course." I couldn't have been more surprised.

I had zero idea what he might want. I backed out of the way and Van stepped inside my house and I closed the tall, heavy glass door behind him. And then we were standing together in the foyer. Alone.

Every light downstairs was dimmed low and it was much darker inside, away from the hot spotlight beam on the front

steps. The entire house looked like a setting for a candlelit dinner. If Van thought this was strange, he didn't say a word. I sensed
his eyes adjusting. My eyes adjusted as well and I saw him look
at what I was wearing—a V-neck T-shirt and shorter shorts than
what I would ever wear to school. My legs suddenly felt extremely
bare.

Van had been a presence in my life but a distant one for
the past seven years. Now he was right here and we were in
that weird interstitial place specific to neighbors: not friends
but not strangers, and in some situations, like family. When
something out of the ordinary happened, it was normal to talk
at 5:00 A.M.

"So you're home alone every night," Van repeated. He
sounded amazed, which made me feel defensive.

"Nurses work at night."

"I know. I just didn't know she did." He shifted his stance and
smiled slightly.

"What?"

"It's just funny that I have Kevin watching me like he's my
jailer and you're the complete opposite across the street. No one
is watching out for you. Wait, you know what I mean—no one is
watching your every move," he corrected. Van glanced up at the
ceiling briefly as though he was kicking himself for what he'd just
said. This was all around becoming the strangest encounter. Van
Tagawa was in my house and not getting to his point.

"Why is Kevin acting like your jailer? Besides just liking to
bust kids in general." I thought of Kevin on Halloween, on his
bike, notorious for chasing after kids with backpacks full of eggs.
I was prolonging things. It could be the one and only conversation I had with Van for the rest of high school and his adorable
nervousness was a side of him I hadn't seen. It was cheering
me up.

"I got caught sneaking out in the fall." Had he snuck out to see a girl? Max and Wilson?

Usually I was okay with long silences. I found other people would rush in to fill them. But Van made me nervous and I searched for things to say. It was still dark but technically morning. "Do you want some coffee?" I stared at the scarlet remains of my weeks-old pedicure as I waited for his no. It seemed like a long time ago that I'd reluctantly let Izzie paint my toes while she recounted her spring break.

"Sure," Van agreed.

Oh. "Okay. This way."

As soon as I brightened the kitchen lights, I deeply regretted that I'd asked him to come farther into the house. Izzie came over now and then but I was always uncomfortable. I didn't like anyone noticing things. And pointing out what was obviously broken. As if I didn't know.

But Van didn't react to the sheer emptiness of my house. Or its condition compared to his bright, lived-in, über-stylish home that kept up with the times.

I guesstimated the right amount of coffee as I shakily dumped it into the filter, spilling grounds onto the white counter. When I turned my head, Van was over at the kitchen windows, gazing out at the wild, brambled yard. The sooner Van went home, the sooner I could relax. I hated how much other people in my home put me on edge. Especially Van. I didn't want to care what he thought.

Van turned back to me and I was struck again by how familiar and unfamiliar he was. I wanted to stare at him up close without him knowing so I could see all the small ways he'd changed since we were young.

"Earlier, you thought you saw someone in the backyard?" Van asked. "At the house next door, I mean."

I poured water into the coffee too quickly and it splashed over the sides of the well. He walked over to me and grabbed the gray-striped dish towel folded neatly next to the sink and began to mop up water. I was completely aware of his arm accidentally grazing mine. I was sure he was oblivious.

I could finally ask him. "Yes. And last night, I thought I saw a lamp turn on. Exactly at the time when you and I . . ." I didn't know how to put it.

"You mean when you and I looked right at each other from our bedroom windows?" His voice was teasing.

I blushed for sure. "Yes."

"So what happened?"

"A light went on in the window and then a second later it went off. You didn't see it?"

"No." He shook his head.

I shook my own head, brushing the entire, made-up incident away.

"Show me," Van said. "Walk me through what you saw from your window."

CHAPTER EIGHT

There was no way I was taking him to my bedroom. He wasn't about to see the dilapidated upstairs of my house.

"It was probably nothing. The doctor said I might see halos around lights for a bit," I backtracked. But I hadn't been staring at a light. All the lights in my bedroom had been off.

"Let's check it out."

"Oh, no, seriously, don't worry about it."

"I guess—" Van stopped midsentence and, frustrated, dragged both hands through his short hair. When he met my eyes, his looked wary. Or guilty.

"What?" I lowered my chin. *What aren't you telling me?*

"So." He paused, readying himself for a confession. "Max, Wilson, and I used that house."

"Oh," I said in one long exhale. "It's just you guys over there." I really didn't know Van anymore if he could have broken into a neighbor's home and stolen from them.

"No. After the family left, we only went over there a few

times, weeks ago. No one would go there now, ever since it's been robbed and the cops have been inside. But when we were there everything was still in the house. The TVs, the speakers. And we left it that way." Funny how he knew what I'd been thinking.

"What were you doing there? Why didn't you just party on the greenbelt?" I faced him, crossing my arms. Van paused and I realized the V-neck of my shirt had slipped, revealing a crescent of cleavage. I straightened, arms back at my sides.

"We know the trails so well, but the woods scare other people. Also, I don't like mixing the two. The greenbelt feels kind of sacred, you know? But the house was a place we could go. We kept it really small . . . just us at first and then we invited Caroline and Seba," he said, slightly apologetically, like it had been so intimate, which was why I hadn't been invited.

Van peered at the coffee maker and then shook it gently. I'd forgotten to turn it on. I pressed the start button and ten seconds later, we heard the hiss of it coming to life. Van wandered over to the windows. With his back to me, he looked thinner than usual. Tall and thin but with muscular, soccer-player legs.

Van faced me again. "The last time I was there was kind of a weird night."

"Weird how?"

"It's hard to explain. I thought I saw some stuff."

I'd forgotten how Van had this frustrating way of not spitting it out, that he could take forever to get to his point. The slow responses had always made me crazy because I was such a fast mover.

I waited Van out and finally he said, "I thought I saw two people come from the greenbelt into the backyard."

"Like tonight! Who were they?"

"I don't know. They were there, I blinked, and then they were gone. Maybe I just saw shadows."

"But did you tell the police?" This was sounding more alarming, not less.

"No."

"What? Why not?" I wanted to shake him. If he'd told the police what he saw, maybe they wouldn't have thought I was just seeing things.

Van took a long, deep breath and my impatience made me want to kill him at that moment, just like when we were kids and he had a secret. But I'd felt free to shove him back then.

"I was lit." He rubbed his eyes hard and it was clear it was a tactic to avoid looking me in the eye.

"Like how lit?" I asked. I kind of didn't want to know.

He dropped his hands and met my eyes. "We were hanging out at Max's. I took what we'd found in the medicine cabinet at the house—some Oxy and Xanax. And then I drank."

"Oh," I said, trying to keep my sudden leeriness out of my voice. I didn't know he was doing that.

Van's eyes were slightly desperate. "I'm not doing that again. I blacked out. I don't remember blocks of time."

I knew how haunting it was when you couldn't remember a stretch of time.

Van looked out the window, like he might locate his memories there if he stared hard enough. "There were things I thought I saw but I'm not sure. It could all be a vivid dream. But then some parts feel like they actually happened."

I knew what he was talking about to an extent—that indistinct line between awake and dreaming. But usually the line sharpened seconds after waking up. It didn't stick with you and make you question what was real. "What do you think you saw?"

"It's like a series of scattered images and feelings. I woke up in Max's basement, and I was all alone so I went looking for everyone. I don't even remember crossing the street from Max's to the house but then I was inside and following the sound of voices to the back. I was standing at the sliding glass doors looking into the yard when two people suddenly emerged through what appeared to be a solid wall of trees and bushes. It looked so surreal, which makes me think I was dreaming. You know—we grew up back there. We know all the trails. I've searched since but there's nothing there except overgrown woods." He laughed at himself, blowing it off, but it was a strained laugh.

Van slowly turned to face me again. "But then this part feels very real: Through the window, I thought I saw Max, so I went outside on the deck. He wasn't wearing a shirt and he was standing close to a girl. They were angry-whispering and then, she yanked away and took off toward the greenbelt. I swore it was Caroline. I started to follow when suddenly, someone—maybe Wilson—blocked me. He pushed me into the house, like there was something out there I wasn't supposed to see. He pushed me all the way down the hall, where I remember broken glass at our feet. Then I don't remember anything until the next morning."

"What! You thought it was Caroline?"

"I thought it was her but she said I walked her home."

"What do you think?"

"According to all of them, I'm making this up. They said no one was at the house that night. I told Max and Wilson every single detail of what I remember and they said I was passed out in Max's basement. So I let it go. I decided to trust them and I told myself it was a dream."

Van fidgeted with the zipper on his sweatshirt, dragging it up and down, up and down. There had to be more to this story.

"Did something else happen?"

Van seemed to waver. Then, "Caroline distanced herself for days afterward. She'd only say, 'You don't remember what you did?'"

"What's that supposed to mean? Why won't she tell you?"

"I don't know. She's acting like I hurt her somehow. But she won't tell me anything. All she's saying now is 'Let's just forget about it.'"

I couldn't imagine Van physically hurting Caroline, but what if Van changed when he was high? Van said that night had been weeks ago. Since then, I'd seen the two of them at the diving meet, at his house, and at the awards dinner. They'd seemed completely into each other.

"Do you think you hurt her?" I asked.

"No! But I don't know!" Van looked shaken. "When I woke up, I believed what I thought I saw. The part I was concerned about was why my girlfriend was huddled up with a shirtless Max and why I was fighting with Wilson."

We were both quiet. Then, the only thing I could think to say was, "It's shitty to feel like your head isn't quite right."

"Oh god. Your concussion is the first thing I should have asked you about."

That was kind of sweet. "No, I'm good. Really. So you didn't tell the police about the people coming from the woods because you weren't sure if it really happened?"

"Yeah. And since I wasn't sure, I really wanted to avoid the hell I'd have to pay with Kevin and my mom if they found out."

"But then tonight happened," I filled in.

"Ever since that night, I can't sleep," he said. "It's killing me that Caroline might be accusing me of something, but she won't say what it is. And the little I do remember I'm being told didn't even occur." I noticed Van stopped short of saying the obvious: He was worried his friends were lying to him. I sensed he was getting to the point of his visit.

"From your window, you have the best view of the neighbors'.

It's a total long shot that it will help me remember that night but what I wanted to ask is, can I look out your bedroom window?"

Van blushed. It was dark but I could tell. He'd put me on the spot and he quickly backtracked. "It's so late. Or early. You probably want to go back to bed."

The silence stretched. I didn't know what was wrong with me—the need to help him overrode my plan to ignore him. I could run ahead and pick up the underwear on the floor. There was just something irrational in me that thought it would mess me up if he crossed this threshold.

Van probably thought my hesitation had something to do with not wanting a boy in my room, or that I was following my mother's rules. I opened my mouth to speak, when a harsh rap on the front door startled us both.

"I'm sure that's my mom. Wondering where I am. I gotta go." Van exited the kitchen before I could walk him to the door. I heard the front door click shut behind him.

From the living room windows, there were hints of the sky growing lighter. I re-bolted the lock while my injured brain sorted the series of improbable events. I replayed the sight of a girl running into the dark.

Later, in the shower, the water as hot as I could stand, I knew I had to find a way to tell Van to come back.

To calm myself, I reiterated that my life wasn't changing. *Everything is still the same.*

CHAPTER NINE

I remembered everything about the day of my first dive: the marbled pastel bathing suit I wore, the chlorine smell of the swim center, the dark hallway that opened to the vast deck with stadium seating. First, I noticed the swimmers rapidly traversing the lanes like cars. Then, in the distance, in a separate pool, I saw the divers. I barely had an idea of the difference between the platform and the springboard. I'd only seen a diving board at the country club where we sometimes met friends of my parents.

I lagged a half step behind my father when he introduced me to a coach. I could still trace the motions of my first dive—a simple closed pike. First the coach had another child demonstrate it for me, then I climbed the wet ladder and did just what they'd shown me. I grinned underwater and wanted to do it again. I did the next dive they explained and then another. After each one, I was met by the coach while my dad stood off to the side, his back against the painted cement bricks, a self-satisfied look on his face.

I understood that look. It said maybe I had potential. Just maybe I took after him.

When my dad took me to dive that day—on my seventh birthday, just as he'd promised—it was like he handed me a shiny new piece of myself that I hadn't known was missing. Sometimes I thought of that day when I needed a way to calm myself.

Tonight, I was using the memory to distract from the fact that I was perched on the roof. I was so desperate to rest that I'd climbed out of my window thinking that if I confronted my fear about next door I might finally be able to sleep. Now that I couldn't sleep, I was overly aware of the abandoned house. All of the hiding behind curtains and locked doors had only made me more afraid, which in turn made it harder to sleep. The roof itself didn't scare me. Being up high was where I felt safest. On the diving board, nothing could get to me. Until recently.

On the rooftop deck at my house, there was a built-in cement bench and a planter behind it, filled now with depleted, cracked dirt instead of an array of curated succulents. If you stepped up on the planter, it was only one bigger step to the flat roof. I looked over one shoulder again at the brown puddles that dotted the expanse of roof behind me, thick with pollen and dead leaves. At my feet, a stray plastic flowerpot lay on its side in the dirt, left behind instead of discarded. Now that I was spending more time at home—and awake—I saw these details I'd previously walked right past. There were so many of them—artifacts from another time.

It was 1 A.M. and all was quiet below on the cul-de-sac. I'd been waiting for a perfect moment like this. I was calm and maybe it was time to replay the dive that had sidelined me.

I closed my eyes. First, I saw the kiss between Van and Caroline, how her wrist draped over his shoulder while he pressed his hand to her bare lower back exposed by the deep half circle of her swimsuit. She had taken a few steps up into the stands to greet him. The kiss was quick—Caroline immediately raised her head to check if she'd been caught by Coach Mike.

"Look at them," Alix breathed. Alix and I stood together, shoulder to shoulder, unexpectedly witnessing Caroline and Van's kiss.

Caroline trotted back to the deck and rejoined the team. We were never supposed to leave the deck during a meet. Coach Mike walked away and Caroline held out a hand to stop him. Like me, she probably knew it was better to get the lecture over with before he stewed.

Next, I was climbing the ladder and then at the end of the board and I had the sensation that I'd suddenly awakened from a long, beautiful dream. A layer had been stripped away and I could feel eyes on me where before I'd been oblivious and confident. There was the realization that the situation was totally unsafe. A voice in my head said with pity, *Oh, little girl, you were so stupid to believe it was that easy.*

I couldn't remember diving. It was supposed to have been a reverse two and a half on the three-meter springboard.

Despondent, I flipped through my internal index of other advanced dives and there was nothing. The worst thing? It was right there; all of that knowledge was in my head but my brain was playing a game with me. I wanted to scream in frustration— why was this happening? Why was I holding myself back? Was this really about Van? Worry about failing Coach Mike?

I kicked the empty plastic flowerpot hard, accidentally propelling it off the roof and two stories down where it made three horrible, hollow bounces. Loud enough to wake the neighbors.

I held my breath and waited for lights to pop on. One second, two, ten passed. Van's was the only light that had been on. Now he walked over to his window to investigate.

I'd expected him to turn away immediately once he saw it was me. But he continued to stand and watch.

After a few moments, he left the window and then his bedroom light went out. I exhaled with disappointment.

It had been one day since he was standing in my kitchen with me, and since then I'd only seen him across the classroom. If I didn't know it was ludicrous that he'd care enough to bother, I'd suspect he was avoiding me.

I wanted a do-over. It sounded far-fetched that a view would jog his memory but, on the off chance that it did, I wanted to help him. I just didn't know the right way to get that do-over. Walk up to him at school? Knock on his door?

"Ingrid." I heard the faintest stage whisper.

I leaned forward to look down. Van was directly below, tucked against my house in the shadows.

"Come up!" I said louder than he had spoken, and I could almost feel him cringe. Not everyone had parents who were absent at night.

My heart tripled its beat as Van lightly climbed the spiral, black metal staircase against the side of the house. He stood on the roof deck and looked up at me.

"Hey," he said softly.

If I had to admit it, that's when the incomplete, unfinished feeling I'd carried around with me since we were nine years old disappeared.

*

"What are you doing on the roof?"

Waiting for you. "I can't sleep."

Van laughed humorlessly. "I wonder why." He stood below me and paced nervously. Then, decidedly, he took the step up onto the planter and then the bigger step up onto the roof. He came to sit down next to me but scooted a few feet behind me, safely away from the edge.

"That's right, you're scared of heights!" I said.

"You remembered," he said dryly.

"We can go to my bedroom," I said.

Van laughed in surprise.

"You know what I mean! I want to help. I just didn't want you up there the other night because . . ."

"Don't worry about it. I get it," he interrupted quickly. "I barged in."

"There were clothes thrown on the floor. . . ." I kept going.

"Hey, you saw worse when you came into my room," he joked.

His reminder of Caroline dampened my relief at getting the opportunity to explain myself. I didn't know what to say or do next and I hated the feeling. Until last week, I had always been so sure. Nothing scared me.

We were quiet as we took in the view of the street and the wilderness beyond. The night noise of crickets rose in undulating clouds from the greenbelt. Simultaneously, we dropped our heads back to watch an airplane traverse the sky above us, the taillights winking.

"Okay, let's go inside," he said. "This is making me nervous."

I wasn't sure if he was referring to the house next door, his fear of heights, or me.

✳

"It's exactly the same," he said with a little bit of wonder in his voice.

I was on edge. It was only when someone new came over that I could really see my surroundings. There was the stained, golden jute carpet with the giant dark spot where I'd spilled juice, the faded yellow everything, thinned-out bedding with pillows that had lost their plushness, the wallpaper more appropriate for a little girl, and then all the medals and awards made me look like an egomaniac. He could see all of me and I hated it.

"Over here," I said quickly. The sooner he looked at the view, the sooner he could leave. I thought about what he would tell Max and Wilson: *Everything is shabby compared to how it used to be. She was so nervous having a guy in her room.*

"You look like him now," Van said. He was studying a framed photograph in my bookcase. It was of me and my dad dropping fall leaves over my mom's head. Her eyes were closed and her face was upturned, laughing. I was a kindergartner when the photo was taken. "In a girl way, I mean. It's a compliment." Both my parents were great-looking but maybe he assumed my mom was the one any girl would want to take after. She was blond, after all. Like Caroline.

"I mean, you have his eyes. Man, I was so scared of him. We all were. He'd give you that stare."

"That's funny. When I was little, he was the softie compared to my mom."

I watched Van take one hand from his pocket and, like he couldn't help himself, he quickly adjusted the frame so it was in line with the others. He shoved his hand back in his pocket and slowly faced me.

"He was so cool. How he'd play music for us when he was home. Well, I guess he wasn't that cool . . ." Van trailed off awkwardly. "I never saw any of that coming, but I guess I was only nine."

I had to blink rapidly. I'd never been so sensitive before the accident. I used to be better at letting things bounce off me. I also wasn't used to anyone talking about my dad. It was weird when something that went unspoken 99 percent of the time in my house was so easily said by Van. It was also weird to suddenly remember how well Van had known him.

"Yeah, there was a ton of fighting in the garage. They thought I couldn't hear but, of course I heard everything." I surprised myself by continuing.

"What did they fight about?" Van asked.

"The amount of time my dad spent in LA. When his career really took off he wanted us to join him and even though we'd moved here because of him, he was annoyed my mom was taking so long to move us. She wanted me to finish elementary school here. Then, I guess Brooke became his client and he stopped asking." I cleared my throat. "Do you remember your dad?"

"Just bits and pieces. Him lighting candles on my birthday cake. Chasing the dog in the backyard."

Van's expression didn't change but I instantly got a lump in my throat. I didn't want to say, "I'm sorry," that seemed so inadequate, so instead I abruptly changed the subject. "The other night—this was where I was standing when I saw the light."

Van made his way around the foot of my bed and came to stand next to me. His presence made everything in the room look so much smaller. He smelled like fresh deodorant and the faded scent of dryer sheets. I glanced sidelong and saw how flat and hard his chest was under his gray T-shirt, and I had an urge to lean against him and feel how solid he was.

I couldn't imagine he was attracted to me in the least. In his eyes, I was the tomboy I'd always been. And now, except for suddenly having a chest, I was tall and lanky with a lot of straight lines. Boyish compared to Caroline, whose curvaceous body was the open envy of the girls on the diving team.

The last time Van had been up in this room, he had been just a little kid. So much had happened since then. So many new experiences and firsts for him. But for me, it had been dive after dive after dive; that was my catalog of firsts. I could tell anyone in detail about my first two and a half on the three-meter, scoring amazingly on my tuck list at Nationals and placing in the top three in the fourteen- and fifteen-year-old division. I should be happy to know so much about one single thing. But at this moment, I felt young compared to Van. And so different. Like Coach Mike said, I wasn't a normal teenager. I couldn't be. I had to choose.

"Right here," I blurted, and pointed.

Van leaned to look and his shoulder brushed mine. He didn't seem aware. I held perfectly still while he took in the partial view of the cedar fence, the runway strip of Bermuda grass now thick with weeds, the untouched trash cans next to the tan brick house. There were two windows on the side of the house, both flanked by colonial-looking black shutters.

The house was like a poor, innocent sleeping giant that should be left alone, a traditional family house. Bad things shouldn't happen in the same space where the little girl had played and her home had been her entire world. Where the hell was she now? Was she okay?

"Tell me again what you saw?" Van became aware he was leaning a bit close to me and took a step to the right. He continued to gaze long and hard at the view.

"I was sitting at my desk chair and, when I looked over, there was a lamp on in that window. But one second later it went dark. You didn't see it? It was literally one second."

"No. I didn't catch it from the front view. It wouldn't be as obvious from that angle." We stood side by side, quiet. I was glad Van wasn't placating me, telling me maybe I was making it up.

I turned to face him. "What do you think is happening inside? Just random break-ins? People sleeping there? Is someone trapping women inside?" I made the last sound like a joke but I was serious. I was looking for reassurance that there was still order in my world.

"I don't know, but everything about that house, that night is messing with my peace of mind . . ." He trailed off.

"Hey, do you think they could all be lying to you about that night?" I asked. My voice was soft but I couldn't think of a gentle way to phrase the question.

"I—" Van didn't continue and it was obvious he wasn't ready to answer the question. These were his best friends. I didn't press and we stood silently, watching from the window.

"Well," I said finally, expecting Van to make his excuses to leave.

Instead, Van sat down on my bed.

I noticed the bruising beneath his eyes. Van always had that teenage-boy thing going on where he looked like he'd just woken up. But now he looked tired on a whole different level.

"You said you've had trouble sleeping since that night you blacked out?" I asked.

"Yeah, it happened once before. Insomnia, I mean. I was five."

That was how old he'd been when his dad had died. It was also the same year his mother remarried Kevin and they'd bought the house across the street.

"What about you?" Van asked. "I've seen your light on a lot lately."

"How long did your insomnia last? When you were five, I mean?"

Van's face registered disappointment that I hadn't answered his question, like he'd offered something and I'd rejected it.

"A while," he said. I didn't like the sound of that, like I might now be on an endless loop.

Nervous, I gathered my hair in one fist and smoothed it over one shoulder. Why wasn't I telling him? There was no good reason. Here he was sharing his problem with me. Maybe I could share mine. "Yeah, I'm having trouble sleeping."

"When did it start?" He leaned back on his hands.

"Since last week. The accident. It's just strange. I'm so tired but I can't sleep."

"And then you get kind of manic and it gets harder and harder?"

"Exactly." I nodded.

"What are you worried about?" he asked.

Ha. That was funny. Screaming women fleeing the house next door, my diving career, money, him. I shrugged one shoulder. "As soon as school gets out, I have Regionals and then zones and then Junior National Championships. Now is the worst possible time to be out for a month. I've got to sleep. The doctors say it's the best way to heal."

Van looked like he was thinking hard about something. Finally, he said, "Misery loves company. Since neither of us can sleep and your mom's gone, do you want to hang out at night? Maybe we can ride out our insomnia together."

What?

Van shifted on my bed and broke eye contact. "I've learned a lot about the subject lately." His eyes cut back to mine. "I also have Ambien."

"You wouldn't get in trouble?"

"I know how to sneak out." Van consulted his phone. "I gotta go." He stood to leave. "Just let me know."

It was exactly what I shouldn't do. But something inside me seemed to loosen, like a door opened. And I stepped right through.

"That sounds great."

CHAPTER TEN

"Are you getting a hotel room for prom?" Collette asked Izzie.

"You mean as a group?" Izzie looked unsure.

I traced one finger through the yellow pollen on the side of Izzie's burgundy-colored Honda Civic, half listening to my friends talk about prom in the parking lot after school. Izzie was there, as well as Preeti, Colette, and Molly. I streaked my finger along the car and a scratch in the paint slit my finger. I brought it to my mouth and tasted metallic blood while I watched Wilson and Max round the opening of the wilting chain-link fence like movie stars presented in slow motion, the low-ceilinged buildings of the school in the frame behind them.

"Oh my god, speaking of hotel rooms, did you hear that Anna B's mom got caught having an affair? She was in the Hilton parking lot on her lunch break with someone from her law firm," Collette was saying.

"That is such a rumor," Molly said.

"My mom told me. She said there's no place to go for privacy.

Everyone gets caught. Eventually. I think she was trying to scare me."

While I pretended to listen to the conversation around me, I surreptitiously followed the boys with my eyes. Max wore a crisp black T-shirt and black Ray-Bans. His red hair was getting long and beginning to curl at his collar. Wilson's outfit was more preppy: an untucked button down and jeans. He was cultivating a rich kid-vibe: very skinny, stoned eyes at half-mast all of the time, slouching like he was a puppy with limbs too long for his body. I spied loafers on his feet—the buttery soft, beaten-up kind. His glossy black hair had also grown long with his curls stretching out.

The boys had become self-aware this year. They knew how cool they were. I'd seen them go through a metamorphosis over the past several months and it was easy to guess the influence: Seba.

Seba was stationed by his BMW, holding court, everything staged around him, drawing the beautiful people and closing the circle to everyone else. Sebastian, aka Seba ("Sayba") was skinny with short curly hair, quoted '90s films and didn't talk to anyone he deemed not worth his time. He'd shown up at the beginning of the school year because, word had it, his private school had caught him cheating. There were whispers about rehab.

I knew him from elementary and middle school and he'd been exactly the same except now he owned his short stature. I'd disliked him ever since second grade when he'd said he hated Jewish people.

Seba snickered, probably at someone else's expense. The others laughed and Wilson, apparently the butt of the joke, pushed Seba's shoulder. This school year, it was like the boys had absorbed some of Seba—Wilson's loafers, sunglasses worn in the classroom, an attitude with a layer of cutting watchfulness. There were rumors of cocaine parties at Seba's parents' lake house. I wondered how much Van was involved in all of that.

Izzie leaned into me and whispered, "You're staring."

I gave my head a little shake. "I was spacing out, I guess." I'd forgotten my sunglasses, which I wished I could hide behind now. I was so rarely in the parking lot after school where everyone checked out everyone else. Usually I was long gone. I would have been having private sessions with Coach Mike by the time the final bell rang.

"They think they are so cool. They are so cool, I guess," Izzie said wistfully. I watched Iz watch Max for a moment. She'd had a thing for him since sophomore year when they'd flirted non-stop in Chemistry. He'd even come to watch her play the Baker's Wife.

"Here comes Caroline and company," Izzie said.

I couldn't resist and aimed my gaze at a group on the opposite side of the parking lot—the seniors. Caroline was walking toward the senior corner with two other girls, one with long shiny hair named Skyler, and another who wore very short cutoffs. How had Caroline moved to Austin only a couple of years ago and integrated so effortlessly? The girls in her grade had made room for her. The alpha males instantly wanted to date her. As Izzie had once said, Caroline had that popular gene. What I couldn't get over was how, even though she wasn't nearly as competitive as the top divers on our team, she still excelled at diving, a pretty cutthroat sport. And she'd only taken it up since quitting gymnastics. While I knew it was useless to compare myself, in my mind, she had it all.

She had diving and a boyfriend. *The* boyfriend.

The car singed my thighs where skin touched paint but I let it burn. It made me feel present. Since the accident, I trudged through a fog with a dull headache that felt like being under a foot of warm, gray water.

Seba left his post and jogged to catch up to Caroline and her friends. He tapped Caroline on the shoulder, and when she whipped around to see who it was, he came close, into her personal space. Seba didn't even glance at the other girls. I saw him cock his head, grin, and then say something to Caroline. The other two girls laughed in disbelief at the boldness of whatever he'd just said. Seba then reached out to gently adjust the charm on Caroline's necklace so it fell once again just above her cleavage. Caroline caught his hand and seemed to hold it for an instant, looking into his eyes. Then Caroline took a step back but laughed and rolled her eyes, expertly handling him like she was used to aggressive male attention and didn't want to cause a scene. Seba grinned and put his hands on his hips, watching as the girls walked away from him. He was the asshole—the very charming asshole—who flirted with someone else's girlfriend for everyone to see. I knew Seba and Caroline were friends but that Seba made no secret he was into her. I'd seen Seba socializing with Caroline even before he was hanging out with Van and the boys. Maybe Seba had made the introduction. He couldn't be happy Caroline and Van were together.

"Did you see Max and Wilson's tattoos?" Preeti asked in her high, singsong voice, as if she'd ever spoken a word to either of them.

"What did they get?" Izzie asked. She didn't look up from her phone.

"The same one, both of them. Kind of small, tribal sort of? Wilson's looks infected. Ew. Van probably has it on his upper arm now, too," Preeti said.

I didn't comment. I was brought back immediately to the touch of Van's bare arm against mine. That was one thing about my new waking state—my mind could wholly disappear from one moment into another.

I lifted my sleeveless T-shirt away from my body, trying to unstick it. The sun was unrelenting. That moment, just after Preeti said Van's name, he appeared like magic. His long gait, head down, maybe to avoid the blinding reflection off the white concrete. He had a quiet confidence and wore his popularity naturally. It was just who he was. He had also been born with that gene.

"Tagawa!" Seba called.

Van waved in greeting but, to my surprise, he strode past his friends toward Caroline's group, wordlessly hopping up on the open bed of a silver truck. Caroline immediately leaned against his legs and he wrapped his arms loosely around her shoulders. She tipped her head backward and he kissed her forehead. Nausea crept up my sternum.

In the background, cheers erupted from the baseball field.

If I wasn't crazy and hadn't made last night up, I'd see Van tonight. He'd left without a word about where we were going to meet and what time. When we'd sat across the room from each other just twenty minutes ago in class, we'd had zero communication.

"He's so into her," Colette said. "He was all about hookups but no girlfriend, and now look at him."

It was true. I'd never seen Van so attentive. I'd also never seen him dismiss his friends.

"Ingrid."

"What?"

"That look on your face," Colette said, sizing me up.

I was having problems bringing Colette into focus. She seemed too close to me and her dainty features hadn't sharpened into view.

"What do you mean?" I asked. From her auburn ringlets to her short stature, everything about Collette fit the word "cute." She was cast as the lead in every school play.

With dawning knowledge, a slow smirk spread over Colette's face. "Like total longing. I have never seen you look at a boy that way."

"No, I'm just out of it."

In our group, Colette and I were the least close. She and Izzie had gone to school together since kindergarten, and she was possessive of Izzie. Colette was also smart in a way I hated—she had x-ray vision when it came to seeing people's weaknesses. I'd had enough of her laughing when Izzie's Israeli mom would say something not quite right in English.

There was zero way Colette could know I had any feelings for Van. Colette was the reason I'd never even hinted to Izzie that I had a crush on him. Izzie once told me Colette was intimidated by me because I was pretty and I didn't give a fuck. Izzie's words. I doubted it—on both counts—but I wanted to kiss Izzie for saying it. I liked the idea of hiding the real me. There was a lot of respect to be had when you came off as being invulnerable.

"Hey, by the way—any more break-ins next door? It's so weird because it's a good neighborhood. I thought it was . . ." Colette remarked.

"The last one was a few weeks ago," I said.

"How many have there been now?" Izzie asked.

"The police have been called three times? No, four? Three, I think." I just wanted to go.

"What if someone is using the space for something? Not just stealing stuff. Like they've set up shop?" Colette said.

I watched Caroline hold her rose-gold phone up to her ear and wander away from the group to talk. Without consulting the time, I knew she was late for practice. Van watched her closely.

All at once, like a herd of elk, Caroline's group across the parking lot seemed to sense they were being watched and turned their heads in our direction. I jolted away from the car and quickly gave them my back—anything to look like I wasn't a voyeur.

"Izzie, you still good with giving me a ride?"

CHAPTER ELEVEN

Still up?

The text was from a 512 area code and when I saw the unknown contact light up the screen, it felt like a piece of precious information falling into my lap. Now we were connected.

Still up.

Was that too curt? I hit send before I could overthink it.

The bubbles appeared onscreen and tantalizingly wavered. I pushed higher up in bed, my heart in my throat.

Should I come through the back door?

Front door. Back gate is loud.

The typing bubbles appeared again for a full minute. He was typing a lengthy response. Then they went away. And nothing. No message.

I'd kept my overhead light on all night so there was no mistaking I was awake if he was paying attention. I'd been stressing since around 10 P.M. about how we would get in touch or if we would even meet again at night. Maybe it had been a suggestion he'd made on a whim and forgotten all about it.

I liked Van even more now that he'd followed through with our tentative plans. But one second later, I had a new terror—what would we talk about? Also, Van was used to girls adoring him. Would he assume I was also trying to hook up with him? God.

I couldn't stand the tension of waiting for his next text. I re-read Coach Mike's text from earlier, hoping that this time I'd feel a thrill from his compliment: *It's so hard to explain perfect form and execution. It's much easier to just have the kids watch you.*

Instead the text still made me anxious.

I wasn't supposed to take Ambien but maybe if I could sleep tonight, tomorrow, I could pull my attention back to training.

I went into my bathroom, still humid from my shower. I put my palms on the gray-and-white marbled vanity and leaned my weight into them, lifting my heels up while I checked myself out in the mirror. Hair brushed, makeup that didn't look like I was wearing makeup—some beige concealer to hide the dark circles and a little mascara. The kind of makeup your friends would immediately know you were wearing but no guy ever would.

When I saw my reflection in the mirror, it was jarring and then reassuring that I was still here, still whole. So much of me felt like it was floating away these days. Losing focus. Seeing myself helped me put everything back into order, into a container.

I'd given it a minute. I went back to my bedroom and picked up the facedown phone from the pillow to check for a message, trying to expect nothing.

Sounds good. Be there soon.

Inadvertently, I smiled.

I wondered how he got my number.

For one tiny second, I reshuffled my mental deck of cards and pretended I lived a life where this was normal and expected—a boy I liked so much coming over just to see me.

CHAPTER TWELVE

THURSDAY, APRIL 7

Van slid past me into the foyer.

Lights blazed in the downstairs of my house and we looked at each other in the brightness.

"So, you brought the Ambien?" I asked, realizing a split second later how abrupt that sounded.

Van peeked over my shoulder and joked, "You're not a cop, are you?"

I smiled. "I recently retired."

Van laughed. "Can we get out of the aquarium?" he asked, gesturing to the floor-to-ceiling windows.

"Sure," I said. He started toward the staircase. Apparently, Van was coming back up to my bedroom.

When I led Van into my room, he walked directly over to the window—*the* window—and looked down on the abandoned house, silent for a moment.

"Do you mind turning off the light for a second so I can see out?" Van asked.

I snapped it off, shrouding us in darkness.

"Do you see anything?" I asked after a long moment.

"It's quiet," Van finally said. He glanced at me over his shoulder and then, like he remembered I was there, he turned to face me and leaned his back against the wall, legs locked out in front of him. "It's weird how you can always tell whether someone's home or not. Like when people leave on vacation. Even if they leave all these lights on, it's so obvious no one is home. It's like you know if a house is breathing or not." Van didn't wait for my agreement. "If someone comes back, we'll be able to tell. Even if we can't see them."

Tonight? Another night? The way he said it made it sound like a commitment—like we'd be doing this again.

I turned on my desk lamp and then watched as Van dug in his pocket and produced a pill. "You're much lighter than me, so I would take half." He brought it over to my desk, sat down, and sliced through one pill. Both of us hovered over the desk like we were performing surgery. Van handed me the half. With a *What the hell?* shrug, he popped the other half in his mouth, then glanced warily at the window that faced his own home.

I definitely wasn't supposed to take it, but I was so desperate. Just this one time. My next neurology appointment was coming up and it was so important that I present a good face. I needed this rest period shortened, not extended.

Grabbing the water bottle next to my bed, I washed the pill down. "Want some?" I asked, holding out my used water bottle. I should have run downstairs to get him water instead of acting so familiar. He wasn't going to want my germs.

He held out his arm and we both stretched long to pass it. "Thanks." Van took a long swig and then held on to it, fidgeting with the screw top.

I sat down primly on the end of my bed. He stayed in the

swivel desk chair but swung it to face me fully. He wasn't exactly making himself at home; his body language was tense, ready to leave any second.

"So, you know, my doctor said you should turn off all your lights at least thirty minutes before trying to fall asleep," Van said.

Van switched off the lamp. We were thrust into darkness. My eyes adjusted and I could see the outlines of Van, illuminated by my screen saver, a multicolored, dissolving triangle that wiped hypnotically across the screen.

"Sorry, is this weird?" Van asked, laughing.

"I don't know. Everything is weird right now," I said.

"That is true. Okay, so you're supposed to turn off all screens. No reading on a device, even. Have you tried all of this already?"

"Sort of. The first week, I had to take a 'brain break.' Dim lights, no screens, no reading."

"That's perfect."

"What about you? Your light is always on." No. Things were coming out of my mouth unplanned.

Van raised his eyebrows in surprise. "Yeah. I'm failing. It's too hard to pass the night in the dark, without entertainment. I read on my phone all night."

"You don't try to sleep anymore?"

"I seem to nod off when I'm reading or watching something on my computer. The second I make it a thing—set the stage— it's too much pressure. But then again, I haven't had a good night's sleep in three weeks."

"What else did he say?"

"She. Anyway, she said it could be a number of things: stress, PTSD, depression, a shift in sleep patterns at our age. I asked her if taking recreational drugs could do it, thinking maybe that one night messed me up. She wasn't sure. But she said something else is overpowering my need for sleep. She said if you have anxiety at night, the stress response takes over and overrides your circadian rhythm. You're flooded with cortisol, your blood pressure spikes, and now you're in this flight-or-fight mode and your brain is on the lookout for potential threats."

Damn, he was well-informed. And smart. I could relate to everything he was describing because that was exactly what was happening to me. There was a lot of comfort knowing I wasn't alone, that this was a common phenomenon. Maybe I wasn't losing my mind.

"But don't worry. The doctor said exhaustion catches up to all of us."

That sounded ominous. "And there are sleeping pills," I said.

"Yeah, the doctor didn't really want to give them to me but after she sent me home, telling me to turn my room into a spa and recommending yoga, my mom called the office five days later and insisted on drugs. SATs coming up, all that." He shrugged.

Grades, college applications around the corner, I silently filled in the rest. Diving competition wasn't the only reason why spring of junior year was an especially bad time to stop sleeping.

"But the Ambien didn't work?"

"Not really. I mostly feel hungover after I take it. But it should help you." When Van quickly said that, I knew he completely understood the mental game of falling asleep—you couldn't psych yourself out because then you wouldn't sleep. No jinxing yourself. If you visualized it and believed in it wholeheartedly, it might actually happen. It was all about maintaining low stress. When the frustration hit, then it was over.

"So, anyway, don't be like me; put your screens away, all that." Van smiled and a dimple appeared in his cheek.

"Why did you quit trying?" I asked. "To sleep, I mean."

"The last time I fell asleep, or more like passed out, something happened to me. Or it didn't. I don't know. Everyone is telling me I'm crazy. They could be right. . . ." Van drifted off and looked up at me, self-conscious. He placed both hands on the black plastic armrests as if to come to standing. And to leave, presumably.

"What if you aren't crazy?" I said. I thought of Van's strained interaction with Max and Wilson at school and the fact that I never saw them together anymore.

Instead of getting annoyed that I'd insinuated his best friends were lying, Van's eyes seemed full of questions, waiting for me to say more. Wanting me to say more.

"I don't know what I'm talking about," I said quickly. "I just know there's got to be a connection between what you think you saw—the girl disappearing into the greenbelt—and me seeing the very same thing. You obviously weren't imagining it. Unless I was, too."

Van leaned his head back on my desk chair and glanced toward the window again.

"When I walk up, they stop talking," Van said suddenly. He stood and walked to the window, staring out into the night. For a long moment, I didn't think he would say anything else. Then, slowly, worries he'd been holding on to began to come out. "But why would they lie to me? Could Max be hooking up with Caroline? Did he hurt her? Sometimes I think maybe they're trying to protect me from something—like there's a secret video that's about to surface. I can't tell if it's me or them, but since that night, things haven't been the same."

I joined him at the window, not wanting him to feel alone. "I've thought about it," I said, "and there's one thing I think I know for sure. I highly doubt Caroline would ever cheat on you with Max. Or Wilson. Or Seba. Or anyone."

"Ha! Why do you think that?"

"I can't imagine her choosing one of them over you. I mean,

the boys at our school are pretty silly, and cocky, and immature compared to you." I realized I'd gone too far and Van was looking way too interested in what I had to say about him. "Look, I'm sure at least part of what's going on is that you're dating Caroline now. They're hanging out with Seba. Everything changes. Eventually."

Van turned his full attention on me. There was something about the way he looked at me that made my stomach flip, like he was really seeing me.

It made me remember that we were in my bedroom together. But somehow, Van was making it not strange. It was again that feeling of recognition between us. And now we had a bond because we had the same problem.

"Are you getting tired? I should go and let you lie down," Van said. But he didn't make a move to go.

"It will probably take a few more minutes to kick in," I said, not wanting him to leave. We stood next to each other, quietly watching the house. The patterned curtains twitched and stirred but when I refocused my tired eyes, they were still. It must have been the branches of the oak tree. I crossed back to the bed and sank down into the mattress, my limbs suddenly languid.

"Tell me about what happens when you try to sleep," Van said.

I propped myself up on my elbows, dipped my head back, and felt the effects of the Ambien taking hold. A light-headedness, more relaxed, liquid.

"I can't sleep. That's it," I answered.

"I mean, do you drift? Are you wide-awake?"

"I'm lying there trying to remember things. And to forget others."

I realized I'd spoken out loud.

"What do you mean?" Van didn't seem freaked out. More like intrigued.

I raised my head. "Nothing," I backtracked. "Dive-related stuff, mostly. The accident."

What I didn't say: *I'm trying to remember my accident and I'm trying to forget how bad it felt when I saw you kissing Caroline.*

But there was also another category altogether: something I was trying to both remember and forget. A push-and-pull. A gray area. I'd kept so busy that I'd never had this kind of time to think. It was a vast, formless ocean of time. If I didn't stay vigilant and grounded, it felt like it was going to pull me under and I'd be lost.

"That's why we call them accidents," Van was saying. "We all make mistakes."

It was such a kind thing to say and Van was the only person who had said it. Beside Mike's initial words at the hospital, people seemed to assume I didn't need reassurance. "Thank you." I smiled at Van. Somehow eye contact was easier in this looser, relaxed state.

Then abruptly Van turned away like he wanted to break contact. He went back to the window, watching.

"Is the house breathing yet?" I asked.

Van gave me a half smile, knowing I understood what he'd explained earlier. "Not yet." Then, "Try to sleep. I can let myself out."

When he got to my bedroom door, Van tossed over his shoulder, "See you tomorrow night."

CHAPTER THIRTEEN

After Van left and I lay in my bed, I started to drift off multiple times. But every time, I became aware that I was falling asleep and I'd startle myself awake. I must have finally slept for a couple of hours because I woke up to the sound of my alarm, with a dry mouth and a heavy head.

By English class in the afternoon, I still felt out of it.

"No, no." Izzie playfully swatted Sam's hand away when he reached out for her homework to copy. He sat back in his desk chair, smirking. Everyone was dying for Izzie to ask Sam to prom but she was being stubborn, waiting on him to ask first.

My peripheral vision was trained on the classroom door. I hadn't seen Van yet today.

We'd ignored each other for so long and now I wasn't sure if anything would change between us in public.

The bell rang and still no Van. Maybe he was cutting last period and had left early with his friends. Or more likely he was with Caroline. I found that whenever Van skipped class and there wasn't that electric presence on the other side of the room, the hour went 100 percent more slowly.

As the class settled for an extra minute while we waited on stragglers, I put my head down on my arms, less self-conscious since Van wasn't in the room. My head was throbbing and my nose was running. For just a moment, I'd rest in the dim space.

Once I cut out the outside stimulation, Izzie and Sam's conversation rang loud and clear in my ears.

"Hey," Sam said.

"Yessssss?" Izzie said. I felt her antennae go up.

"Are you going to prom?"

Long pause. "Why do you ask?"

"Want to go?"

"What do you mean?"

Oh my god, Izzie. Put him out of his misery.

"Do you want to be my date to prom?" Sam enunciated every word, annoyed.

"Sure," Izzie said easily. She kicked my chair. I smiled into the one-inch space above my desk, feeling my warm breath.

My fingertips touched the outsides of my bare arms. Thoughts drifted to diving. It had been days since I'd worked out. I was losing muscle. I'd read somewhere that it only took three days for atrophy to begin.

"Ingrid!"

My father was calling my name. Waking me up for school.

"Ingrid!" I heard some laughter. I was suddenly delivered abruptly and terribly into time and space.

I lifted my head and my hands quickly, self-consciously went to my hair to smooth it back from face.

"You're sleeping in my class." Mr. Brandt was glaring at me.

My expression may have been unreadable but I knew my face was red. Every single eye in the classroom was on me.

"Turn off your phone."

It was so quiet you could hear a pin drop. I was confused until I heard the chime. I'd forgotten to silence it. And then there was another chime. Someone was insistent about getting in touch with me right away. With the class watching me, I riffled through my brown leather bag covered in ballpoint pen stains. The texts were all Coach Mike. *I have the name of another doctor. Second opinion? The longer out of the water, the harder to get back in.* From the look on Mr. Brandt's face, I stopped there and quickly turned off my phone altogether.

"This isn't like you."

He hit a nerve. Nothing was like me anymore.

"She's recovering from a concussion," a male voice said from across the room, loudly. Firmly.

My gaze snapped toward the voice. Van was staring down Mr. Brandt. When had he come in? When I'd fallen asleep. Wonderful.

Mr. Brandt resumed discussion and I relaxed slightly, though my heart still pounded in my ears.

Thirty seconds later, when everyone had moved on, Izzie kicked my chair again. When I glanced back at her to acknowledge the incident, I knew Van was trying to catch my eye. Embarrassed, I kept my eyes averted.

When the bell eventually rang, I bolted. "I gotta go!" I said to Izzie.

I was halfway down the hall, on my way to the parking lot and the safety of my car, when Izzie caught up to me.

"Ingrid, wait!" For a second, I wondered if I could ignore her. I slowed.

I was such a jerk. I'd forgotten all about prom.

I turned and smiled, ready to discuss Sam,

"What was *that*?"

I looked down into her concerned brown eyes, her stick-straight hair grazing the neckline of her pink tank top.

"Which part?" There was no point pretending.

"Van Tagawa just defended your honor."

"Oh, whatever."

"*He did.*"

"He was there, remember? When I got the concussion."

"I thought he was sort of . . . I don't know . . . too cool for everyone else, I guess. But that was really nice of him."

Here was my chance to tell Izzie everything. *I've spent the last two nights with him. He's been in my bedroom. What does it mean?* It would be a relief to get her take on what was normal and what wasn't and to admit to her just how crazy this was making me.

"Izzie," I started. I opened my mouth to tell her. Because then I'd also know I wasn't making it up. I trailed off when I saw Van headed down the hall toward us. Caroline walked with him, their arms touching. Van and I met eyes. It was the moment when we decided if our relationship at school would change. I looked away. I had to, because I didn't want to know that he might look away first.

In that one second, it was determined. We'd stay strangers at school.

I acted absorbed in my conversation. When I was sure Van and Caroline had passed, I observed their backs. Van looked excellent in his jeans and Caroline was toned in her sleeveless T-shirt and cutoffs. From their physical ease, I guessed they'd already had sex. Obviously. Had he really texted me last night? It was like the Van at school and the Van from my bedroom were two totally separate people.

Van and Caroline's progress down the hall was suddenly halted by Seba. Seba ditched an underclassman who seemed to be pestering him—probably for nothing good—and planted himself in front of Caroline, messing with the flow of traffic. With their backs facing me, I could only see Seba's face. They were still close enough that I could hear every word.

"What up, y'all? Hey, beautiful," I heard him say to Caroline.

"Who are you? Where did you come from again?" Van asked sarcastically.

"When are you finally going to admit you want something else?" Seba looked serious for a second, his eyes trained on Caroline's.

"Move," Van said.

Caroline gave a peal of fake laughter. "Seba," she said indulgently, condescendingly brushing him off. Seba quickly altered his expression into a sly grin. He nodded at Caroline, walked backward for a few steps, and then turned around.

Then, without a word, Caroline disentangled her hand from Van's and caught up to a group of seniors. I saw her breeze past Max. They didn't make eye contact, as if they didn't even know each other. Was it on purpose?

"What?" Izzie said.

"What?" I repeated, distracted. I caught sight of Wilson. He lounged against some lockers, one foot on the ground, one leg propped against the row of maroon metal behind him. As the crowds flooded by in the halls, he was motionless, watching me. Watching me watch Van and Caroline. I looked away, rattled.

"Oh my god. Tell me!" Izzie demanded, her eyes flashing.

"It's nothing. Let's talk about your prom date."

CHAPTER FOURTEEN

"Hi."

Caroline rolled up next to me in her black Volvo, tinted window at half-mast.

"Hey." I gave her a quick smile. I was walking home while everyone drove past. I'd forgotten my mom was using my car today while hers was in the shop.

"Want to ride with me? Stop by practice? Everyone wants to see you. Especially Mike."

Did she know I'd been with her boyfriend for the past three nights? Did she want to confront me?

"Come on," Caroline coaxed. "You should show your face. Show everyone that they can't forget about you. It'll be good," she said definitively. "When you stay away, it makes it too hard to come back."

Looking at her porcelain face, I saw she didn't know a thing about Van and me spending time together. She genuinely wanted to help me.

"Hop in. I can drive you home after."

It was a bad idea. I hated being trapped. But she'd hit a nerve about the importance of showing my face. And I simply wanted to hang out with her.

The car's buttery leather interior smelled like heaven, as did her fresh perfume. "Throw that in the back. Wait, let me see it." She took her gray woven leather tote bag from the passenger seat as I got in. She rummaged through it while distractedly pulling out of the high school parking lot. We passed Van, Wilson, and Max's hangout area and I saw Wilson and Max take note that I was in the passenger seat as the shadow of the car played over the boys.

Caroline dug in her bag, steering with her knees, focused mostly on the contents neatly packaged inside: folded black cotton sweater with a few blond hairs stuck to it, an AirPod case and a heavy, brick-like paperback of *Middlemarch*. I worried she was going to kill us both until, thankfully, she found what she'd been looking for—a small Louis Vuitton pouch. She unzipped it and took out a breath mint.

"Want one?"

I reached into the tin. They were some kind of fancy herbal mint I'd never seen. Everything she owned and touched was interesting and beautiful. *Including her boyfriend*, I thought. It was like Caroline operated on every cylinder and excelled at every aspect of life, no facet left unconsidered: her hair, her gear, her brain, her athleticism. When I marveled that she could listen to podcasts on 2x speed while doing her homework, she modestly shrugged and said she was just weird, that it was like her brain always needed to be stimulated. All I could focus on was diving, then homework. I didn't pay enough attention to what I wore, blogs, art. I wasn't jealous, exactly. I always learned something when we talked. Who knew you could go to a small, walled village in France for spring break and study lavender production through a program she'd found online?

Caroline took a left, choosing the slower route to practice, passing through the thick of downtown. At a stoplight, I watched grackles hop up on empty tables outside a café, nabbing remnants left behind.

"You quit gymnastics because of your injury, right?"

Caroline's expression closed off. For a moment, I didn't think she was going to answer. "It started that way. Then when I was gone, rehabbing, I grew. I was like this giant freak compared to everyone else. I was treated differently after that. Then I overthought everything and got in my own head and pretty quickly fell away. It just sucked. It had been my entire life."

I understood completely but didn't know what to say that would be right. I didn't want Caroline to think I felt sorry for her but I could see her disappointment. Most athletes had complicated feelings about their sport and how it took over their lives, but it was clear she had loved being a gymnast.

"Anyway," she said. "I know how weird these breaks are. My advice is, don't think too much. Just get through it. Keep picturing yourself picking up where you left off."

"Thanks," I said. I hoped she knew I really meant it. Caroline nodded and kept her eyes on the road.

"You look good, by the way. Are you wearing makeup?" She had put on a pretend-shock voice that I resented a little. I had, in fact, put on some makeup. It was because I looked exhausted otherwise.

"A little."

The music on her stereo was all Van's influence. She played the same three songs he was obsessed with. I noticed there was a pair of men's shower slide sandals, the kind swimmers wore, on the floorboards of the backseat. I couldn't picture Van wearing them and wondered if they were a gift from Caroline.

"What are you working on at practice?" I asked, trying to keep up my end of the conversation. It took so much work. It was easier to space out these days, hope to rest my head against a window and close my eyes. The perfume scent in the car that I'd loved so much at first was more cloying than I'd thought.

"Same shit I've been working on forever, it feels like." Caroline wasn't forthcoming.

"Are you excited to dive at USC?" I asked.

"I'm excited to get the hell out of high school, but diving—it's not my sport. I'll give it a try when I get there but I'm not sure where I'm going with it." Said like a kid who had college paid for. "Is the AC too cold for you?"

I had my arms crossed stiffly. "No," I said, and shook my head to try to relax. "I'm good."

At a stoplight, Caroline checked her phone, holding it loosely in one hand. Then she read something of interest because she brought her phone closer and hovered her head over the screen, intent. Then, very unexpectedly, she chucked the phone in the backseat of the car.

"Ugh!" she exclaimed. A dark expression descended over her features.

"What's wrong?"

Caroline thumped her head against the back of the seat and squeezed her eyes shut as though my question and me being in the car had suddenly aggravated her. A car behind us honked and Caroline gave it a dirty look in the rearview mirror before starting to drive. She cleared her throat. "It's my parents. They're all over me because of my grades. Until I get them up, I'm only allowed to use my car to get to school and practice."

So that was why she walked to Van's. "I thought your grades were good!" I thought this because she'd said the podcasts didn't interfere with her work.

"They were. I slacked off once I got into USC. Senior slump. Spring fever. Whoops," she said dryly.

Whatever her parents had said, Caroline seemed really upset. Her forehead creased and she began chewing her thumbnail. I wanted to ask if she was okay but a storm cloud had gathered on her side of the car.

"Is it killing you to sit on the sidelines?" Caroline asked abruptly. It almost felt like she was putting me in her sights. If she was unhappy, maybe she wanted to know someone else was, too.

"Yes," I said. Because that was what I was supposed to feel.

Caroline waved her parking pass and swooped into the parking garage when the yellow gate swung up like a guillotine.

"It's rattled the team, you know. If it can happen to you of all people, it can happen to any of us. And Mike has been out of sorts. He pushes you so hard, but it's like his favorite child is missing."

I dismissed that with a shake of my head.

"You know what I mean. You're important to him. You've made his career." Caroline parroted what my mom had said. "You helped him rise from the ashes."

He had made my career, too. We were both from families with reputations and we were the outliers. I knew what Caroline was referring to; unlike two other members of his family, Mike hadn't gone to the Olympics. He didn't make it past trials. He was the less-talented member of a diving dynasty, which hit all too close to home and was probably why I'd instantly liked Coach Mike. But now he wasn't even thirty-five and he was working toward building a center where kids from all over the country came to be coached by him.

"Just make sure you come back. We miss you."

"I will. I miss you guys, too."

When Caroline and I strolled into the chlorine-scented entrance and waved to the college student working the front desk, Caroline gave me a quick nod, then headed to the locker room to change, her heavy swim duffel flung over her shoulder.

The swimmers and members of my diving team had all arrived for practice, bodies filling in the lanes and milling on the deck by the three platforms and springboards beyond. Caroline always ran late. I was never late to practice but if I were, I would have been so nervous to face Mike's reaction.

When I walked onto the steamy deck, I felt that familiar click. I could breathe again. It was like I was close to something I fundamentally needed. The sting of chlorine, damp swimsuits, the people talking louder and louder over the splashing and echo. It felt like home even more than real home. The chemical smell stayed in my nostrils long after I'd left the center and I used to hear the rhythmic din of the swimmers in my sleep.

When I drew near the divers, I saw Devon on the springboard in a practice suit and Coach Mike, in his usual board shorts and T-shirt, coaching her from the deck. Devon stared straight ahead, closed her eyes for a pause before jumping twice and then launching herself at that perfect angle we all wanted to achieve—about 10 percent away from vertical—then tucking and blindly flipping backward, toward the board, doing a reverse one and a half.

I knew she had been working on her reverse dives. Devon was the second-best diver on the team and of course Mike would be working closely with her in my absence. I both wanted to be Devon at that moment and I never wanted to be Devon again. The thought of doing a reverse and not knowing how far I was from the end of the board was terrifying. As I'd learned, the price of missing those dives was high.

Coach Mike noticed me and pointed. "Hey!" he yelled. "New kids sign up with Ashley!"

"Ha, ha," I said, joining him at the side of the pool.

"What's up? I didn't expect you today."

"I came with Caroline. To say hi." Coach Mike scanned the deck for a moment, presumably for Caroline. Maybe he'd give her a break if he thought I was the one who had made her late.

"Did you see my text about getting a second opinion? Hey, Marta." A little girl from the younger division ran up, wordlessly gave Mike a hug around the waist, then scurried off.

"I did. I'll talk to my mom." There was no way I would ask her to take me to more doctors, let alone pay for them. Mike was usually sensitive about my mom's availability and resources. He'd even stopped the movement to have team bags monogrammed because he knew that was just the kind of thing that would be tougher for some families.

Mike trained his eyes back on Devon. With a start, I realized that without a purpose here, I shouldn't take up his time.

"I better leave you to it," I said, trying not to feel the sting. What had I thought? That I was the best member of the team and would walk in and be treated like a queen? Embarrassed, I realized that was exactly what I'd thought.

"Are you going to watch for a bit? Next time you come, you're going to be suited up or at least dressed for dryland workout, okay?" Mike kept his eyes on the pool.

"Yes, sir!" I teased.

I backed away. Mike folded his arms and I watched him watch Devon.

I knew without me he'd have to focus more on my teammates. But the feeling felt familiar, from even before the accident. I realized that he'd been doing this lately—not quite focusing on me the way he used to. Or maybe it was that he'd pull away and focus on others, especially Devon, as soon as I faltered.

After her next dive, when Devon exited the pool, Mike met her. "Hey!" He sounded brusque. "Why didn't you tell me you could dive like that?" Devon grinned ear to ear. "That's exactly what I want to see from here on out."

Devon was leveling up. I heard my mother's refrain about her own job play in my head: *Everyone is replaceable.*

"Ingrid!" My teammate Carrie came up. Then Alix. They patted me on the back and I was cardboard. Smiling automatically. Quickly answering their questions.

"It's so weird to see you in clothes!"

"Hey, can you tell Caroline I took a rideshare home?" I said suddenly.

"She's late again," Alix said when Caroline sauntered onto the deck.

Mike turned his stern look on us and the small group around me dispersed. Life went on. I was left standing alone, conspicuous.

I felt someone staring at me. Tate and Heidi, two divers my age, stood in front of the plans for the grand expansion to the diving facility tacked up on the wall. When I looked their way, I thought I saw one of them elbow the other, and they stopped talking. I touched the back of my head and then swiftly turned to leave practice.

To reach the exit, I had to cross the deck, as endless as a football field. At the last second before the tunnel that would lead to street level, I changed my mind and slowly climbed the stairs to the stands, picking my way higher and higher up until I could almost touch the ceiling. I wanted to watch for a few minutes, unseen.

Mike's intensity at practice was at a level I hadn't seen for a while. Like he was newly recommitted. Was it because of my accident? Was he creating as many backup plans as possible? There was less joking around. The usual crew of girls circled him, teasing him, but he gave them his back so he could conference with divers one-on-one. The girls had no choice but to drift away.

I understood why the girls thought Mike was attractive, but it was hard for me to see it. He was like family. I propped my chin on my hand and thought back on the actual day, in this building, when Mike told me he would be my family and I'd tacitly accepted.

I remembered it was the winter I turned fourteen. My dad's assistant had called out of the blue to inform my mom that my dad was coming to Austin. The assistant wanted details about my practice the following day so my dad could watch. Of course, the meeting changed, his assistant accidentally canceled his flight, my dad's regrets were conveyed . . .

But I didn't know any of that until later. I waited for my dad to arrive before practice so I could introduce him to Coach Mike and the team. But then practice began and he was nowhere to be seen. I fixated on the swim center entrance for the entire two hours, thinking, *Any minute now.* Then, *Maybe he'll catch the last five minutes.* When practice concluded, I remembered my teammates wandering away in groups, looking like emperor penguins in their long black parkas, and I stayed behind, carefully packing my bag so I could be alone.

Mike was preoccupied with wrapping up practice so I didn't think I needed to say a word about my dad being a no-show. I thought Mike had forgotten about the potential visitor. I was almost out the door and about to cry like a baby when I heard, "Ingrid."

I waited for Mike to call out something for me to work on at practice the next day. Instead, he came over to me. Very firmly, Mike said, "You don't need him. You have a family."

I nodded stoically, trying to keep my eyes emotionless, wishing he couldn't see my chin quiver.

"You have your mom, me, and Laura."

Mike had no idea how often I thought about those words. At the time, I didn't know I wouldn't see my dad for another three years and counting. The only power I had was to let Mike fill his shoes.

Was I still Mike's family if I didn't dive?

Probably not.

Below, the tiny figures continued to dive. Less than two weeks ago, I'd been mindlessly doing my thing at practice, unstoppable and confident, a machine. Not thinking about anything else besides diving. Confident in my place.

I wanted that girl back.

Why did I feel like I needed to find something else before I could find her?

My eyes landed on the half-worn-off sticker stuck to the metal railing: PERSIST.

CHAPTER FIFTEEN

It would be so easy to stare at my ceiling all night. I listened to the crickets and the empty quiet of the house, telling myself to rest. To finally let the thoughts go.

But, if tonight was like every night since the accident, the worries would become obsessive.

I began to make snow angels on top of my bedspread, my arms and legs making whispers across the fabric, debating.

Or—

I flopped over onto my belly. My fingers flew over the screen, typing the quick message, casting a line to the other side of the street.

Are you awake?

We were just two friends helping each other out. He wasn't the Van I'd fantasized about. This was the real version and everyone knew reality couldn't possibly live up to the fantasy.

Downstairs, the back door creaked opened. Then I heard

the footfall on the stairs. I counted slowly to ten but my heart wouldn't stop racing.

When Van appeared, I tried to contain the massive smile about to split my face.

Van grinned from my bedroom threshold. "Hi."

＊

Van was once again seated in my desk chair. He'd kicked off his flip-flops and I was perched on the edge of my bed, reporting back on my Ambien experience.

I cleared my throat. "So I felt hungover—"

"That's exactly how it makes me feel—gross."

I'd noticed Van used the word "gross" a lot.

"Have you ever even gotten drunk?" he asked.

"Um," I wavered. Then I conceded, "No."

The problem with my room was my bed was disproportionately large, which kept putting Van and me too close together. I had a good view of his dark eyes, which constantly changed color. When he was amused—like right now—they lightened, orange penetrating the brown. I was having a hard time finding a balance between not staring and not making eye contact at all.

"What do you and your friends do for fun?"

I was surprised he wanted to know. "Hang out. Go to parties. Same as you and your friends."

"What about you? Do you go to those parties with them?" He was watching me now. I brushed my hair back over one shoulder and he looked away again, dragging one foot back and forth through the carpet.

"Not usually. Sometimes."

"I never see you," he said.

"My friends go to different parties than yours." I'd noticed that when we talked, we got off track a lot. Van always seemed to stop me in order to ask questions—about my friends, myself.

There was a pause and before he could consider the high school caste system and where I fit into it, I continued with my Ambien report. "So, anyway, I'm not even sure if I slept. But then tonight I read something that said insomniacs actually sleep more than they think they do."

"I don't know," Van said skeptically. "I think I can account for every hour."

"You must be sleeping sometimes. Otherwise you would have died by now."

"The weekends have been better for some reason. Maybe because alcohol's usually involved. I guess we could try drinking every night."

"I have to get back to diving. Not ruin myself in the meantime."

"You don't think the break will be good? Go back stronger."

"It's the kind of thing where a break can mess you up. Make you think too much about what can go wrong."

"No, not you. You've always been unstoppable."

He'd surprised me with his compliment. "Ha. I wish," I said.

Van sprang up and stood like a sentry at the window again. He rested the side of his head against the wall. In profile, you could see a glimpse of the man Van would become. Strong, eye-catching. A lot like his elegant father in the entryway photograph. Sometimes I thought of the word "lonely" when I observed Van but it was hard to imagine. He was always surrounded by people.

"It seems like everything is quiet over there."

"It always does," he said.

That gave me the chills because it was true. Besides the one night I'd seen and heard the girl, it was always silent.

"Do you remember anything more?" I asked.

"No. Nothing. I just have this really bad feeling that sits over me, like the hangover from that night never cleared."

Initially, Van told me he wanted to see the house to help him remember. But now it seemed like we were just watching the house and waiting for something to happen.

"Hey, do you want to get out of here?" Van asked suddenly.

"Where do you want to go?"

*

The elementary school playground was four blocks away, under the cover of live oaks and out of street view. Van and I sat on the swings next to each other, swaying gently, both of us holding onto the cold chains.

At first, I was anxious at the thought of leaving my house, but then I realized I had no reason to worry. No one was waiting on me. It had never occurred to me that I could come and go as I pleased.

After pestering Van with questions about where we were going once we set off on the streets, he had said, "Damn, for someone who leaps from a billion feet off of a board into water—not to mention, backward—you act like you don't like taking risks."

"Shut up."

"I should be the one who's scared," he said.

"To sneak out? Why aren't you?"

"I am. But I promised you I'd help you sleep. And maybe a walk will help."

I couldn't tell if he was serious or not. All I knew was it was a lot easier to talk when we were next to each other, walking or swinging rather than facing each other in the close space of my bedroom.

"God, what if we never sleep again," Van was saying, bringing me back to the playground. "I guess it wouldn't be so bad. Look at this. It's beautiful." We both took in the gentle mounds of the greenbelt in the distance. The dark disguised the worn and dated condition of the school built in the 1960s. "I'm starting to think maybe people who don't sleep get to have two lifetimes. The one at night and the regular, boring one during the day. At night you can do whatever you want."

"Don't even joke about it. I have to get it together."

"You have it together, Ingrid," Van said pointedly. "Besides crippling insomnia, you completely have your life together."

"I did. I think I may have developed a case of stage fright. In diving we call it a block," I said, casually.

The steady creek of the swing next to me slowed. I kept swinging lightly, as if that would also make light of what I'd said.

"What do you mean?"

I could smell the iron of the chains. "I'm supposed to go back in a few weeks, but I may not be able to. I can't remember that last dive and I don't think my body will obey if I can't see the moves in my mind. And my mind is refusing to see them. It just stopped cooperating. I've been told what went wrong but I can't remember exactly what happened. And I'm really scared to get back up on that board until I do."

"I'm sure the block is because you got hurt, right? It's because you're scared."

"That's what I'm trying to figure out. It's definitely why I can't sleep. Who knows? Maybe when the concussion heals, all the memories will come back."

I'd told him too much and dreaded that he was about to say the wrong thing and I was going to feel foolish. I hadn't told anyone. Not Coach Mike, not my mom, not Izzie, not the neurologist. Why bother? Only I could help myself. I began to swing higher.

"I don't blame you," Van said. "From what I've learned, diving is about getting as close as you can to hitting the board. So basically, as close as you can to getting injured."

"Pretty much. It's a crazy sport. It's also about getting the perfect angle to maximize speed and height. A coach can help but really, no one can explain it to a diver—how you get there. I can't tell you why or how but naturally, I can do it. Could do it."

"You can still do it."

"I like your confidence."

"Do you like your coach?"

"He's really good. You need someone to push you and to coax you and to be in your head so they can convince you that you have it."

"Didn't you say before that it's mainly about trusting your instincts?"

"Yes and no. There are different types of divers: the type-A ones and then the thrill-seekers who need the adrenaline."

"Which kind are you?" Van asked. For a second, I thought he was joking. I thought it was all too clear.

"The type-A kind. I don't like leaps of faith and just trusting myself. I like careful practice."

"Yeah, I know." He agreed, like he knew this about me. "But you wouldn't have the guts to do it at all if you weren't a little bit of the other type as well."

I looked over at him and gave him a little smile. Van cleared his throat. "I'm not your coach, but maybe I can help you."

"Ha! How?"

"Because you need someone objective. You also need someone who's going through the same thing—insomnia. And because I've had enough therapy to last me a lifetime," he stated matter-of-factly.

He'd surprised me. I felt him waiting for my reaction. "You have a lot of knowledge, Van Tagawa."

"I do," he said, and laughed at himself. "When my dad died, my mom took me every week. Then later I struggled with depression on and off."

"I never knew."

"You were gone."

For a moment, I felt like I'd abandoned him. In hindsight, maybe I had. "Did therapy help?" I asked.

Van cleared his throat. "Probably? My mom moved on quickly when she married Kevin. But it was nice because it was like she was telling me I didn't have to move on right away, too. Did you go to therapy after your dad left?"

The mention sent a zing through me like an unexpected electrical shock. "It was just a divorce," I said. "Not *just*, but you know what I mean."

"Tell me what you do remember about your last dive. What happened leading up to it?" Van asked. He threw me by beginning to swing from side to side, getting too close to me, and I didn't like being out of sync.

I tipped back in the swing so I could make out the playground's black mulch and metal fencing beyond. It instantly bothered my head so I hauled myself up to seated. "Everything was normal. I saw other divers, Caroline, I saw my coach, the crowd. Then I walked out to the edge but I don't remember anything after that." A more complete description would have included the person next to me, with his hand on Caroline's lower back and my incomprehension that he was even in the building.

I knew I sounded deceptively unemotional. I could feel Van studying me. I steeled myself for more questions, but he backed off, gently saying, "Take it easy on yourself. What you need more than anything are delta waves, that deep sleep. That's the only way you'll feel rested and heal up."

"Then what are we doing out?"

"Trying to relax. Break the loop. What's keeping us awake is stress about losing sleep." After a second, he said, "It's funny that we've both mentioned Caroline."

"What?" We didn't talk about school. But now we were talking about her?

"It's nothing. Just a coincidence that she was in both of our stories about when we stopped sleeping."

CHAPTER SIXTEEN

"What are you so happy about?" Colette asked. I'd just sat down at the table to join my friends in the cafeteria. Our table was located beneath the giant painting of a knight, our school mascot. Without asking, Colette moved my backpack from the bench next to her to a greasy spot on the floor.

"Nothing," I said, a little too defensively, shaking the dressing into a prepackaged salad. It was extremely loud, kids eating and filing in and out, but hearing my tone, Izzie and the other girls stopped their conversation. It was rare for me to show any kind of edge.

"Did someone ask you to prom?" Colette smirked, knowing the answer full well. My former possibility had moved on. He'd asked a tenth grader named Harper Brandon.

Before I had to give her the answer she wanted to hear, I saw Colette lift her eyes to someone behind me. I recognized the perfume just as I felt a tap on my shoulder. I tilted my head up and saw Caroline standing above me.

"Hey! Just wanted to see if practice was okay yesterday. I saw you talking to a few people and then you left." God, even her voice was sweet. She was wearing a white cotton V-neck sweater that showed a shade of cleavage.

"Oh, it was great. I touched base with Mike. And I got to see everyone. You were right. Thanks again."

"Of course. Anytime. Sorry you had to get a ride home."

"It was fine."

"Cool. Maybe I'll see you at Connor's party tonight?" Caroline said, referring to someone from her class. Of course, I hadn't heard of any party. I was suddenly stuck on the realization that it was a Friday night.

Caroline wasn't really waiting for my answer. She was just being polite. She smiled and gracefully crossed the cafeteria, turning a few heads in her wake. A band geek made a rude gesture behind her back and when he saw me catch him, I narrowed my eyes and he looked away.

A shadow passed over my mood.

What are you so happy about?

Colette was right—I had been happy. Too happy, I knew. Last night had been the best night I'd ever had.

(A) I'd never stayed out until three A.M. with a boy.

(B) I'd never spent time in the company of a boy who was the number-one person I wanted to spend time with.

(C) It may have been a mistake telling Van about the stage fright, but it felt like a tiny, tiny weight off my shoulders.

Without permitting myself to admit it, a stupid part of me was looking forward to this evening with Van. But I'd forgotten tonight was a weekend night. Undoubtedly, he would be busy. With his girlfriend.

"Which one is that?" Colette asked, gesturing with her chin to my salad. Her refusal to acknowledge my friendship with Caroline spoke volumes. The rest of the table looked like they had questions.

I hadn't even registered what I was eating. My brain was sluggish when I stared down at the label, working to make sense of the lettering. "Santa Fe barbecue chicken," I obliged Colette.

"Watch out. That one has a billion grams of fat."

CHAPTER SEVENTEEN

Early in the evening, Coach Mike texted: *Pizza? Our place? You can come watch and laugh at us old people trying to put together a crib. God, I think I was still skateboarding when you first met me.*

I wanted to sink into Mike and Laura's couch and feel taken care of, but I had to get myself in a better place before I faced Mike. Mike would want to talk diving and he would know instantly that I was off. He'd pull it out of me that I was scared. He wasn't good with scared. He was good with strong.

Instead, I whiled away the early hours of the night at the movies with my friends but, later, I only remembered snatches of what we'd seen. After the movie, on the drive back to Izzie's, Colette said, "Anyone up for a stop at Connor's party?" That got my attention.

"We could," Izzie hedged. "I'd have to lie to my mom about where we went after the movie."

"Text her," Colette said. "Just keep it simple. That's the key to lying. And always include a grain of truth." The car went silent, contemplating Colette's wisdom.

When I looked out my window, at first, I was confused by the sight of trees blurring together like an impressionist painting. Then, my vision telescoped and I couldn't see the road ahead. It was what I'd once felt on a tire swing as it twirled and twirled, the chains entwining endlessly above me, while Van and Wilson screamed with glee. Panicked, I'd launched myself off the side.

I was on the verge of making a scene in Izzie's car, to do anything to get them to let me out.

"Nah, we don't know him. It would be weird," Izzie, the unspoken leader, concluded. "How about that street festival downtown?"

I began to breathe again. Relieved but shaken, I remained uneasy in the back row. It was terrifying how close I'd come to losing it in front of everyone.

Soon I was spit out at the hot, crowded festival. I slapped at mosquitoes as we maneuvered through swarms of people. I scanned the vendors' jewelry with my friends, not really seeing it. The girls' chatter faded as I walked into a cloud of music.

"Oh my god, look who it is!" Izzie said.

It took a second for the song to take form for me. Then I saw the live band performing, the downtown skyline in silhouette behind them. There were four guys onstage. My eyes were drawn first to the massive, dark sweat rings under the arms of the lead singer's T-shirt. But then I realized the lead singer was Van— standing center stage, a little farther out front than the others, microphone in hand.

Izzie was yanking on my arm. I realized I was standing, frozen, watching him.

That gravelly singing voice had become more mature. And sexier. I'd seen Van play before but it had been with his high school band and he'd been the best one by far. This band was good. And this was a big festival. Why hadn't he told me he was in a "real" band? From what I could tell, he was the youngest member. The others were in their early twenties at least.

Izzie tried to pull me up front to dance. I resisted and shook my head. But I met her smile and found I couldn't stop.

God, that voice. And the crowd. I scouted for Caroline but didn't see her. Or the boys.

At the end of the song, Van chugged a bottle of water, then lifted the tail of his shirt to wipe off his face, exposing his lean stomach. And a six-pack.

It was almost funny how Izzie and Preeti gasped.

I couldn't remember the last time I'd felt this happy. The energy from the crowd was so alive.

"Van is *so* good!"

"Oh my god, and that drummer is so hot!"

Later, when we drove home, Izzie said, "What if they get big?"

It was possible. I had the random thought—my dad would have been really proud.

✳

Izzie tried to convince me to spend the night. Her sweet mom had chimed in, worried about me being alone so much. I'd made my excuses. If I couldn't fall asleep in my own bed, it would be impossible in someone else's.

Late that night, I rolled onto my side, still fully clothed on top of my bedspread, eyes wide open, wired from the evening's turn of events.

The phone shook on my bedside table. I flipped it over, hoping but not expecting.

You awake?

It may have been my favorite text ever.

✳

"I think you just fell asleep."

"What are you talking about? No, I didn't."

"Then how come I can do this?" Van dodged right, tore past me, and made a basket.

"You are such an asshole."

"You know you love it!" Van laughed, taunting me.

We were back at the playground and Van had brought a basketball. We'd started an impromptu game and Van wasn't really taking it easy on me, and I was feeling a little competitive. I hadn't expected to hear from him because I thought he'd be doing rock-star things, like going out with his band, hanging out with his girlfriend.

On the car ride home, I'd texted him: *I was at the festival and saw you onstage! You were so good!*

All I got back was: *New band. You should have said hi.*

Now I slapped the ball out of his hands and dribbled in place. "Why didn't you tell me about the band? You guys are so good!" There was a thrill at having him all to myself after seeing him onstage.

Van had showered since the performance and wore a clean black T-shirt. "I don't know. It's a newish thing," he said quickly, a little self-consciously.

"I couldn't believe the crowd!"

"Yeah, well, they're still auditioning me. They aren't psyched I'm in high school."

"From what I saw, they'll keep you around. By the way, how do you have the energy to play basketball?"

"I definitely can't sleep after that."

Van suddenly stole the ball and made another basket.

"Hold on," I said, ready with an excuse. "My hair is in my

face." I walked backward and shook it from its ponytail. Van followed me and came a step closer.

I scooped my straight hair back again while he watched. It was like this with us. One second it was easy; almost as if we were the best friends we had been when we were eight. The next second, there was an awareness of who we were now and we were both overly conscious of everything. At least it felt that way for me.

As soon as I was done I lowered my arms and snatched the ball from Van, catching him off guard. I tore past him and made a basket. Van picked it up and started dribbling, swaying back and forth, back and forth.

Van sped past me but this time I used my body to block him, sick of him running over me. He was bigger and taller, and his chest was hard and solid when I slammed against it. I tripped backward and Van used a hand to catch my back and right me before I creamed myself on the pavement.

"You are not allowed to wipe out," he said, somewhere close to my ear.

My entire body was flush with his and I could hear his heartbeat thudding in his chest. I stood still, caught off guard at the sensation of being close to Van.

We stood like that while we both caught our breath.

Van took a step back first and, wanting to seem unbothered, I grabbed the ball and zigzagged around him. This time the ball hit the rim and bounced off.

"Stop!" he said. "I could have reinjured you. You're such a great athlete I forgot for a second that you're supposed to be recuperating."

My head was in fact not liking what I was doing. I realized that only once the fun and games were over. I bent to tie my shoe and collect myself.

"You okay?" Van came over and put his hand on my shoulder.

"Yes!" I straightened and his hand fell away. "I'm fine!" He kept touching me tonight and I liked it too much. Van consulted his phone. "It's really late. Or really early, I guess. It's four."

"Seriously? We've been here that long?" It was still a night sky, low clouds hiding the stars.

"Yep. Come on. I'll walk you home." Van bounced the ball a couple of times but when we hit the streets, he held it tight. One car passed us and we both kept our eyes straight ahead.

We took a right onto our cul-de-sac. One of the neighbors' grown daughters, a beautiful, twenty-something Asian woman, wearing only a black sports bra and small black shorts, jogged past us, her long, straight hair flying behind her. She didn't seem to think it was odd that we were all out on the streets so early.

Van abruptly stopped.

"What?"

"It's my dog." He jogged ahead.

I expected to see Stella but it was Heidi, the old black Lab Van had had since I first met him.

I caught up to him. Van had squatted down next to the dog, holding her graying head gently in his hands, checking Heidi over, making sure she was okay. Her tail wagged, but otherwise she seemed blind, her eyes glazed over with a filmy light blue. She was ancient.

"I didn't know Heidi was still alive! I haven't seen her in so long." I knelt down next to Van and stroked Heidi's back, so happy to see her even though her scent was overpowering.

"She's barely alive. But she's like Houdini—a total escape art-ist. Or Kevin left a door open. I think he's actively trying to get rid of her." Van rose and Heidi stepped to the side, skittish. "I better get her inside. You okay getting home?"

"I don't know. It's so far away."

"I'll watch and make sure you get inside."

"Van! I'm fine."

"Ingrid!" Then, "There could be something going on next door."

I looked at the house now and felt a strange twinge, like I'd been avoiding something because I was too happy, too preoccupied with Van to want to deal with it. The house seemed to mirror my own state—fine from the outside but inside, something was off.

"Hey, look, Mary's up," Van said.

Sure enough, a backlit Mary Seitzman, wearing a nightgown and a headband with cat ears, stood in her picture window and unapologetically watched us while she ate from a tub of ice cream.

Van stepped in front of me. "Hey, Mary, want to take our picture?"

"Shhh. Okay. I'm going," I said.

"Okay." He smiled.

"Good job tonight, by the way. That was a great show."

I split off and walked across the street, knowing he was watching my movements. I used my key as seamlessly as I could and, before I closed the door behind me, I looked across the street to where Van stood with Heidi, his hand holding her against his leg as if to comfort her with his presence.

When I was with Van, it was like we existed in a different world. A kind of dream. Right now, it even looked like one.

The sky was still dark, but there was a shift in the air, a bridge to morning.

I gently closed the door shut behind me.

Not so long ago, I had dreaded night. Now it was better than day.

CHAPTER EIGHTEEN

"Come on in," Van whispered. He held a toothbrush in one hand. "Hold on." Van leaned into the powder room and spit in the sink. He placed the toothbrush down and quickly rinsed his mouth. "Sorry. Did you get wet? Here, let me take your umbrella."

"I'm fine." There was something oddly intimate about seeing Van brushing his teeth.

I swept past him into the mudroom and took off my dripping tennis shoes. Snacks of goldfish crackers and pretzels and flats of six-packs of sparkling waters lined the shelves. A basket of neatly folded laundry sat on top of the washer. The dryer-sheet scent in the air reminded me of Van.

Van had texted at 1 A.M. on the dot: *How do you feel about coming over to my house? I'm babysitting tonight.*

That was how I found myself being led into a den/media room. A plush gray sectional draped with folded cashmere throws dominated the room and faced the most enormous flat-screen TV I'd ever seen. Beyond the sliding glass doors, the light blue pool was set aglow by underwater lights and shimmered as raindrops broke the surface.

The rear of the Moores' house was mostly floor-to-ceiling glass. Their house backed a cliff, a limestone shelf pockmarked with shallow caves that rock climbers or drunk people on the greenbelt would climb up to. One time a girl, high on something, had scaled the cliff all the way up to Van's backyard and wound up waking Lisa when she pounded on the glass with bloody hands.

"Watch out for the Legos," Van said as he scooped up a pirate ship and a nerf gun. Then he fell back onto the sectional and stretched out his legs in front of him. He quickly moved over to the part without the leg rest. "Here, you take the money spot."

I took a seat next to him, still curious and looking around. I saw a vintage Evel Knievel pinball machine in one corner of the room next to a bar with a built-in refrigerator stocked with drinks. Van saw me notice the bar and stood. "Here, let me get you something. Diet Coke, sparkling water?"

"I'll have sparkling water. Thanks."

"Watermelon, lime cranberry, mango . . ." Van trailed off.

"Mango!" I laughed.

"What?"

"You have a fun house. This room is new. The pool."

"Kevin moved to a hedge fund and things got nicer around here," Van said, matter-of-factly, a little bit like none of it was his. I glanced up at a family portrait on the wall behind me. It was hard not to notice how different Van looked from his family.

Van saw me take it in. "Max calls me the foreign exchange student," he said dryly.

"He must think he's really funny."

"Oh, he does." Van smiled. It was the first mention of Max in a while. But then Van's smile faded, as if he remembered again that things had changed. Max wasn't joking around at Van's house anymore.

"Where are your parents?" I asked, changing the subject, and accepting the drink from Van. We accidentally touched fingers and a shock traveled through my hand. It happened each and every time.

"My mom and Kevin?" I noticed Van correct my use of the word "parents."

"Staying downtown overnight. There was some event for Kevin's work."

"That's awesome that they trust you."

"My mom trusts me. She shouldn't, but she does. Kevin's all over me but he can't say anything."

"Why shouldn't your mom trust you? From what I can tell, you're not out crazy-partying."

Ugh. Instantly, I wished I could take it back. I wasn't an expert on Van. I was well aware that I had zero idea why he waited until 1 A.M. every night before he texted me. His main life took place before then. I was reserved for the time when nothing was going on because the rest of the world was asleep.

Van gathered a throw in one hand, sank into the sofa next to me, and tossed the blanket over both of us. That was a first, being under the same blanket as Van.

"That's true. I've been tied up with band stuff." Van angled himself so he was facing me a little bit and he moved his legs over to my portion of the sofa with the leg rest. Once again, we were touching. Just a little bit.

"You've been really busy?" I asked, distracted. I scooted a half foot over so I could face him more naturally. I rested my elbow on the arm of the couch, which inadvertently put me in a suggestive position, thrusting my chest out. Van's eyes glanced down and back up lightning quick. I would have moved but then I wouldn't be as comfortable so I decided not to worry about it. Van steadfastly kept his eyes on mine.

"Yeah, now I have practice on Tuesdays and Thursdays and shows all weekend. I'm rambling."

"Are you blushing?" I asked.

"No."

"You are! Why are you blushing?"

"Because you're sitting like that."

"Like what?" I teased. Were we flirting?

"I don't know . . . all . . . I'm not used to . . ." Van said, uncharacteristically flustered.

Now my face felt warm. I moved my arm and folded my hands in my lap.

"Never mind," Van said, backtracking and regaining the unruffled composure he always had. "It's fine."

Whatever had just happened, I decided to ignore it and never, ever accidentally flirt with him again. I obviously did it wrong.

"So . . . how'd you find them? The band, I mean."

"It's actually thanks to Caroline. She met this guy at a coffee shop who was looking for a new lead singer. What?" he asked self-consciously when I stayed quiet.

"Nothing! I was just thinking you're a really great singer."

Van seemed to be taking in what I was saying about him like it was the most important thing in the world. "I don't know about that," he said, "but thanks. Kevin's always saying I'll never make any money as a musician, but this . . ."

"Don't listen to Kevin. You're talented."

"Thank you," Van said, and nudged my foot with his.

"You're welcome." I stared back at him and smiled. What was going on with us tonight? All of the eye contact. The rain pounded hard outside, we were cozy under a blanket together, and it felt like we were the only two people awake in the world. I leaned my head back on the sofa.

"You tired?" Van asked.

I raised my head. "I'm always tired. What about you?"

"I am always tired. But I can never sleep. Want to watch a movie?"

Just then we heard the padding of footsteps. One of the twins showed up at the doorway, holding a stuffed penguin.

"What's up?" Van asked.

"I don't know. Where's Mom?"

"Remember? I'm babysitting all night."

"Oh yeah." The twin, Anthony, stared at Van like he was an unappetizing selection. "What's Ingrid doing here?"

"Keeping me company."

"Oh."

"Want me to tuck you in?"

"Okay."

Van stood, knocking the blanket away, and scooped up his half-brother to carry him off to bed. Anthony laid his head on Van's shoulder. My heart expanded just a little bit more, seeing this side of Van.

I finished my drink and anticipated Van's return. When I leaned forward to place the empty can on the coffee table, my movement jostled Van's phone next to me on the couch. The phone lit up, showing his lock screen—a picture of Van, Max, and Caroline in the hot tub at Van's house, a stunning view of the greenbelt behind them. Caroline wore a tiny floral bikini and had a spring break tan. Max's pale, freckled arm was slung around her, curving Caroline into his body. He was looking into the camera, smiling. Caroline was glancing toward Van, on her other side. Van was laughing and saying something to the person taking the photo. Most likely Wilson.

"What are you doing here?" Van's fourteen-year-old brother Adam stood in the doorway, his lip curled. He looked identical to Kevin and already his body was thickening.

I didn't know the correct way to answer, when luckily Van saved me. He showed up and pushed Adam aside. "Go to bed," he said dismissively. Adam bumped into the wall, sending a picture frame nearly crashing to the ground. Van swiftly caught it with one hand.

"You are in so much trouble."

"Go to bed," Van said more loudly.

His brother sneered at him. He sauntered away, disappearing down the Saltillo-tiled hallway.

"I should go."

"No!" Van said, insistent. "No one is going to get mad that you were here."

Because I was nonthreatening. I wasn't really a girl in any of their minds.

"He reminds me of Kevin," I said, gesturing with my chin to where Van's younger brother had just been.

"Exactly. He's his mini-me." Van sounded distracted.

"I'd be careful of him, Van. He's definitely going to report on you to Kevin."

"Don't worry," Van said, covering us with the blanket again and picking up the TV remote. "Kevin can't touch me."

Van's hand lingered on the remote but he didn't turn on the TV.

"What's up?" I asked.

"It just occurred to me—remember I told you how, that night, I thought Wilson pushed me back in the house? And there was broken glass? What if I went over there and looked for glass on the floor? Then I'd finally know if I was in the house that night."

"But there could just be broken glass from the break-ins."

Van shrugged. "In my memory or dream, my *recollection*, Wilson pushed me from the patio down the hallway. I could look for something there."

I folded my arms across my chest. "You really want to sneak back inside the house?"

Van was quiet for a long moment. Then he spoke slowly and directly, like he wanted me to understand. "Sometimes I think everyone is acting completely normal and sometimes I think they're acting like something is up. Caroline was angry and now she's not. I hate that feeling of not knowing what's real and what's in my head. I'm looking for anything about that night. Or something that will help me let it go. I think about it way too much."

I realized that even though Van had seemed in a good mood every night we'd spent together, his deep anxiety had always been just beneath the surface. "I get it. Okay. When should we go?"

At my use of "we," Van's lips broke into a small smile, one corner hinting upward. He glanced upstairs to where his brothers slept. "Soon."

CHAPTER NINETEEN

After the rains, the next day was crisp and beautiful. Sunday was my mom's day off and it was a lovely spring evening. It was new to not look forward to my mom's night off. It had always been my favorite day of the week.

Maybe it was because I felt guilty lying at my neurology appointment on Friday after a short lecture from the doctor on the importance of being honest about my symptoms. My mom had stroked my ponytail while the doctor went through a checklist. Any sleep disturbances? Headaches? Any concentration or memory complaints? I'd said no each time and passed his tests with flying colors.

Tonight, my mom and I ate our frozen dinners together in the big, empty kitchen and she announced she was going to pick up an extra shift. I started to tell her she was crazy, that she needed to have a life, that now I'd really never see her, but then I stopped talking. It was because of the cost of my accident.

If I could go back in time and jump farther out . . . I knew my mom would never want me to feel ashamed but I had trouble looking at her after that. I felt less guilty about lying at the doctor. I didn't want her to worry and it was my job to get back to diving. Especially when she made so many sacrifices for me to do it.

My mom began clearing our dinner. "Hey, what movie do you want to watch tonight? Or we could start a series?" My mom's blue eyes were happily expectant and her face was relaxed for once.

"Oh, Mom—I'm sorry. I have to finish an essay for Spanish. I should have worked on it all weekend."

She glanced over her shoulder at me as she started washing dishes in the sink. "But it's our thing. You can't start flaking on me!" she teased.

"Never." I meant to give her a quick half hug on my way up to my room. My mom surprised me by turning around in my arms. She gave me a long, firm hug, holding her soapy hands away from me. I relaxed into her briefly, wishing I could give her my weight and not worry about being so self-sufficient. Instead, I pulled away first, smiled brightly and headed upstairs.

Coach Mike had texted: *Hey kiddo, how was your appointment on Friday? You ready to do this thing? What do you think of the recovery plan I sent you? Ready to start wading in?* My stomach pinched. In his mind, the resting period was over. Mike wasn't going to baby me anymore. Tomorrow. I'd get on top of it tomorrow.

At 1 A.M., my phone came alive in my hand.

Ready?

What was I doing? Helping a friend by breaking into a house? This crush was hopeless and it was even more of an unhealthy obsession now that I was spending time with him.

I typed that my mother was home, that I couldn't get out. Her sleep schedule was so off that I knew she would have trouble falling asleep. Then I erased it.

✳

We met in the shadows of the home deepest in the cul-de-sac, the farthest down the block from our two houses. After almost having a heart attack from sneaking out for the first time in my life, I couldn't believe Van did it every night. I had expected my mother to appear at any moment and catch me. But her door stayed shut and I kept going. There was still the matter of getting back in. My heart was calming but the adrenaline was still coursing.

"Mary Seitzman's window looks right into the yard. Maybe we wait until she's at her dad's?" Van seemed reluctant.

"I think she's there tonight. She goes on Saturdays and Sundays. What are you scared of?" I asked, hands on hips, staring directly at him.

Van gave me an *Isn't it obvious?* look.

I realized I was standing and sounding exactly like my coach. I smiled to myself. Some things were drilled into you.

I softened. "I don't mean that in a mean way—okay, maybe a little—but what's up? Really."

Van didn't break eye contact. "I don't know. Maybe I'm scared to remember."

"No matter what, it will help you move forward. The only way out is through."

"Sometimes there's not a way through. What happens stays with you."

I didn't like that sentiment. I'd been taught to focus on what was ahead of me.

"Okay." Van stared at the house, sizing it up like they were enemies.

"We can't stay for long. I'm worried about my mom catching me."

"Let me walk you home, then. I don't want to get you in trouble."

"No. That's not what I meant. It's fine. Come on." I had déjà vu, recalling all the times I'd once said *Come on, Van* when he'd wanted to hang back.

"This isn't you daring me to try some stupid skate trick. This is breaking and entering."

"Van, I won't let anything happen to you." It slipped out but I meant it. I'd always been the fearless one.

I thought he would think I was mocking him. Instead, Van smiled at my use of his name. "Okay, *Ingrid.*"

Van walked ahead of me back onto the sidewalk, out of the shadows. I followed, having to take quick steps to keep up with his long, fast strides. Van noticed and slowed his pace.

The temperature was precipitously dropping, an irrational dip in the April Texas weather. "Let me give you my sweatshirt," Van whispered.

"I'm good."

"Here!" He unzipped it and thrust it at me. I swiftly put on the gray hoodie from Van's old sleepaway camp and was wrapped in his scent.

We took the gate on the opposite side from my house, next to Mary Seitzman's. It opened smoothly. We cut through bristly weeds that had grown up tall in the pea gravel and lined the path leading to the wide backyard. Van edged around two lawn mowers pushed up against the side of the brick house. I was surprised no one had taken those, too.

My shin accidentally connected with an old sprinkler head

and my foot caught. When I tripped, I put out my hand and accidentally touched Van's back. He startled.

"You okay?" He reached a hand back to me.

"Fine," I breathed. Van dropped his hand to his side.

We paused at the sliding glass door, listening for a heartbeat inside the house.

"I don't think anyone's in there," I said.

Van waited a moment longer before seeming to agree with me. "Okay."

The police had most likely locked it and we could turn around. Now I wasn't sure about doing this. The vibe of the house was strange, disturbing.

Van tried the door and miraculously, it slid open.

We walked directly into a tiled room that held residual heat. The odor was musty and sour, like soiled, old furniture had baked in the sun and released the scents it had absorbed. A TV was missing in the corner—all that was left was the partially ripped-out arm mounted to the wall. Wires hung from two corners where someone had jacked the speakers. I caught sight of Disney princesses on DVD case covers scattered on the tile by an old pool table. A dog bed was tucked into one corner.

Van crouched low and used his phone to light the floor. "From the backyard, if I was pushed, it was through this room, down this hallway."

"Careful with the light," I said.

The light didn't catch any sparkles of glass on the smooth tile.

"This way." Van took the two steps that led up to a narrow hallway covered in shag carpet. He shone his flashlight but the carpet was thick and could have disguised anything except the largest shards. Van began running both hands through it before sitting back on his haunches. "Nothing." I couldn't tell if he sounded dejected or relieved. "Hey, sorry I dragged you in here," he whispered.

"Beside the things that were taken, the house looks untouched," I said, looking around.

With our mission over, we sauntered to the front of the house where there were more windows and moonlight. I moved the curtain aside and had a new perspective on my house. Even through the thick oak trees, there was a partial view into my bedroom.

Van came to stand next to me. "Could you see me when you came here?" That was back when I could sleep.

"No, your lights were always out."

He'd checked.

I saw the rest of the room as my eyes adjusted.

Everything in the house looked worn, like the family had moved their same furniture from house to house. I again wondered if they were part of a church that had maybe given them this mismatched furniture. They hadn't removed the ancient carpet when they'd moved in. They hadn't repainted walls. But because of its location, the house itself was worth a small fortune. And there was so much packed into every corner: toys, movies, instruments. Beside the sheer amount of stuff, the family had never made the home theirs. It was like they had lived here tentatively.

"What are you thinking?" Van asked.

"It's more sad than scary to me. What about you?"

"That, I guess," he said. Van exhaled slowly.

"Hey, maybe we just learned that nothing happened and you were just passed out. That's a good thing, right?"

"Then why won't Max look at me?" Van said, frustrated. He put his hands on his hips and looked all around.

I sucked in my breath. Van saw it at the exact moment I did. A light had come on in my house. We both edged into the narrow, train-car kitchen. It was where the sour stench was coming from. I wanted to believe it was the garbage but it was an overpowering smell, like something had died in the walls.

My mom was up. She came to the window and looked out, her long gray jersey nightshirt clinging to her narrow body. Van and I ducked at the same time, crouching down together. I wasn't used to getting in trouble. My mom treated me like an adult so I didn't know what her reaction would be if she caught me sneaking out. Not knowing somehow made it worse.

"You okay?" Van asked.

"Yeah. But I'd like to not get caught."

"Just get in the house. If she catches you downstairs, pretend you were in the kitchen. Get through the back door quickly, then you're good. Even if she thinks you're lying, she can't prove it."

He reached over and touched the back of my hair, sliding his hand down my ponytail. "Mess up your hair, look like you've been sleeping."

I shook out my hair. The moonlight glowed through the kitchen window and I could see him clearly. His eyes held mine steadily.

The light went out. Van slowly stood. "Come on." Van reached down for my hand. I took it and his warm fingers grasped my wrist to gently pull me up.

We walked down the bedroom hallway. Van paused at the open doorway to the master bedroom.

"Let's go." I wanted to get out of there. There was something exposing about the bed being unmade, a corner of the fitted sheet and mattress cover yanked up, baring the shiny blue mattress beneath.

Again, Van reached his hand out to me before quickly replacing it at his side.

Just before I opened the sliding glass door, willfully ignoring the evidence of rats, I twisted back to Van.

"You go. I can get back into my house on my own."

"No, I'll walk you. I'm the one who convinced you to sneak out."

"I'm the one who said yes."

We were quiet for a second, our whispering almost feeling romantic.

It was rare to let someone help me. I did everything scary alone. Diving was all about doing a scary thing all by yourself. Van's offer felt good but I didn't want to lean into it. I'd learned not to lean on something because it wouldn't be there to stay.

I carefully slid the door open and we made our way into the wild backyard.

The light in my mom's bedroom flipped on again. Van grabbed my arm and we swiftly headed for the dark cover. Straight ahead, deep in the backyard, toward the greenbelt.

We were knee-deep in brush and there was some ominous skittering next to our feet. Van looked behind us, trying to find a gap in the bramble wide enough for both of us.

"Is there any way we can push back into the woods? Get out of plain sight?"

"No. You remember—there's the chain-link fence behind all this. You can only get on the trail by Wilson's."

Van was so close. We were in a tight space. Waiting. Van shifted and put his hand on my upper arm to position me. There was no room except closer to him. We stood, chest to chest, on the edge of the woods, frozen. I could feel whenever he inhaled. Our breathing synced up.

I wanted to joke. To say *This is ridiculous* and *What are we doing?* But I didn't. If either of us got caught, we wouldn't be meeting again anytime soon.

Staring for minutes on end at one point of light became hypnotizing. I was a zombie, not awake, not asleep. Just so heavy everywhere. My mind, my body. At this point, I didn't know what amount of sleep it would take to make me feel rested again. A week to seriously recover?

"I'll make sure you don't get in trouble," Van whispered.

"You won't get me in trouble."

"Your mom will think I'm a bad influence."

"No. She likes you."

We quit talking. Maybe only five minutes passed, us staring at my mom's ominously lit window, our breath rising and falling. There was more rustling not too far from our feet and I leaned closer to Van. An owl hooted above our heads. A moment later, there was an answering call.

I bowed forward to see if any lights upstairs had been turned on. Van pulled me back just as I saw all was dark. He kept his arm around my shoulders.

I quit breathing when he did that. He was so close. For a moment, I imagined being Caroline. I saw their kiss right before my dive but, this time, I pictured myself being the one curving my hands around his shoulders, standing on tiptoe, and tilting my face up to his while he smoothed his hands down my lower back. Ashamed, I peeled his hand away. When I did that, Van put as much space between us as he could.

My mom's light went out again.

"Let's go," Van said. I noticed how careful he was to avoid touching me. Then he stopped so abruptly, I slammed into his back.

"Ow. What?"

"I think it was a picture frame. Maybe I knocked a frame off the wall and broke it. I told Wilson I remembered shattered glass that night. So, if they really wanted to, they could have cleaned it up. But there could still be a broken frame inside."

I felt bad for him. He sounded like he was grasping for straws. "We have to look another time," I told him.

"I'll go in real quick."

"No. I'm about to get caught. Not now, but soon. Okay? When my mom is working."

"Fine," Van said, sounding reluctant. "Let's get you home."

CHAPTER TWENTY

Hey! I went to a sports psychology seminar in Fort Worth. There's a new, slightly weird therapy that might help get you back quicker. Doesn't require getting wet. Call me.

"Hi! Look what I bought you." Like a game-show hostess, my mom presented a pair of floor-length gossamer curtains cradled in her arms and draping down to the floor.

My brain was behind, still stuck on Mike's text, and I could tell my pause was unexpected, that my mom had looked forward to a positive reaction.

"Thank you!" I scrambled off my bed to take them from her and behave like a normal person.

"Do you want some help hanging them?"

"Sure!" They were what you'd find at a motel, a flimsy insert in front of the heavier curtains that was supposed to lightly obscure the view and the viewer. My mom's head was bent as she went about ripping off tags. When she wafted the length of semi-sheer polyester, she looked like an old-fashioned bride, or a bridesmaid straightening the train of the bride's dress.

When the curtains were hung, they changed the light in my room. It was shadier but the light was also more yellow, ethereal.

"You can still see through. I'm sorry. But it's better than nothing." My mom gave me a Mona Lisa smile I had never seen—kind of wistful, like she was appraising how grown up I'd become. For a moment, I wondered if someone on the cul-de-sac had said something to her about the inappropriateness of being able to see me at night.

"Thanks, Mom."

"How's the head today?" she asked.

"It's fine!" I lied.

Recently, we had been like two ships passing in the night, only crossing for Sunday's brief dinner. When I got home from school, she was always sleeping. I had lain down next to her once since the accident, hoping that being so close to the person I had always wanted to be close to would lull me to sleep. It made me anxious instead; the blackout shades, the gentle up-and-down of my mother's chest in rhythm to the tick of the clock. I used to feel like the child in our relationship but since the accident, I felt more like the adult. Maybe because I'd realized, after the accident, how on my own I was. Or maybe it was because I was keeping secrets.

"You look like you haven't slept," my mom was saying. "Your eyes are all pink."

"I was up late with Izzie. At the movies, then her house." There was a grain of truth in the lie. All of that had happened, but days ago.

She appraised me for a moment. "I trust you."

"What's that supposed to mean?"

"Nothing. Just, I trust you. I couldn't do any of this—my job, our lives—if you weren't you. You're not an ordinary kid."

To me, that wasn't a compliment.

✳

Later that day, I stood at my new curtains, watching the activity on the street. The obfuscation made me bolder and I observed for more than an hour, mesmerized by the show.

It was afternoon and bright and beautiful. The cul-de-sac looked as American and healthy as could be. Kids wheeled by on bikes, Mrs. Kitchen was planting her vegetable bed and various service trucks parked at intervals. Two men on opposite sides of the street used their blowers to push dust, debris, and the confetti of fallen white blossoms farther down the block. Between the noise of the blowers and the pop music from wireless speakers, it was almost celebratory.

I caught sight of Mary Seitzman on the sidewalk below and I raced downstairs and out the front door to catch her. Mary sat on the curb in front of the abandoned house, wild grasses and weeds crowding the base of the mailbox. She laced up her roller skates, happily humming to herself.

"Mary!"

"Hi, Ingrid. I saw you the other night! At first I thought it was Van's girlfriend—I always see her—but it was you."

Oh, great. Well, of course she saw Caroline on our block. Just because I never saw Caroline didn't mean she'd stopped going over to Van's. "We're just friends," I said quickly. "Hey, I was wondering, do you know anything about the break-ins here?" I pointed to the sad house behind us. "Did you ever hear anything? Or see anything?" After all, I'd seen her awake at dawn.

It had just now occurred to me that maybe Mary had a piece of the story that could help Van.

Mary stood, adjusted her black-and-yellow knee socks, then began expertly snaking backward on her skates. "No. It's so weird! Every time the police have been called, I've been at my dad's."

Mary skated to the middle of the street, twirled like a ballerina, and then returned to my side. "Do you think they'll come back?" she asked.

"Who?"

"The family."

We looked to the house at the same time and paused for a moment, as if we were both wistfully imagining a happy family, together, inside.

"I don't know. But I somehow doubt it."

Mary nodded to herself a few times, as though reluctantly accepting reality, and then she skated away.

I saw Wilson and Max exiting Wilson's house. They were both looking down at a large digital camera. Max held it but Wilson kept consulting the instruction booklet in his left hand and then would point out a feature. With knitted brows, they both toyed with the black camera. I was surprised Max didn't tell Wilson to back off and give him some physical space, but Max and Wilson were so intertwined, they were apparently used to being in each other's business. It used to be that Van was right there, too.

I knew nothing about cameras, but the way Max was cradling it, you could tell it was valuable. Expensive new clothes for Wilson, expensive new camera for Max, new tattoos. They were trying to keep up with Seba. I thought about asking Van if he had noticed but he didn't seem to want to talk about Max and Wilson. If Van missed their friendship, which he had to, he never said a word.

I realized I was staring. I made my way back inside and up to my bedroom but once there, I felt the pull of the view and returned to the window.

The opening of the Moores' front door caught my eye. Van came out first, trailed by his three younger brothers and his mom and stepdad. Behind Kevin, one of the twins rolled a black hard-shell suitcase, getting it stuck between each and every paver before laboriously hauling it up again. The entire family waited in the front yard amid their Georgia O'Keefe–inspired landscaping. Van stood a bit apart from the family, off to one side under a mesquite tree, sleeves of his hoodie pushed up to his elbows, hands shoved in his pockets. He froze when he noticed Max and Wilson, watching them for a few long moments. I bit my lip and waited for him to call to the boys, but instead, Van lowered his gaze to the ground and subtly turned his back.

A sleek black Mercedes pulled up and the driver got out, shook Kevin's hand, and immediately loaded the suitcase into the trunk. The twins clung to Kevin's legs and he jokingly pretended to shake them off. Then Kevin put his arm around Adam. Adam's madras shorts made him look 100 percent more country club than Van. Kevin was shorter than Adam but he managed to pull his son's head down to plant a kiss on top of his blond curly hair.

In a messed-up family tableau, the five Moores stood together while Van was a distance away, now typing on his phone. In an attempt to include him, Lisa called Van over to come say good-bye. Kevin waited, seeming to want to say goodbye to Van. But by the time Van looked up, Kevin was lowering his large frame into the luxury vehicle. Lisa walked over to Van and tried to place an arm around him, but Van was too quick and already heading back inside.

Van had never been a fan of Kevin's. But I hadn't thought of Van as a loner in his own home. It made sense why Wilson and Max—and formerly me—were like his other family. But now Wilson and Max had drifted.

I glanced over to see if Wilson and Max were still outside. When I focused out over the entire block once again, I saw Max's camera in Wilson's hands and aimed directly at my window.

CHAPTER TWENTY-ONE

All day, I waited for night.

Pieces of dives were coming back to me. Still not *the* missing dive but it was a sign that the block was loosening. It was a miracle given the fact that I was in bad shape sleep-wise. Maybe Van had been right—distraction was good.

It was a joke that Van would ever help me sleep. He was keeping me up at night, which I had to admit was wrong but, if I was getting dives back, something about it also had to be right.

A voice in my head screamed about getting too attached to Van but, from lack of sleep, from neurons constantly firing, it was like I was taking speed. For once I wasn't stopping to think. Not that I could hold my train of thought for that long anyway.

I sat at my desk, a massive travel mug of black coffee next to me. I refocused on the dirty computer screen. We had an English paper due—a long one—and I couldn't work on it to save my life.

The only motivation I had was to compete with Van. He had bragged one night that he was getting all As this quarter, his soccer coach was playing him more, and he was staying up every single night with me. How was it that he was maintaining every aspect of his life—excelling, actually—and making it look so easy? I wasn't diving, my friends had stopped inviting me anywhere since I kept saying no, for the first time I'd forgotten a test, and I'd thrown away my house keys at Chipotle.

There were more worrisome things, like how I'd run a red light yesterday and how I'd end up at a destination but not remember a thing about the drive. I still owed Mike that phone call. I had two missed calls from him since he'd asked me to call him. His voice mails were kind and encouraging, urging me to give this new therapy a try. It was so unlike me—every time I picked up the phone, I found an excuse for why it wasn't a good time to talk.

I had once been the strong one, just one of the boys who teased Van from the higher perch in a tree. If this was a competition to see who could survive on less sleep, he was kicking my butt. But if he could do it, I could do better.

Some of the air went out of my sails when I went back to my paper and attempted to figure out where I'd left off. I closed my eyes and let the adrenaline roar through me. Even if I wanted to sleep, it would be hard to come down now. I was tired but never sleepy.

I heard the swoop of a text land perfectly on time.

Change of plans tonight. You up for a party?

We didn't go to parties together.

Where? I typed. There was a tremor in my hand.

Guess.

It was like when a neighbor has to invite you to their party because they know you'll hear the noise.

Maybe things were getting back to normal with the boys—Max and Wilson were partying that night and Van wanted to join. He wouldn't want me there. I declined Van's invitation and then I had to sit with that.

I stood at the window overlooking the lonely, silent ranch house. Around 1:30 A.M., I saw two figures expertly sneak into the back gate, getting around the loud scratch I knew it made. If I hadn't been watching, I wouldn't have known anyone was there.

My phone buzzed, illuminating my room.

Come on.

I'd thought he'd accepted my answer and moved on.

I don't want to go back inside, I wrote, and hit send. I also didn't want to see him with his friends, getting high. I didn't want to interface with popular, partier Van. Of course he would act different.

I don't either. Just come. I want to look at the frames on the wall. See if anything is broken.

Fine, I relented.

I'll meet you outside.

He was going to escort me.

※

I traded out sweats for a pair of jeans and Converse. I stood in my bra, unsure of what to wear on top, when I heard the downstairs door open. I snatched a random shirt and hauled it over my head. When I looked down, I saw that it was a Swedish soccer jersey my grandfather had sent me last Christmas. *Great.*

I skipped down the stairs and headed through the kitchen where Van stood inside, the back door closed behind him. He was a sight for sore eyes. Today, it felt like I'd had to wait forever to see him, my sort-of partner.

"I didn't want to let the bugs in," he said in greeting. "Nice shirt."

I opened my mouth to explain and then decided to let it go. Van most probably saw me as his sporty neighbor friend, so it didn't matter what I wore or that I was embarrassed.

One hand on the chrome door handle, Van put a finger to his lips and I rolled my eyes, gesturing to him that of course I knew to be quiet.

Van and I were out the door and I was closing it behind me when Van drew up short. Wilson was standing on my property, watching us.

"What are you doing?" Van whispered.

"Seeing where you went," Wilson said in a normal, if not overly loud, voice. He looked from me to Van, as if he was trying to figure this out. Van shushed him. "What?" Wilson said. "You were the one who said Kevin was out of town."

Van shook his head and walked ahead. I glanced at Wilson, who made an *After you* gesture.

Tonight there was only a sliver of moon, and it was so dark, I had trouble making out Van's back. When he opened the sliding door to the abandoned house, it was only moderately brighter inside. Wilson brushed against me. "Pardon," he said. Then he placed a hand gently on my back, urging me into the house.

It didn't smell any better. But now that I knew the layout and that others were present, the house wasn't as creepy, as if there was safety in numbers.

Wilson moved ahead of us so he could lead the way down the short, dark hallway. Van slowed. He gave me a quick backward glance over his shoulder and pointed to one wall. There were framed photos, just like he'd mentioned. It was a Christmas series. From when she was maybe kindergarten age, it was the little girl sitting in Santa's lap at the mall, the little girl standing in front of the Christmas tree, and the little girl next to a dollhouse with a red bow taped to the top.

I took a step closer and gently touched a fingertip to the glass on each frame. They were all intact.

Van and I locked eyes. Then he shrugged one shoulder and shook his head, indicating *I guess it was nothing.*

"What are you doing? This way," Wilson said. Van led us into the front room. With its low ceilings and painted brown walls, the room was a dusty, depressing cave. A phone flashlight was turned on, aimed at the ground but lighting our way. It belonged to Max, who sat low to the floor on a shiny red beanbag that reflected the light. I saw his red hair, and a younger girl I recognized from school sat draped over his lap. Their heads were close together and at first, they didn't seem to notice us, they were so involved in one another, their noses nearly touching.

It was hard not to stare, witnessing Max act so un-Max-like. He wrapped the girl's dark hair around his fist and then dropped a kiss on her nose.

Max and the girl looked up. "Oh hey, Ingrid," Max said with a slight question in his voice when he saw me. "This is Nina." Nina held up a hand in greeting.

"Nice to meet you," I said.

"Hi," Van said simply. He didn't let on if he was surprised by this development in Max's love life. Max had a girlfriend. Or someone he was hooking up with. And she wasn't Caroline.

Wilson scooted past me and sat down in the middle of a tweedy brown-and-green sofa, immediately reaching for the lone bottle of vodka in the middle of the coffee table.

My eyes searched for Van. He sat in an armchair and gestured for me to take the only other empty space, on the sofa next to Wilson.

"What's the occasion?" Max asked Van.

"What do you mean?" Van asked.

"It's been a while. Since the last time we were in this house," Max said. "It's good to see you." Max didn't sound sarcastic. He sounded like he meant it. I didn't know about Van but I started softening toward the boys. They seemed to genuinely want things to go back to normal with Van.

"Yeah, I've been busy with band stuff," Van said, his tone more open.

"You guys want a drink?" Max asked, nodding to the bottle of vodka in Wilson's hand. Wilson held the bottle, momentarily distracted, listening for something. Van took it out of Wilson's hand and poured straight vodka into a Solo cup. He handed it to me and then poured one for himself.

The only advance warning was the whisper of the sliding door. Then, like she had materialized from thin air, Caroline abruptly strolled into the living room, at home even in the dark. It must have taken her eyes a moment to adjust because she carried herself like she thought she was alone and didn't know we were there, sprawled on every available piece of furniture. She drew up short when she made out our figures in the dark.

"Hi . . . ?" Van said, a question in his voice.

"Hey, everyone!" Caroline said brightly. She stood stock-still, taking each of us in. Her eyes landed on me and the drink in my hand. "Hi, Ingrid." Caroline actually sounded let down, like she'd had higher hopes for me.

Van stood up and walked over to greet her. He slipped his hand around her waist and leaned close, whispering something in her ear. She removed the red Solo cup from his hand and took a long drink.

Caroline would never tell anyone on the diving team that she'd seen me here but it made me aware of what I was doing: drinking, not training, not sleeping. Seeing myself through Caroline's eyes was a reminder that diving was all I had. These weren't my friends. Van wasn't my boyfriend. In fact, his girlfriend was standing right in front of me.

I stood up. "I better go," I said.

"No! Stay," Wilson said emphatically, and grabbed my arm. I saw Van take note and give Wilson a strange look.

"What's up?" Van asked Caroline, questioningly.

"Seba let me know you guys were hanging out," Caroline said. Van dropped his hand from her waist.

"Wow. How's it going, Max? Wilson? Things look awfully PG-13 in here." Caroline and Wilson held eyes. Wilson looked away first.

Caroline took a step away from Van to consult her phone. She turned away to type something and then faced us again. "Seba's on his way."

Van murmured something I couldn't hear and Caroline nodded. The two disappeared down the hall and I heard a bedroom door shut tight. We all watched them go.

"Well, they're about to fight or they're about to—" Nina said.

Max looked to Wilson before clearing his throat. Wilson slid farther down the couch and dropped his head heavily to the back. I noticed the beanbag had exploded at a seam and plastic beans spilled out over the floor.

Why had Caroline, Wilson, and Max all seemed to immediately go on edge when they found themselves in the same room together? Maybe she made them tongue-tied and nervous simply because she was Caroline Kelly. Or maybe they just resented the hell out of her because, even tonight, she monopolized their best friend.

"Ingrid?" Wilson said, waving his hand in front of my eyes.

"What?"

"How've you been?" Max asked.

"Fine. Good."

"We heard you had an accident. You okay?" Wilson asked.

"Yep. I'm good now."

"Van said you had a concussion." Any second someone was going to say I pulled a Greg Louganis but so far Wilson in particular had been almost courtly.

"A minor one," I lied. My brain was swimming with what could be happening in the room down the hall. An ache spread in my chest at the thought of them in a bedroom together. I stood again. "It's so late, I really better get back home."

"Oh, wait, let me show you something." Wilson stood, too, and scrolled through his phone. I saw photo after photo of nature shots from the greenbelt. It made me wish we had pictures of those long, golden days when the four of us explored around the creek. Wilson finally found what he was searching for and leaned in close, not seeming to mind that our shoulders were touching. "Look at this one. I took it accidentally when I was trying out lenses. I swear, I don't usually point the camera at your window."

"He thinks he's a professional photographer now," Max scoffed.

It was a photo of me standing at my bedroom window—big surprise. It must have been just before I caught Wilson aiming the camera in my direction. Even I had to admit it was a good photo. It was me in profile. My arms were loosely crossed and I was brushing one cheek with my shoulder. I was almost peaceful, staring out onto the street, most definitely at Van.

"I promise you I was not being a stalker," Wilson said, getting a little nervous when I didn't say anything in response.

"Wow. I mean, it's weird that you took it," I said, joking, "but will you send it to me?"

"For sure."

What was up with Wilson being so sweet? "Can I give you my cell phone number?" I asked. Wilson handed me his phone. His cell had the same lock screen as Van's—that image of Van, Max, and Caroline in the water. Max and Caroline noticeably skin-to-skin. With Max and Nina across from me, I saw the photo differently this time. And I could see how it might be misinterpreted. Max was probably only posing for the camera.

I was putting my number in Wilson's phone when someone appeared at the end of the hallway. We all looked up, alert. The figure paused, watching us, then stepped into the room. It was Seba, trailed by two girls I didn't recognize.

"The party started without me?" Seba asked. He was slightly breathless.

"It's all good," Max murmured, shifting Nina on his lap so he could sit up higher.

"Sorry it took me so long." Seba crossed to the other beanbag next to Max and Nina. I saw Seba kick Max's leg out of the way. Hard.

Seba slouched down into the beanbag and let his gaze drift from Wilson to Max, slowly shaking his head. He seemed to be in a foul mood. Finally, Seba stopped staring mutely and bent his head to light a joint, shielding the flame with one hand. He tipped his head back and blew a plume of smoke to the ceiling. The room seemed to relax, hoping the tension had melted away with his long, continuous exhale. Seba passed the joint to one of the girls who had settled near his feet. Then he produced a second one and handed it to Max. I was thinking how Seba clearly liked the role of Mr. Generous, passing out joints, always playing host, when he pulled yet another one from his shirt pocket. He offered it to me.

"Ingrid," he said. Though we'd gone to school together for years, I was still surprised on some level that he acknowledged me. One of the girls kneeled behind him and began to rub his shoulders. As Van would say, *gross.*

"Actually, I need to get home. Here, take my seat," I said to the girl at Seba's feet.

"Okay, then." Seba half laughed. "Enjoy your night. Take care, you hear?" he said, sickly sweet. Perhaps his bad mood hadn't passed.

"You too," I said automatically. But Seba had already lost interest and was deep in his phone, ignoring everyone completely.

I began navigating my way around the coffee table.

"Hey, Ingrid," Max called out softly. I spun around.

"Yeah?"

"Why did you stop hanging out with us?" Max asked.

The question surprised me so much I found I didn't know how to respond. It sounded like Max actually cared.

Then I saw Van had quietly reentered the room. He leaned against the wall, also waiting for my answer.

Everyone was watching me, including Seba and his friends.

Caroline appeared behind Van. When Seba saw Caroline, he immediately rose to greet her, knocking the girl's hands off of him.

"Walk me home?" Caroline said softly to Van.

"What's up, Van," Seba started in, sauntering over to them.

With everyone's attention diverted to Van and Caroline, I slipped away without another word.

CHAPTER TWENTY-TWO

Back in the absolute stillness of my bedroom, I closed my tired eyes. I could hear the sounds of dogs barking, the muted wail of sirens, and the forlorn bells of a distant train crossing.

I opened my eyes and found my discarded pajamas, then stripped off my shirt. A sudden creaking sound set my teeth on edge. I heard the back door open. Clutching my shirt to my chest, I didn't move. I listened.

I heard some loud, intentional throat-clearing carry from the empty downstairs.

I'd been so confident that Van was occupied that I'd even changed out of my clothes. Quickly, I reached for an old sweatshirt to cover up, hurriedly putting it on and struggling with an inside-out sleeve as I walked to the top of the stairs to meet Van. What could he possibly have to say? He needed to get back to his girlfriend.

"Wilson!" The shocked surprise in my voice shattered the quiet.

"Is it okay that I came in? Van comes in through the downstairs door, right?"

I realized my hand was clutching a handful of the front of my tattered gray sweatshirt. "Oh my god. You gave me a heart attack."

"Sorry, sorry."

There was an awkward moment of silence. Wilson stood tentatively at the bottom of the stairs while I stood at the top.

"Can I come up?" Wilson asked. It was like déjà vu from one of my initial conversations with Van two weeks ago.

Did he *like* me? For a millisecond I tried it on—hooking up with Wilson. Would that same illegal feeling, that Johnny Cash/June Carter ring-of-fire feeling I had about Van ever apply to Wilson?

No.

But I was seeing him in a new light. He was hot; you couldn't argue with that. His body was perfect in that skinny, ectomorph, every-muscle-defined way. Wilson looked like he'd had dinner out with his parents earlier. He still wore a preppy dress shirt but he had changed into long soccer shorts. And the dress shirt was open one button too low. Whether that was intentional or not, I wasn't sure, but it added to his lazy-rich-boy-who-smoked-too-much-weed vibe.

Yet there was a tinge of sweetness in how he was battling shyness at the moment. Clasping his hands behind his back, Wilson looked both nervous and intent, waiting on my answer.

What would Van think if something happened between Wilson and me? Hypothetically, it was interesting to play out.

"Ingrid?"

I was saved by the sound of the back door opening again, presumably Max coming to fetch Wilson.

"Hey!" Van appeared in the shadows behind Wilson. Van

looked to me and then back to Wilson. "What are you doing here?" Van asked Wilson point-blank, an irritated note in his voice.

"I wanted to talk to Ingrid about something," Wilson responded in a *None of your business* tone. Then, "Where's your girlfriend?" Wilson asked pointedly, wanting Van to leave.

Van had been put on the spot and he didn't answer right away, only making me more curious about how he was going to explain his presence.

"I walked her home," Van finally said. But he made no move to leave and made no excuses for being at my house. Whatever the hell they were communicating, it was nonverbal. To me, it felt like a territorial standoff. I waited for Van to have no choice but to turn around and go.

I started down the stairs to do something to defuse the cloud of testosterone.

Van stepped up onto the lowest stair, positioning himself between me and Wilson. Van whipped his head around and looked up, his eyes scanning my bare legs, no doubt noticing my pajama shorts. Then he looked back and forth, like he was imagining Wilson and me together and trying to understand if it made sense.

There seemed to be a moment of indecision in Wilson's expression and I wondered if Wilson really did want to talk to me about something. But just when I was about to tell Van to go away, Wilson said, "I better get back. Pry Max and his lady apart. Night."

"Night," I said. Van didn't say another word to Wilson. The back door slammed a little too loud and we both tensed.

Van turned around to face me.

The wooden stairs were smooth and cool on my bare feet when I pressed them hard into the floor, making my toes turn white as I waited for what was going to happen next. I realized how much more relaxed I was with Wilson gone. Van trotted up the stairs. He brushed past me and proceeded to my bedroom, the smell of clean laundry and pot smoke from next door following in his wake.

Part of me was incredulous in a *Who the hell does he think he is?* kind of way.

When I joined Van in my room, I sat on the edge of my bed and thought about what to say. I bounced one time on the mattress, then settled on, "What's up?"

Van seemed a little manic. He was pacing and running his hands along the spines of the books on my shelf. Not answering me.

We'd just gone out in public together and look what had happened. All kinds of dynamics were short-circuiting.

I lay down on my back. I felt Van's eyes on me. I didn't care that I was wearing pajamas. I was too exhausted and sick of being on an emotional roller coaster. Whether or not they were getting along, tonight I'd seen him and Caroline together. A sighting of the two of them had become rare for me, but they had to have their private patterns of communicating and meeting up: texts, evenings spent together before 1 A.M., ways of being a couple that were outside of the prying, public eye.

"What was up with Wilson being here?" Van spoke at last.

"I don't know. He just let himself in."

"You didn't invite him?"

"No!" I said a little too emphatically. I opened my eyes.

Van's face had relaxed, like we were friends again. "Really? That's bold."

"Why? You do it every night."

That stood between us.

"Do you mind? That I come over every night?"

"I've been counting on you teaching me how to sleep."

"And how's that going?" Van said, laughing.

"You're a shitty teacher. More like a bad influence."

"You think I'm a bad influence?" Van asked, suddenly humorless, and I knew I'd struck a nerve. He didn't like that I knew about the drugs he'd taken. Even though he'd been the one to tell me.

"No, no, of course not," I backpedaled.

"It's not like I'm corrupting you. Well, I guess I did take you to a party tonight. But back to Wilson," Van said.

"Yes?"

"He wanted to hook up with you."

"And?" I was getting offended. Was that so unimaginable?

"Is that what you wanted? Because I just realized I interrupted."

That was some revisionist history. He'd known exactly what he was doing. "Yeah, you got in the way of that."

"Seriously, if that's what you want, I can make it right."

I closed my eyes again. "Don't worry about it."

"Don't worry about it?"

"Yes, don't worry about it."

"As in 'don't do anything about it' or 'don't feel bad about it'?"

"Oh my god, Van! You're making me crazy!"

"You're making *me* crazy!" he said.

I turned my head on the bedspread and opened my eyes.

"I mean, just tell me if you want me to do something or not, because I don't want to screw things up for either of you," Van said.

"I'm not interested in Wilson," I said, watching Van closely.

"Okay." Van exhaled. "Thank you for answering the question."

My phone lay on the side table but I resisted checking the

time. My guess was it was around three. I was thinking about how dehydrated I was, how gross I felt, how crazy. I wanted to make Van feel self-conscious about what had happened down-stairs but I'd suddenly lost my ability to form a coherent thought.

I fished for information. "You walked Caroline home?" It was a dumb question. Van had already mentioned it.

"We broke up."

"What? Why?" My voice got a little loud.

"We never saw each other," he said casually.

I tried not to smile. I heard the whisper of Van sliding a book from the shelf. I opened my eyes again to watch him flip through an old yearbook.

"Which one is that?" I asked.

"Freshman year. Look at you!"

"What?" My mind was reeling from the news about the breakup. Maybe they'd broken up when they went off to one of the bedrooms, or maybe on the walk home. Who had broken up with whom? What was the catalyst?

"You're not even smiling in the picture. Ha, Max looks like such an idiot."

I heard the yearbook slip back into place on the shelf. Another came out. I must have nodded off for a second because Van's voice startled me.

"You look older in this one. From last year."

"Obviously. I was two years older."

"You look good." He closed the yearbook. It made a small puff and he put it back on the shelf. He pulled out another one.

"Are you just going to read yearbooks all night?"

"Yep. Damn, some of this feels like a *long* time ago." Van drew out the word "long."

Then it was silent. I closed my eyes again. The silence stretched and I realized something in the air had changed.

I sat up. Van was looking at one yearbook intently, attractively biting his lower lip.

"Which one is it?" When he didn't answer, I ducked to see the cover underneath.

I dove for the yearbook. Van immediately held it up high so I couldn't get it.

I leapt at it. My entire front connected with his chest, startling Van, who bumped a step backward.

"Give it to me."

"No. But you can keep trying to come get it," he joked.

"Van." My voice was angry. I felt the blood leave my face.

"What is this?" He splayed the eighth-grade yearbook so I could see the spread.

I'd guessed correctly. It was our eighth-grade homeroom photo. Van's individual photo had a giant heart drawn around it. Then there was beautiful cursive writing in fine-tipped, turquoise felt pen: *Ingrid & Van, Ingrid & Van, Ingrid & Van.* And the worst: one mortifying *Ingrid Tagawa.*

"Nothing. I had a crush on you," I said nonchalantly, in a whiplash change of persona.

"You just tried to take me down for looking at it," Van pointed out.

"It's embarrassing!"

Van wasn't laughing. He was staring at me like he was seeing me for the first time.

"What? Why are you looking at me that way?"

There was a long pause. Finally, he said, "Because I thought you hated me."

"When? Eighth grade?"

"Every year."

"Why would you think I hated you?" I asked.

"Why do you think?" Van asked, incredulous.

"I held your hand. Obviously I didn't hate you."

"You took your hand away."

"No, you did."

We stared at each other. I couldn't believe we had just actually acknowledged the incident. That he even remembered it.

"You never answered Wilson and Max tonight. Why did you stop hanging out with us?"

Finally, "My dad. I was embarrassed."

"Why?"

"That whole scene when he left. And then everyone knew about his affair. It's fine now. But back then, it was mortifying."

"We were your friends. We wanted to be there for you."

For a second I thought about what would have happened if I hadn't missed a beat and played with them the next day. Now I realized, too late, my relationship with my friends would have eventually returned to normal and probably been the most stable thing in my life.

"It wasn't me? Me and the boys, I mean?"

"God, no. Maybe Max. I thought he might say stuff."

"I wouldn't have let that happen."

I shrugged. I wanted to joke and say something sarcastic like, *My hero*, but my throat had constricted.

Van held up the yearbook. "Tell me about your crush." His voice was light and joking.

"Nothing! I can't remember."

"'Ingrid Tagawa.'"

"Shut up." I sat back down on the edge of the bed.

"This entire time, until you walked into my bedroom two weeks ago, I thought it was me. That I'd done something. You realize you walk around like I'm dead to you, right?"

"You have so many friends." I wasn't sure what to say. I couldn't believe he'd even noticed.

"No one likes it when someone hates them. Especially someone like you."

"If you were worried about it, you could have spoken to me! It's not like you were coming up to me."

"You really think I was going to go up to you? You're scary, Ingrid."

"How in the world am I scary?"

"You're an elite athlete, you're not friendly. You could probably kick my ass."

"How could I hate you, Van?" It came out a little husky.

Van walked over to the bed and I held my breath. He kicked off his shoes and lay back on the bed, putting his head on my favorite pillow.

"Lie down."

"You're ordering me around."

"Just lie down."

"Why?" He didn't mean . . .

"I don't know. To try to sleep, maybe?"

"Don't you have to go?"

"I don't want to go this second."

"Okaaay."

"In a few minutes, I'll leave. I'm so fucking tired."

I lay down next to him, the usual foot of space between us. When had it happened that it wasn't weird for Van Tagawa to tell me to lie down next to him in my own bed? Also, he knew my vulnerability—that I'd had feelings for him—but he was making me feel like everything was normal and natural.

And who knew that for all these years, he'd actually cared.

CHAPTER TWENTY-THREE

"Ingrid."

When the shaking started, I was in the deepest state of sleep. The mattress was firm but my muscles relaxed into it, letting go of everything.

The continuous jostling pulled me up slowly, like being extracted from cement. The left side of my body was tucked against someone.

"Ingrid! It's six." Van loomed over me, his forearm propped near the top of my head. I rolled onto my back and stared up into his eyes. In the lamplight, they were like liquid amber.

I blinked a few times and then stretched full-length. Van touched my head as if he was doubly making sure I was awake now. Then he sat up and threw his legs over the side of the bed.

I sat up quickly, too, and watched his back. I couldn't get over that I was seeing him in my room in the daytime, as if, finally, I had proof that those dreamlike interactions were real.

Van rubbed his face with his hands and shook his head. Then he turned to look at me over his shoulder.

"I have to go, get back into my house."

"Okay," I said, still so dull at the edges.

"Oh my god."

"What?"

"We slept." He gave me a smile that could have launched a thousand ships. It was amazed and relieved and grateful. And even excited.

"Wow. We fell asleep," I said. I'd forgotten what a miracle it was. Sleep was all I'd wanted, and every night for the past two weeks I'd beaten my head against a wall wondering why I couldn't do it. But this morning, before my usual defenses were in place, my first thought had been, no matter what, I'd had last night with Van.

Van located his Converses and quickly tied them on. "We just slept together," he said, and laughed.

It was a joke. It was also true.

Then he looked alarmed. "I shouldn't have woken you up. I'm sorry." He switched to whispering. "Go back to sleep." What I'd once thought of as his rock-star indifference wasn't accurate. He was so caring.

Van halted his rush and paused, looking down on me as if he wanted to hold the moment for one more second. He gave me a half smile. Then he left.

✳

By the time I was dressed, I felt like a million dollars. In the mirror, my eyes were bright and my skin had plumped out and looked clear again. Apparently, some renewal process happened when you slept. Without it, you just kept withdrawing from the bank.

My mom came in from her shift just as I was grabbing my school bag. Amazingly enough I had located my keys in no time at all, remembering they were in my shorts pocket from the day before.

"Hey! You look happy." My mom put a graceful arm around me and pulled me close for a quick squeeze.

"I am. I slept really well," I said. I reached up and stretched, pointing my fingers as if to touch the ceiling.

But my mom was already distracted, doing three things at once as usual. She shimmied her purse off her shoulder onto the countertop, put her sunglasses in the junk drawer, opened the dishwasher and put her travel mug inside, only to find the dishes were clean. She stepped back, took off her stethoscope, and began to unload.

"Mom, go to bed, I'll do that when I get home." She glanced up at me and, for a second, it was like looking at my own reflection, she was so tired.

With a clatter, my mom collected a stack of royal-blue plates. "No, no. I've got this. Your job is to go to school, get As, and place at Nationals."

She reached up and put the dishes away on a cupboard shelf. When she lowered her heels to the ground, she looked over, surprised to see me standing there, frozen. She smiled gently. "Go, I'm making you late."

✳

Izzie and I met in the hallway just before lunch. I experienced a wave of such intense well-being, I linked my arm through Izzie's. She gave me a funny look.

As our hall converged with a tributary of traffic from the west wing, Colette, Preeti, and Molly seamlessly joined us, our small cluster swimming its way to lunch.

I'd worn my hair down for once and just as I brushed it from my face, I saw Van coming from the other direction, walking toward us, his characteristic slight swagger back in place. He saw me just as I saw him and instead of looking away, we continued to very obviously hold eye contact. He gave me a self-satisfied smile and I found myself grinning in return. We were both proud we'd finally beat the thing that had been beating us. If either of us were high-fivers, that would have taken place. Even as we passed one another, both of us continued smiling, me even turning my head a little over my shoulder to watch him pass while he did the same.

I faced forward again, my smile still in place.

"What the hell was that?" Colette asked.

I realized the girls were looking at me.

"Nothing," I said.

"What? That wasn't nothing," Izzie said. "That was Van Tagawa."

"He's my neighbor," I said dismissively.

"You told me you don't even speak to each other. That he's too snobby. Is this why you've been acting so weird?" Izzie asked, on the verge of sounding pissed.

"No." I shook my head. "Trust me. It's nothing." It wasn't a lie.

Izzie stopped inspecting me so closely. "Man, Van Tagawa is everywhere today. I heard he and Caroline broke up."

"Seriously?" Colette asked. "Did she break up with him?"

"I don't know but I want to find out. Who's Van going to prom with now? It's only two weeks away."

Colette archly raised one eyebrow. "Ingrid's still looking for a date."

CHAPTER TWENTY-FOUR

from: Alicia Roth Sandberg
to: Ingrid Roth
date: April 14, 12:38 pm
subject: Nationals

Hi Ingrid,

Your mom said you had an accident?! I'm so sorry to hear that. I totally get it—once, right before Regionals, I injured my ankle. I just wanted to drop you a note and let you know we're all pulling for you and hope you're on the mend.

The kids are interested in the family sport but we don't have a decent program here, much to your father's disdain. He hates that they are swimmers! Let us know if you qualify for Nationals. We'd love to come and watch this year. Maybe your dad would want to meet up with us. Any chance you've been going to temple? Ha, ha. I know, I know. I can always hope.

Love,

Aunt Alicia

My fingertips lightly brushed the keyboard while I thought about what to write to my aunt, my only vague line of access to my dad. Whatever I said might get back to him since they were close. I tried not to entertain the thought of my dad coming to watch me compete at Nationals. When I was a little girl, that had been my secret dream—that if I was good enough, he would come to watch. It took thirty minutes of gazing absentmindedly at my medals before I settled on:

Thanks so much for your email. I'm doing great. Back to training and excited for July. Would love to see you and the family.

✳

"Now you've been with the same crowd at the same house as the night I blacked out. So I'm crazy, right?"

We coasted down the slight incline on our bikes, side by side, picking up speed. Wind whistled loudly past my ears and ruffled Van's hair. It was magical being out this late on bikes. We owned the streets. Van was single.

"Well, Max seems to have a girlfriend," I laughed.

"It's about time," Van said.

"Does that make you feel better? Knowing he and Caroline were probably never hooking up?"

"It does. It also makes me feel like a lot of the stuff I thought happened didn't. You saw those pictures in the hall-way, too? I don't know what I was thinking. Maybe everything is fine."

"Tell me what you remember again," I said.

Van pointed and we took a right, me falling slightly behind him. He slowed until I was right next to him. An elementary school stood on the right and a line of bungalow-style homes to the left. The school's marquee was lit with a dim yellow bulb and advertised a chili cook-off.

"Not much," Van said. "It's more like screenshots. The sliding glass doors and looking into the backyard. Those figures coming out of the greenbelt. And then Max, standing there shirtless, close to a girl who may or may not have been Caroline. Wilson shoving me so I couldn't see. What I don't remember is walking Caroline home and what I could have done to make her ghost me for days."

"Okay. Well, what are some possible explanations?"

"I walked Caroline home and I have no recollection."

"That's one."

"I was passed out and all of this was a really, really vivid drug-induced dream."

"That's another explanation. Also, I've seen the lock screen photo on your phone—the one of you and Max and Caroline and you've obviously been swimming. Wilson has the same one and it reminded me: In it, Max is shirtless and he has his arm around Caroline. You see it every day, constantly. Maybe you mixed that into a dream?"

Van sounded happy when he said, "That's totally possible."

"And with the shove? That night you could have been staggering around, so messed up, that Wilson wanted you to lie down. Where did you wake up?"

"On the floor in my bedroom. In vomit."

"Oh, wow." I had to duck so I didn't get smacked by a tall Pride of Barbados plant arching into the road.

"Careful! Sorry to be gross. Just giving you the full picture."

Van's voice was unconcerned and almost joking. It had been a theme, though—a few comments here and there about how shocked I must have been by his behavior.

"You know I don't think you're a delinquent, right? Max and Wilson, I wouldn't necessarily say the same," I half joked.

"Yeah, I can't keep up."

I almost mocked him—he was out every night between 1 and 4 A.M. But I let him save face. It was his excuse for why his friends were getting ahead of him.

"Do you mind—that Max and Wilson are, I don't know, I guess 'changing' would be the right word?" I held my legs out to the sides as we traveled down a small hill, feeling like a kid again.

"If I could go back in time, I would. To before Caroline, even before the band. When things were normal."

After weeks of saying very little, that said it all about how much he missed his friends.

"I also care that Wilson is showing up at your house uninvited."

I looked over at Van. He was on his bike next to me, his eyes on the broad city street up ahead, glowing signage in the distance. We'd almost made it out of the neighborhood. It had been his idea to go biking, and it took pressure off the awkward question of whether we wanted to try to sleep with each other again.

"Why do you care if Wilson comes over?" I finally asked.

Van's brake squealed as we slowed our speed to a stop and waited for the light to turn. "Did you want him to come over?"

"No! I mean, he's Wilson."

There was a long pause before Van answered. He fiddled with his gear. "You were our best friend. It's weird." He stared straight ahead at the red light on the other side of the crosswalk.

I went quiet and found I couldn't immediately recover.

When the silence was on the cusp of growing awkward, Van jumped in to fill it. "I'll back off if you want me to." Now he sounded weirdly formal. The light turned and he took off on his bike ahead of me.

Because of my celebrity adjacent-ness to the famous stepmother I had never met, I was used to a bit of excessive interest. And I was good at knowing when people were checking me out.

But I never knew with Van. Even when he'd held my hand in eighth grade, I had never picked up on him having a crush on me before that. I had zero radar when it came to him. But now I finally knew how he saw me: I was the friend. I mean, that should have always been obvious so I hated my disappointment. What had I thought? That maybe he was interested in me now that he was single?

Just to piss him off, I didn't comment on what he'd said about not interfering. Let him think I was having second thoughts about Wilson. I liked that it bothered Van. I cleared my throat and caught up to him. "Back to what we were talking about—Max and Wilson are changing, we're all changing, but do you really think they would lie to you?"

"I thought they were acting like something was up, but lately I've been thinking maybe Wilson and Max were just being assholes because I was spending all my free time with either Caroline or the band."

"Then why do you keep watching from my window? What's still bothering you?"

"That I may have hurt Caroline and I don't know what I'm capable of. That feeling that everyone around me is lying to me. Oh, and the feeling that I saw something I wasn't supposed to but I can't grab hold of the memory."

It struck me that what Van said last was exactly what I'd been feeling.

"But, again, maybe insomnia has made me paranoid," Van said, shrugging lightly.

"I think it was the drugs. Now it's the lack of sleep. Maybe we just agree to let it go because we both can't fully trust our minds until we sleep. For instance, I saw a light go on in that house, you didn't. The brain is the ultimate unreliable narrator. It's a mystery." I had the thought: *Or maybe we don't want to know the truth.*

"You're right. I got messed up on something I'd never taken. Then I mixed it with alcohol."

"The house right next to us is creepy. We focus on it because we're awake."

"So, there's nothing going on?" Van's tone was joking but he was also asking permission to let that night go and trust his friends.

"It's just a vacant house that was broken into a few times. Nothing more has been going on there. We would know," I said. "And Caroline is strong. She wouldn't have stayed with you if you'd done something bad to her."

I was aware that we were building a case designed so we could quit worrying. One that provided easy explanations and turned things right-side up and sunny again. Neither of us mentioned the girl who came tearing from the house and into the greenbelt, who, in addition to terrifying me, also vaguely corroborated Van's vision.

"What about us?" he asked.

"What do you mean?"

"There's still the mystery of why neither of us can sleep," he said.

Except for last night, with each other.

"It's a coincidence. Not a mystery," I said. "People can't sleep all of the time."

"You don't think it's weird that it's happening to us both? And started around the exact same time?"

We pedaled in silence for a moment. I listened to the tick of a loose spoke.

"You ready?" Van asked as we passed an empty Shell station.

"For what?"

"The race to the karaoke place!" Van took off ahead of me.

"You know I'm going to beat you!" I yelled after him. He had me smiling again. I pedaled at full speed. He won, but only because he got a head start.

*

The all-night karaoke spot was sandwiched in a mini mall between a dance studio and a check-cashing place. Van flung open the door and stood aside, gesturing for me to go in first. I'd never been and I was skeptical because, when we entered, it looked like a dental office replete with blond wood floors and fluorescent lighting.

"I don't want to sing, Van."

"Come on now! No, seriously, you're back diving in two weeks? This is all going to end soon. We gotta make the most of it."

He'd kept track. My hiatus was more than halfway over. My aunt's email coupled with Coach Mike's now-daily check-in had played in the back of my mind all night. I didn't blame Mike for his increasing intensity. As my coach, he thought it was his responsibility to help me turn the accident around. I couldn't keep making excuses for why I wasn't training in the slightest. I wasn't totally sure why I wasn't. For a second, I imagined standing on the board in front of everyone, then turning around, climbing down, and becoming a cautionary tale.

"Just for a little bit," Van coaxed. "I love this place." His eyes sparkled and he seemed happier and lighter than I'd seen him since he'd first showed up at my front door, paranoid as hell.

Van insisted on paying and I waited, reading the quote on the wall behind the welcome desk: MUSIC. IT'S WHO I AM.

A host who looked like an exhausted K-pop artist led us down a hallway with numbered doors to our tiny room lined with two floral couches and a coffee table squished between.

The microphone stand and karaoke machine were tucked in the corner. When he asked us what we'd like to drink, I had the feeling they'd serve us whatever we asked for.

"Two Cokes," Van said. I looked at him quizzically when he ordered for me. The server disappeared.

"Coke is going to keep us up for sure."

"Just wait." Then he proceeded to ignore me while he flipped through the song catalog. I leaned my head back against the sofa and closed my sandpaper eyes. When the server delivered the drinks and clicked the door shut behind him, Van extracted a flask from his backpack and poured brown liquid into each glass. "I stole Kevin's Japanese whiskey. I'm just going to give you a little bit. I know you're not supposed to drink because of training."

"Really?" I asked.

"It helps. With the singing. And we rode our bikes."

"We can order fried chicken. They have it delivered," I said, scanning the menu card.

"Nah, it's tradition to go to the diner after this."

I sipped my drink and then I sipped some more when I realized it mitigated my preoccupation with my aunt's email and the dread that came with telling lies. I sat back and watched as Van began to show off his considerable karaoke skills. He goofed around, making sure I knew that he knew every word of every song he chose.

"Wow, you're really bringing the house down," I said. My heart caught even as I crossed my arms and teased him. He was impressive.

"Let me have my small moment of glory."

My limbs began to feel liquid and then I was laughing a whole lot. Van kept offering me a turn and I'd shake my head. But I was so happy and felt light as air. Then, when Van took too long to select yet another song, I stood up, wordlessly elbowed him out of the way, and picked one at random.

"Give it to me." I grabbed the microphone from Van, leaning heavily against him in the process.

Next thing I knew, I was singing "Summer Nights" from *Grease* and doing both parts and I couldn't keep up or keep track and I doubled over laughing. We were friends, right? Why be on good behavior. I was sick of perfect behavior. When I straightened and wiped sweat from my forehead, Van was watching me and he wouldn't look away.

"What?" I demanded. My laughter slowed.

Van seemed to shake himself. "Nothing."

"Did I put you to sleep?" I teased.

"I'm just admiring your terrible singing skills." He quickly sat up. "My turn."

I collapsed on the couch and put my feet up on the laminate coffee table. Van, Mr. I'm the Lead Singer of my Band, had the best voice and now I got to hear him and watch him, up close.

Earlier in the year, back when Van only played with his high school band, my school friends had invited me to a party and mentioned Van's band would be performing. I'd actually made up an excuse and told Coach Mike I couldn't stay after practice. For once, I didn't want to be left behind while I watched everyone else go off to have fun on a Friday night. I wasn't disappointed.

So sexy playing his bass guitar, Van with his calm was in total contrast to his three other bandmates jumping up and down and going crazy. I'd stayed in the back where no one would notice me studying him closely—this boy I'd grown up with who'd transformed into someone so talented and self-possessed. And seemingly untouchable.

I was preoccupied, thinking about that night months before,

when I recognized the opening bars of Dire Straits' "Romeo and Juliet," my dad's favorite song. The smile fell away from my face. I turned my head to look at Van, my cheek against the smooth sofa. Did he remember?

Like stepping into a dream, I was suddenly sitting in the back-seat of my dad's fancy car next to Van, my cheek against that upholstery, looking at my dad in the front. I could see his strong profile as he drove us to the convenience store to buy Popsicles, "Romeo and Juliet" booming from his car speakers. All four windows down, my hair flying around me, my dad sang loudly and joyfully, hands smacking the steering wheel for emphasis and making us sing with him. Van and I sang and laughed, thrilled to be in my dad's universe. My dad told us to get over it and sing the lyrics "made love" or he wouldn't buy us anything at the store.

My eyes were big as I watched Van sing.

The past and the present converged in that moment. The barrier between them fell away, also taking down the one around my heart. It was clear Van loved this song.

When he was done, I knew it had grown beyond a crush from afar. I was truly in love with Van.

CHAPTER TWENTY-FIVE

The nearby twenty-four-hour diner was almost empty except for a large table of college-age kids scarfing down their one order of queso and a bedraggled server whose beard was braided with beads. When he took our order, he sat down next to Van.

After the waiter shuffled off, I stretched out my legs under the table, touching Van's feet with my own accidentally. Van didn't move but I slid my feet away like he was on fire.

"What's up with you tonight?" Van rested his head against the booth and crossed his arms. Then he reached into his pocket and withdrew some ChapStick, gliding it on while he waited for my answer.

"Nothing!" I didn't like the overly bright lights of the diner, where he sat across from me and I had to maintain a poker face. I was in love with him. Now I was looking at him differently and I was sure he'd be able to tell.

The diner was his idea. I would have much preferred sailing next to each other on our bikes, in the dark.

Van studied me and then quickly looked away, as if he had seen something he didn't want to notice. He stared out the window into the black parking lot.

In case something was on my face, I wiped at it with my scratchy beige paper napkin while his attention was elsewhere. "What's up with you and Kevin?" I asked.

Van looked back to me. "What do you mean?"

"I don't know. It seems like you two are in a war."

Van shifted lower down in the booth. He took his napkin and wiped away a ring of coffee on the table.

"I caught him cheating on my mom," Van said dispassionately.

"Wait. Are you serious?" I exclaimed. One of the college kids, a lanky redhead, looked us over. Van stared back until the boy turned around.

"Yeah, I'm serious," Van continued. "Do you want to know how people get caught having affairs? They forget their text messages appear on their computer screen." Van kept scrubbing at the stain, not looking at me.

"Does your mom know?"

Van shook his head. "No one does, except for me. And now you." Van raised his eyes to mine in warning.

"I promise I won't say a word. You know that," I said.

Van nodded. He did know. Over the past several nights, we'd sometimes had moments of understanding and shorthand, a product of growing up together. To me, it felt like an amazing relief, that I wasn't alone after all. It also reminded me how weird it was to be in love with someone I'd known since childhood. But that also made it deeper somehow.

"Yeah." Van crossed his arms tightly. "The text popped up on the family computer. Luckily, it was me who saw it."

"What did it say?" I asked, morbidly fascinated.

"Stuff about a night away." Van shook his head. "What an amazing asshole."

"He knows you know?"

"Yep. So he's pissed and overly focused on me. That's part of the reason why I stopped messing around with Max, Wilson, and Seba. And then Caroline came into the picture and, between her and the band, I had excuses to avoid them anyway. . . ." Van trailed off.

The mention of Caroline made me want to ask about their breakup. But, of course I didn't. "I can imagine how well Kevin's dealing with this."

Van smiled an evil smile. "You can only imagine."

"You won't tell your mom?" I asked, right as our food arrived.

It took a minute for our server to unload the tray. He was so slow he had to have been stoned and Van seemed to have ordered half the menu, unable to decide between breakfast or dinner. Van reached out his fork and took the first bite of my pecan pie. "Seriously?" I laughed.

"You order better. You go for the thing that's probably the best on the menu."

"It's true." I shrugged one shoulder and smiled flirtatiously before I caught myself. "Your mom?" I prompted.

"I just want my mom to be happy."

"But he's a jerk!" In my mind, the story I told myself was that Lisa married Kevin far too quickly after Van's dad died and then became overwhelmed with kids and quit working. Now she felt stuck.

Van picked at his food, which drove me crazy because it was looking to be an incredible waste. His parents' money had in fact rubbed off on Van in certain ways. "I don't want her to lose husband number two. She loves him—which I've never understood, but okay. He's a good dad to his kids. And he's tried with me."

"It's like you have two separate families in one house," I said. "I might be making that up." I retreated quickly, not wanting to let on that I'd been observing their dynamics from afar.

"No, you're right. We do. Kevin has always wanted to parent me and it makes him insane that I won't let him. It'll be fine— one more year and I'll be out of his hair. It will just be his family in the house."

"They're your family, too," I said.

"I know," Van said quickly, unconvincingly.

"What if he keeps cheating on her?" I asked, repositioning my thigh off the sticky duct tape used to patch the red vinyl booth.

"He better not," Van said with an *I'll kick his ass* tone that under other circumstances, I would have teased him for.

"I want your mom to have everything she deserves," I said, maybe a little too passionately. But I really meant it.

Van slid his hand toward mine on the tabletop, his long, elegant fingers stopping just short of making contact. "Me too."

"You know that to the outside world, you guys look like the family everyone wants to be?"

"Ha. Nothing is ever how it appears, right?"

"Do you think we're going to make all these same mistakes when we're older?" he asked a few seconds later.

"No, not us. Not ever." I smiled.

CHAPTER TWENTY-SIX

How many days had it been since I'd slept through the night? I wished I could go back in time and appreciate that last good night's sleep more. But now I was overflowing with endorphins instead of stress.

At school, the hallway smelled like enchiladas. I had taken a different route than usual to my car to avoid my friends. I wanted a break from hearing about prom, smiling politely and thinking about my double life while Izzie looked at me like she knew there was something I wasn't telling her.

"Ingrid," a lovely voice called out my name.

"Hey!" I said in surprise, feeling somehow caught. Why was my first instinct *Oh, shit*? Caroline lengthened her stride to catch up to me. I saw a paperback copy of *The Sun Also Rises* dangling at her side, two of her fingers wedged somewhere in the middle of the book.

"Did you get my text?" She was slightly breathless. She wore black gym shorts and a white T-shirt with a black sports bra visible underneath. Her blond hair was braided and wound into a bun.

"No." I began to dig through my bag to search for my phone. Sure enough, there was a text from Caroline from hours before. *Meet me at the library after school? How about some stairs?*

Did she know about the nights Van and I had spent together? Was she going to confront me? But she didn't appear to be acting any different than usual.

"Did Mike put you up to this?" I asked. "Is that why you're not at practice?"

Caroline looked a bit alarmed. "No! We have a late start today because of the water polo team." She tilted her head and shrugged one shoulder, signaling, *Why not?* "Come on! It'll be fun. We'll do the dryland workout here. You're dressed for it!"

I berated myself for wearing workout clothes to school: black spandex capris and a large gray Adidas sleeveless T-shirt. I knew I always looked like an athlete but my wardrobe was made up of 75 percent gym clothes.

Mike had started emailing workout regimens directly on the heels of the accident. I'd thought it was a joke and ignored it. For no good reason, I'd kept ignoring them even once the staples came out. Even after he'd asked for a training log.

"We'll go to the fields. Come on!" Caroline proceeded down the hallway and fully expected me to follow her lead. She slowed and waited, beckoning me. As if on their own accord, my feet began to move and I walked into Caroline's open arm, which she curved around me. I could not figure out how to say no. Maybe she wanted to work out together because she had made me her project and her motive was entirely benevolent. I knew her free time was precious.

When we reached the fields, you could feel the spring fever energy. It was around seventy-five degrees, clear with a light breeze. A few kids sat on the sidelines and watched various sports, creating little villages. A boy and a girl showed off doing cart-wheels for one another, both of their shirts riding up and neither one of them caring.

Of course the soccer team had to be on the field directly in front of the bleachers where Caroline decided we would work out. Caroline jogged up a few stairs and I skipped up after her. My limbs felt leaden. That was my first warning that my body wasn't going to perform like normal. Now I wondered if I should be doing this. The doctor had said to start exercising slowly and build up. I racked my brain for the right excuse.

Hands on her hips, Caroline turned to face the field, her eyes scanning the players. I came to stand one step below her.

The boys' soccer team stood in a loose grouping to listen to their coach. I spotted Wilson's silky curls and then, of course, Max, who stood right next to Wilson, their shoulders touching like they were conjoined twins. Van was always right there, too, as if the boys had been raised in a litter and they were accustomed to close quarters. But Van wasn't there. I finally spotted him on the opposite side of the group, where he stood with the seniors.

"Just wait," Caroline breathed.

What was this? A ploy to get Van's attention? To remind him of what he'd lost? Sure enough, after a moment, Van looked up. Caroline waved. Van hesitated, no doubt surprised to see us to-gether, then held up his hand. Other players noticed when Van waved and took their attention off the lecture. Like a celebrity used to causing a disruption and then quickly skirting it, Car-oline began to ascend the stairs. With the entire soccer team watching me—with Van watching me—I began to run.

Caroline was like a mountain goat in front of me and I was like an eighty-year-old. I'd always been the best at everything: arms, abs, legs, diving. It was because I worked so damn hard.

And now, I had no idea why I'd let myself get out of shape. I'd had a concussion but it was also like I'd had a mini rebellion. After years of going nonstop, I'd gone on strike.

Within two minutes of jogging up the concrete stairs, close on Caroline's heels, I knew I was in trouble. My chest tightened. When we started round two, my stomach cramped. But no one could know. It was too humiliating to be this winded.

Caroline gave a whoop when we started round three. This was a walk in the park for her. The beautiful day now felt too hot, the sun penetrating and mean. The entire exercise made me aware of how gross I felt physically—no energy, dehydrated, underfed. Insomnia had turned me into a zombie, a sickly night-walker compared to Caroline, the picture of health. On the way down the stairs, I snuck a look at Van and spotted him running fast, his body at a slant as he stuck out his foot to stop the ball. How was he doing it? He kept the same hours I did and he didn't look at all affected. I inadvertently stuck my shoe in a lump of wet, pink gum.

Every part of my body told me to stop. Every part of me burned. I heard Coach Mike's voice in my head: *You get to decide how to end this workout.*

For at least thirty minutes, I shut down my body's panic. I kept going, one beat behind Caroline's path. At a certain point, I blocked out where we were in the workout and went on automatic pilot, not thinking, not talking to myself, just giving in to the rote torture.

When Caroline halted at the bottom and extended a foot up on a metal bleacher to begin stretching, I was almost senseless.

"That was awesome!" She barely had a sheen of sweat on her brow and her cheeks were light pink. "You okay? You're beet-red."

I nodded. "All good."

Caroline examined me, making me uncomfortable. "Pain is

weakness leaving the body," she joked. "I better get to practice." Caroline squeezed my shoulder. "See you tomorrow?" I noticed she didn't spare another glance at the soccer field.

It was a countdown until the moment Caroline was out of sight. When she disappeared behind a rectangular, red-roofed school building, I walked as casually as I could manage down the stairs onto the field, willing Van not to notice me. Less than one second after I'd stepped out of view, I threw up beneath the bleachers.

CHAPTER TWENTY-SEVEN

I stared at the madly buzzing phone, thinking it had to be a mistake that Van was calling me instead of texting. Van had never once called me on the phone.

"Are you awake?" Van used our usual greeting, but he didn't sound like himself at all.

"Of course," I said.

"I need your help."

"What's going on?"

"Can you drive me and Heidi to the vet?"

The clock said 3:45 A.M. For the past two hours, I'd thought tonight was shaping up to be the night Van broke our pattern. When one thirty faded into two, then 3:00 A.M., I'd flipped blindly through a magazine.

"Yes," I said. I wanted to ask a million questions: What had happened? I knew his family was home because their cars were in the driveway. Why wouldn't he wake Lisa? But his *Can you do this or not?* tone didn't welcome any questions.

Van met me in the middle of the empty street. Front porch lights were lit but all the homes were dark inside. The street felt quiet and abandoned, like a set from a TV show about the rapture and we were playing the last two people left on earth.

Van held Heidi and she looked small in his arms. Her grayed muzzle rested on top of his forearm. When I drew closer, I heard the whimpers coming at regular intervals.

"Let's go," Van said. He passed me and began walking to my car in the driveway.

"What's wrong?" I asked, trying to keep up.

"It's time for her to be put to sleep," he said. "She's been crying all night. We knew it would be this week, probably."

Van waited by the door to the backseat until I hopped to and opened it for him. Very slowly, he folded himself in, trying to jostle Heidi as little as possible.

I climbed into the driver's seat, started the car, and began to back out slowly, reversing in front of the abandoned house. My headlights swept over the façade, making the two front windows look like glowing eyes. I put the car in drive and headed out of the neighborhood.

I glimpsed Van in the rearview mirror. He was gently stroking Heidi's back, smoothing her black fur. Van caught my eye. His expression was stoic. I noticed now that he had wrapped Heidi in an old rainbow-patterned beach towel. It brought back memories of her on the greenbelt with us, off-leash, wet from the creek and tearing up and down the steep hills. We would all hug her and kiss her while Van's mom warned us there might be poison ivy on her fur.

"Maybe she's just sick?" I asked. Van still hadn't given me any directions to where we were going.

"She has a tumor," he said bluntly.

"Where's your mom?" I finally asked.

"Asleep. I didn't want to wake her."

This seemed like a strange thing for Van to take on himself at almost four in the morning. But I didn't think to question him. He was acting like this was completely normal, that he was so independent it wouldn't surprise his mom that he'd taken care of this in the middle of the night. That, and Heidi's cries were coming louder and closer together.

"Do you mind driving a little faster?" Van asked, managing somehow to still sound polite.

He directed me to the animal hospital, which was mercifully close, and a vet tech met us out front when she saw the car pull into the emergency parking space. She opened the car door for Van but let him continue to carry Heidi into the building. It was clear she and Van had spoken on the phone.

The vet tech asked if Van wanted to stay with Heidi. Van nodded and followed her out of the small lobby decorated with artificial flowers and pictures of cats and dogs and veterinarians' diplomas. It smelled like a strong disinfectant. They disappeared into the back, leaving me alone in the waiting area.

I sorted through the dusty stack of magazines and waited. And waited. Through the wall, I smelled doughnuts frying at the bakery next door. Which reminded me that morning was near.

The vet tech eventually materialized. She stood in front of me in her scrubs and gently said, "Heidi's passed. Van's just going to sit with her for a few minutes."

When Van appeared minutes later, he went directly to the front desk, pulled out a credit card, and signed the bill. He looked more adult to me than when he'd gone in. Heidi had been in the background of our entire childhoods. Now she was gone.

When Van turned to me, I saw his eyes were red.

We drove home in silence and neither of us mentioned that it was light out. My mom was going to beat me home.

When we pulled into the cul-de-sac, Lisa was out front, searching the yard, madly calling for Heidi. As I let Van out in front of his house, Lisa stopped yelling—surprised to see Van, whom she must have assumed was sleeping upstairs. I watched Van cross to his mom to tell her what he had done.

I pulled into my driveway and got out slowly so I could watch them across the street. I could hear the whole thing unfold. Mrs. Kaplan was dragging her trash cans to the curb and stopped in her tracks at the sound of yelling. The Loves, out walking their two cream-colored standard poodles, inadvertently slowed and the dogs raised their heads upright, at attention.

Lisa was almost hysterically pissed. I heard, "Why did you do that? Why'd you go without me? She was my dog, Van!"

Kevin came out and stood on the grass and began to take over, questioning Van. Van didn't look like he was saying a word in response. Then Lisa walked over to Van's side, the two of them facing Kevin. I heard her say in a *Back off* voice, "It was his father's dog."

"You didn't have to do that alone. You're not by yourself, okay?" I heard Lisa say to Van. She started to cry openly. Then she pulled Van's head to her shoulder and he let her. Kevin walked back to the house while Lisa and Van held each other tight. Belatedly, I realized Heidi was their link to another time, an entirely different life.

"Ingrid?" my mom asked, framed against the open front door, holding herself straight even after a twelve-hour night shift. "What are you doing? Are you crying?"

I turned away from my mom and back to Lisa and Van, unable to stop watching how open they were with their grief and unable to understand why I was jealous.

CHAPTER TWENTY-EIGHT

"Want to take a seat?" asked Dr. Garcia, who had introduced himself moments before.

"Thanks for meeting with me on a weekend."

I'd been in the little meeting room in the swim center only once before, when a parent brought cupcakes for someone's birthday. I sat down in a metal folding chair, across the long, faux-wood conference table from Dr. Garcia.

"Sorry," he said. "This isn't the ideal space." Dr. Garcia had salt-and-pepper curly hair and soft brown eyes. He seemed like a nice enough guy, but I couldn't have been more uncomfortable that Mike was making me speak to a sports psychologist. When I finally called Mike back, I agreed simply to get off the phone.

"I'm not sure how much Mike told you about why he thought we should meet. I use a treatment called EMDR. It stands for 'eye movement desensitization and reprocessing.' The basic idea is to help reprocess a traumatic event. Instead of addressing the memory through talk therapy, we focus on the memory itself and try to change how it's stored in your brain."

I didn't like the words "traumatic event" at all. It made me seem tainted.

I must have looked skeptical because Dr. Garcia gave me a look that said, *Young lady*, and raised his eyebrows. "Hitting your head on a three-meter springboard and having a concussion would qualify as a traumatic event."

He continued, "This is a nontraditional type of psychotherapy that's gaining popularity, especially for treating post-traumatic stress. Obviously, you haven't been in combat or a horrific car crash, but you had a serious accident. What we're learning is that disturbing events can cause anxiety and stress because the memory wasn't properly processed. These unprocessed memories are believed to store the emotions, and sensations that took place at the time of the trauma. When something triggers the memory, you reexperience the alarming parts as well as symptoms related to a traumatic event, like anxiety or depression."

"Would insomnia be a symptom?" I asked.

"Definitely," he said. "Well, before I explain the therapy, if you're willing, tell me a little bit about yourself. You're a great diver, obviously."

"I've worked really hard at it since I was young."

"Mike said you have Olympians in your family?"

What else had Mike told him? "Just my uncle, but my dad was supposedly even better." I realized I'd said that with pride. "But then he quit."

"Why?"

There was nowhere to look in the windowless room. "He left to pursue music. He said he'd figured out everything he needed to know about the sport and was satisfied. One day, he was just done. He 'came to the end of his quest,' he used to say."

"Wow." Dr. Garcia kind of laughed. "He sounds like an interesting guy. Your father must be very proud that you're carrying on the family sport."

I gave him a nod and a noncommittal smile.

"Your parents are married?"

"No. Divorced."

He wrote something down. "I don't know too much about diving. What do you like about it?"

I smiled. "It's pretty thrilling. It's really fast."

"You're a thrill-seeker?"

I shrugged one shoulder. "I think every diver has to be."

"But you also have to have a lot of control?"

"Yes, it's both. You're going so fast but you can control it. It's like you're in this zone, a thrill zone, but you operate it, if that makes sense."

"So the thrill zone and the control zone are sort of the same thing?"

"I've heard it compared to race-car driving. You're going over one hundred miles an hour but you have control and you are also improvising on the spot and relying on your instincts." I was talking more easily to Dr. Garcia than I had to anyone else about diving. Until Van recently, people rarely asked me details about the sport, but I was finding I loved to talk about it.

"Whew!"

"Yeah. It's so fast but at the same time, if you're not patient and you make the next move one tenth of a second too early or tense up, well . . ."

"It sounds scary. You have to be so brave. Do you ever feel fear?"

"You can't think about it."

"How do you do that?"

"By knowing what I'm going to do. You never know how a

dive is going to go but you know how to deal with it. If I mess up, I know how to hip out. Which means I push my hips forward and that positions me away from the board and I avoid getting hurt."

"But you didn't do that this last time."

I scanned his face for judgment but his eyes were kind, even though his words were blunt. "No." I glanced down at a tiny hole in the knee of my jeans and recrossed my ankles, moving my gaze to my checkerboard-patterned Vans. "I must have been slightly distracted. I was so confident nothing like that would happen. That I wouldn't tense up. I was too confident, I guess, and I got reckless."

"What about now? Are you having trouble trusting yourself after the accident?"

Every part of me fought against admitting out loud that this was precisely the case.

"Coach Mike says you just have to believe you can fix the problem," I said lamely.

"You told me what you love about diving. What do you like least about it? Beside hitting your head, obviously." Dr. Garcia doodled a little on the pad of paper in front of him.

"The pressure."

"Competition?"

"The college-scholarship thing." This was safer ground. Everyone was stressed about college scholarships. "There aren't very many full scholarships in diving because diving programs are so small compared to swimming. You can fit, what, ten swimmers in a lane and pool time is expensive. And the colleges have to make sure they give the scholarships to the right people who can perform so their programs keep getting funded."

"What are your hopes and dreams when it comes to diving? Do you see yourself going to the Olympics like other members of your family?"

"No. I mean, when I was young I dreamt about it, especially when I watched the Olympics. I want a full scholarship. It's what I've been working for."

"What would that mean to you? Besides getting into college and having it paid for. Which is not a small thing at all."

"It's been the goal since I started diving. Whether I knew it or not."

"That's a lot of pressure."

"It's also given my life a purpose." I made a face. "I know that would sound insulting to my friends who have more normal lives."

"How have you been doing on the sidelines these past couple of weeks?"

I settled on, "April of my junior year is just about the worst time to be out with an injury."

"Mike told me," Dr. Garcia said gently. "I'm sorry."

Again, I tried to look anywhere but his eyes but there were zero distractions in the bare room.

"Okay, let's chat a little bit about what we're going to try to do today."

It was a long process for Dr. Garcia to take my history and run me through how the treatment worked. Again and again, he said this was unusual, that he usually worked with clients for at least three sessions before using the therapy. But since we knew we were targeting a very specific event we could try the therapy today.

"While you think about the accident, follow the movement of my finger from left to right, right to left with your eyes. You can think of it a little like REM sleep. In REM sleep, your eyes move back and forth and there's a theory that that's how you process the events of the day. In sleep, the movement is involuntary of course, but we can re-create that here.

"I'm going to begin. You follow my finger. Your only job is to be present. You may notice other thoughts, other memories, the movement of your eyes. Just be curious about what comes up."

I watched his finger. I wasn't scared because, honestly, it seemed like a very easy way for a therapist to make money. But I participated. I tried to focus on the memory of the accident.

But, instead of the memory of my dive, a different recollection spun into my mind. I began to relive a morning from seven years before.

I was upstairs in my bedroom, jumping up and down to get into a pair of jeans, wondering why no one had bothered to wake me. Every Saturday morning, I wanted to sleep in, but instead my dad took me with him on a long walk (which I hated). At the end, we would stop at the convenience store and he'd buy me a jumbo-size candy of my choice. He'd hold my hand on the walk and when we got home, we'd play backgammon before he got back on his computer to work.

I wandered downstairs to the empty kitchen. The coffee maker hadn't been started but the sun was bright. I knew my dad was back in town for the weekend, as usual, because I'd heard the garage door the night before, signaling his arrival from the airport. A bunny decoration I'd made sat on the table alongside a bouquet of daffodils. Other than a few pieces of my artwork, it looked like only adults lived in our house compared to neighbors' and friends' houses. Wilson once said my house looked like a space-age airport lounge.

My parents' footsteps came down the stairs. My dad was dressed up, like he had a meeting. My mom trailed after him, still in her pajamas. I'd never seen her face look the way it did— shell-shocked. I stopped moving when I saw it. Just like my mom stopped moving for a second when she saw me.

"Ingrid, go to your room. Now."

"Why?"

When he saw me, my dad said something harshly under his breath but I didn't catch it. He walked past me, into the kitchen, and unplugged a phone charger from the wall and zipped it into his sleek black backpack.

My heart started hammering.

"Wait. Let's sit down and tell her," my mom said.

From the kitchen doorway, I watched my dad stalk down the hall to the front door.

"You are *such* an asshole," my mom called after him. I'd never heard my mom say that before.

My dad continued to ignore her. He swung his backpack over his shoulder.

"Where are you going?" I called after him.

"The airport," my mother said after a long silence. She'd stopped barking at me to go to my room. She stood next to me and rested a hand on my shoulder.

"You're going back to Los Angeles?" I asked in a loud voice so he could hear me, so disappointed.

"No. He's leaving, honey."

"Elsa." That was all he said. Like he wanted my mother to do something with me. That was when I realized he wouldn't look at me.

"Ingrid, he's moving out." My mom stated it bluntly.

"But you live here," I said to my dad.

I noticed the two large suitcases sitting in front of the door. Then, my dad grabbed a small painting off the wall. It occurred to me later that it was as if he'd just had the thought that it would look great in his other home.

"When are you coming back?" My dad's handsome face was becoming blurry. Realizing he was almost out the door, I ran to him.

"Go to your mother."

"Ingrid. Come with me, honey," my mom said.

"No." I grabbed my dad's hand. He shook it off.

"Elsa," he said to my mother. "Get her."

When he flung open the door, there was a black sedan idling in our driveway.

My dad stepped out and managed to half close the door before I stopped it with my foot. I followed him and my mom followed me.

Max, Wilson, and Van were already out playing in the cul-de-sac. *Ingrid!* Van shouted. They'd set up a small soccer goal. They kept yelling for me, gesturing at me to come over and even out the teams. My mom started to cry, maybe because she had given up trying to stop me, and she let me walk down the driveway to be as close to my dad as possible as he handed his bags to the driver. The boys stared. My mom came to stand next to me and reached out at air, as if to grab my dad, to pull him back to yesterday when he was still a part of us. But he was done. He got in the car, closed the door, and they pulled away.

My mom held me in a vise-like grip, tight against her side. In a voice I'd never heard, she said, "Don't let him see you cry. I've got you."

He was there and then he was gone. And everything I thought I knew was wrong.

The finger stopped moving. "Okay." Dr. Garcia sat back. "What did you notice?"

It was like Dr. Garcia had stopped too abruptly and pulled me out of the memory wrong. I felt half in and half out of that time. I had a terrible metallic taste in my mouth.

When I refocused on Dr. Garcia, my only thought was, *I am never, ever doing this shit again.*

CHAPTER TWENTY-NINE

When I got home, I was still in a fog and heavy with a feeling I could only describe as dread.

I placed my head down on my folded arms at the kitchen counter. Why would I ever want to remember what it felt like when my dad left? I was perfectly functional when I didn't dwell on it. The only way out was through.

I was interrupted by insistent knocking on the front door. Worried the noise would wake my mom from her nap, I rushed from the kitchen to open it.

Mike stood on my doorstep. He was wearing a ragged pink polo; light blue, worn-in jeans; and flip-flops. He hadn't given me any warning that he was coming over.

"Hey, I just wanted to check in, see how therapy went?"

He appraised me intently. For a second, I had a glimmer of him standing on the deck below, the last time I was on the diving board. My head still pounded and Mike's visit felt surreal, as if he were a mirage the way my dad had been in the memory. I didn't feel like myself at all since the session.

"But that's supposed to be confidential." It slipped out of my mouth and definitely sounded slightly snotty and I wasn't sure where it came from. I wanted to slap myself to wake up. From the slight rear-back of his head, I could tell I'd caught Mike off guard.

I was immediately uncomfortable. I'd never, ever spoken to an adult like that. "You know what I mean. I just didn't think people told their coaches what went on in their therapy sessions."

Mike took a moment to respond, and then, as if he were carefully choosing his words, he said, "I think that might be the case if it was about your personal life, not about performance."

Over Mike's shoulder, I saw Van's 4Runner zoom into his driveway.

"Ingrid!"

I jumped.

"Are you paying attention to what I'm saying?"

Oh god. I realized Mike had been talking and I'd spaced out.

"Sorry. I was just distracted by my neighbor."

Mike automatically turned to see where I had been looking. Van was slowly unloading his car and making no bones about watching us curiously from across the street. His arms were full with a large box, cords dangling over the side, and Van knocked his hip against the driver's-side door to close it. He sauntered toward the front entrance of his house, looking at us one more time over his shoulder.

"Isn't that Caroline's boyfriend?" Mike asked, still watching Van.

"Yes. Ex-boyfriend. He lives across the street. Would you like to come in?" I took a step back.

While I'd been over to Mike and Laura's dozens of times over the years—to study diving video; for dinner; I'd even been a guest at Laura's law school graduation party—Mike had only been over to my house one time before. That felt like ages ago and also like it had gone by in one second. I could still picture a younger Mike, perched on the living room sofa, hands clasped and elbows on knees, attempting to woo my mom with his enthusiasm for my potential and vision for my future. He was aggressively building his program and had seen me at the pool with my father.

Mike turned back to face me but made no move to come in. "Anyway, you got out of there so quickly. I was afraid you didn't want to be around at practice, that you're dodging the water. Hey kid, if you choose to be at home, I want you doing everything we're doing during the dryland workout but double it."

"Of course." A garage door down the street shuttered loudly as it rolled up. Four small kids on scooters clamored out and began riding in our direction. They stopped in the middle of the cul-de-sac, blocking my view of Van's.

"If your core weakens . . ." Mike didn't continue the troubling thought. "I know you don't feel one hundred percent post-injury but, remember, pain is weakness leaving the body."

I didn't want to hear his warnings because I knew how right he was. My core was undoubtedly weaker and would affect my ability to snap. I was swearing to myself that from here on out my workout regimen would be my primary focus, when Coach Mike said gently, "How about coming to practice tomorrow?"

I was having trouble hearing Mike over the din of the kids in the street. "To watch? For dryland?" I asked.

"No. To dive. It's time."

My entire body locked up.

I watched Van come back out of the house and walk to his car again. I started, "But the doctor—"

"Every coach cuts that time in half."

My eyes darted to Mike's. He had me backed into a corner. What was my problem? Why couldn't I just do what he said?

"Okay? Sound like a plan?" Mike asked, waiting for my agreement.

I either had to dive tomorrow or tell Mike now about the mental block. But once I told him, there would be no going back to how things were between us before the accident.

It was perfect timing when my mom came up behind me, slightly disheveled from her nap.

"Mike!" she said, surprised. "Would you like to come in?"

"Elsa." Mike took a step back. He held out his hand to shake my mother's. "No, thanks. I was nearby and wanted to check on Ingrid. I was telling Ingrid, I think she's ready to practice tomorrow."

My mom shook her head. "I'm going to side with the doctor." My muscles instantly relaxed. I resisted the urge to step behind her.

Mike smiled. "Got it. Okay, we'll take the time. Take as much as you need." His voice was sincere though he obviously didn't agree with what he was saying.

"Let's start managing expectations, though. It's going to be hard to come back after a month. It just will be. You can't expect to perform as well at Nationals as you have because it's coming up soon. But that's okay. There's next year, and you can even take an additional year after high school."

The tough-love approach had launched me into the beginnings of a full-fledged panic. But when I heard Coach Mike's softer, more hands-off plan, it was clear that it was the far scarier one.

"Thanks, Mike. We'll see how she feels." Oh my god, he'd even gotten my steely mother to waver.

Then, in a moment I knew would stick with me for the rest of my life, Mike looked to me and said, "Ingrid, you won't always be the girl who has endless potential."

Mike gave both of us a wave and headed down the concrete path.

When he was out of earshot, I turned to my mom. "I can't believe he said that! *You won't always be the girl who has endless potential.*"

My mom was looking after Mike as he walked to his car. "Don't worry. That was more about him. He's having a baby. He sees his path narrowing."

I watched Mike get into his beat-up gray hatchback smattered with peeling diving stickers, always somewhat surprised that someone I thought of as a god had such a crappy car.

✳

Later that night, my mom called me from her shift, something she rarely did.

"Honey." She sounded breathy, like she was glad she'd caught me. It was 11 P.M. but she didn't ask why I was still up. "I forgot something."

"Sure. What is it?"

"Do you mind moving some money for me? My credit card gets automatically paid at midnight."

I wanted to explain that she could do it from her phone but she probably didn't have the time or energy to figure it out while she was working.

"Of course. Just tell me your password." I put down the canister of cashews I'd been working my way through for dinner and cradled the phone between my ear and shoulder while I washed my hands. I dried them on my jeans and then opened her ancient laptop that sat on the kitchen table. Folding one leg under me, I brought up the website for her bank.

"It's 'Outpost2330,'" my mom said. The address of the house I knew she'd once lived in, high in a canyon in Los Angeles.

"Okay." I took my cell phone back in hand while I waited for the screen to display my mom's account information. "Your computer is slow," I said. I could feel her impatience, various sounds of the Labor and Delivery ward behind her, equipment trills and voices.

"I know. I need to jump. Just move seventeen hundred into checking. Actually, make it seventeen hundred and fifty. Okay?"

"Got it."

"Honey?"

"Yeah?"

"I appreciate it."

"Anytime," I said but she was already off the line. I smiled into the phone. There would always be something in my mom's voice that made me feel safe.

When the numbers of the accounts appeared on the screen, the reassurance fell away.

I was surprised my mom had let me see this. Or maybe she thought it was time for me to see it. I moved the seventeen hundred into the checking account that now contained more money than the savings account. I'd remembered the lone fifty dollars and moved that quickly as well.

I leaned back in the kitchen chair and watched my thumbnail dig into the tabletop, the smallest of details coming into hyperfocus. This wasn't a joke. We were walking on thin ice and I was becoming a person who ignored all the warning signs like a child.

I replaced the laptop near the thin row of glossy cooking magazines from a bygone era. The one facing out was titled *Outdoor*

Entertaining. Next to the magazines was a stack of bills, stamped and ready to be mailed. The top envelope was payment to my diving club.

Outside the wind blew through the overgrown trees and a branch scraped at the kitchen window like a gnarled witch's finger, pointing at me to get my shit together.

I did a sport that must remind my mother of my father every single day. The least I could do was make it pay off for her.

I heard the swoop of an incoming text:

I'm sorry for being hard on you. I don't know how to deal with you being hurt. You know I'm not good at sympathy but I know that's not what you need or want right now. You need to stay strong. Literally. We don't have time for doubts or second-guesses. Everybody has a bad dive. It's what you do next that counts.

CHAPTER THIRTY

"Move over."

Van had suggested we watch a movie together. After what Coach Mike had said in person, followed by that heartfelt text, I knew spending nights with Van was insanity. Van's presence in my room tonight felt illegal.

I'd expected we'd watch downstairs on the sofa but Van arrived in my room with his laptop tucked under one arm.

Now Van was in my bed, legs stretched out on my girly bedspread, one foot away from me.

A very hot sex scene came on and we watched the starring couple make out in a shower. From my peripheral vision, I could see Van simply staring at the screen impassively, no indication that he was uncomfortable. I tried to adopt the same expression. What was he thinking?

"What?" He glanced over at me. For Van, he was extremely quiet tonight. We'd barely spoken.

"Nothing," I said.

Van paused the movie. "Thanks for coming with me to the vet. Sorry to drag you into that," Van said. He sounded like he'd been building up to say it. He unzipped his sweatshirt, balled it up, and stuffed it behind him to add to the pillows.

"I'm happy I was there." When I said that, Van looked me in the eye for the first time all night. His shoulders relaxed. "How's your mom?" I asked.

"She's sad."

"It is sad," I said.

Van nodded and played with a stray thread on my pillow. "Everything changes eventually, I guess."

I thought about how everything had been the same for so long and now, in only one year, we'd be away at college.

"What did your coach say?" he asked.

I slid lower down the headboard and focused on the china figurine of Little Bo Peep that had sat in the same spot, unquestioned, since before I could remember. I cleared my throat and aimed for unfazed. "Kind of a now-or-never speech. He wants me to dive tomorrow. Two weeks early."

"What are you going to do? Or what do you want to do?"

The glow from the computer lit Van's features, making me very aware that we were lying next to each other in my bed. It was almost too much and his questions about my life only made it worse. How was he not worried about leading me on? What did he think girls thought if he lay in bed with them at two in the morning? Did he not know he was attractive? Apparently, he believed I was asexual.

"I got out of practice tomorrow. My mom said no until I get cleared by the doctor. But what do I want? I want to blink my eyes and go back to normal and do my thing without thinking about it like I used to. Oh, and to sleep."

Van half laughed. "Yeah, that would be nice. But think about what we would have missed."

Van had just admitted he thought our nights together were better than sleep, even though we hadn't come close to figuring out the problems that had brought us together. I was still scared to dive and he didn't have any more clarity on his lost hours.

"Why do you think you have the mental block?" he asked suddenly.

It was a question that I may not have been able to answer two weeks ago when I never stopped to think. I moved all the way down on the bed so my head came to rest on my pillow. "Because I trusted myself and then got hurt. I think what's shaken me the most is that I didn't see it coming. I hate not seeing things coming."

Van's eyes grew serious. "Sometimes, if you look back, you see the signs. If you think about it, you see the buildup."

"I have been thinking about it, actually. Maybe two weeks before the accident, I started to make more mistakes. But I'd just correct it quickly by placing myself farther out from the board. In the forty dives during practice, I was still only messing up a few more times than usual. Maybe I'm reading into it."

Van collapsed the laptop and the room went dark. He threw aside his sweatshirt to the floor and scooted down so his head was also on a pillow. He turned on his side to face me. The two of us stared at each other and there was silence for a moment except for the soft in-and-out of our breath.

Then Van said, "I know it sounds like bullshit, but, no matter what happens, you're going to be fine."

"What do you mean, 'no matter what happens'?" I asked, wary. He sounded like he knew something I didn't.

"Just that." But there seemed to be something more that he

wanted to say. Van changed positions. He propped himself up on his elbow, resting his cheek on his palm. When he shifted, Van's other hand came to rest between us on the bed and touched mine.

Did he know our hands were touching? All of my awareness came to that one point of contact, waves of attraction pouring from me. The same thought kept going through my mind: *Why can't I have this?* I bit my bottom lip as if that would hold my feelings back. It was impossible to think he couldn't tell how I felt. But he never gave any indication.

When I'd watched him at karaoke and realized what I felt for Van—that my crush had turned into something real—I'd known I had to get away from him. But here I was, in the dark lying next to him.

Van had taken the place of diving. He wasn't some dumb distraction like I'd first thought when I'd renounced him as my crush, blaming his presence for my fall. He'd become something even worse in the time since. He'd become my adrenaline thrill. Diving was something I controlled. This was even more dangerous because it involved another person.

"Ingrid?"

"What?" I shifted so we were no longer touching.

"Nothing."

If I weren't crazy, I would have thought I'd broken a moment between us.

I cleared my sore throat. "I'm going to try to get some rest." It came out sounding formal and then a long pause hung in the air. We had done everything together every consecutive evening since the police had knocked on my door and neither of us had abandoned the other to try to "get some rest." We'd had a silent agreement that we wouldn't leave the other person alone.

My words had just put a barrier between us, which made

our physical proximity suddenly seem much more obvious and newly awkward. Van's entire body lined up with mine, just inches away.

"Sounds good," Van finally said. I rolled onto my side, facing away from him. I waited for the feel of his weight to leave the bed, the old mattress springing back up to life.

Instead, Van misinterpreted what I'd said—that I wanted to be alone. He drew closer. His entire front just barely touched me, like a seam sewn along my back. Surprised, I whipped my head around to look at him, my loose, tangled hair splayed out on the pillow between us. He ignored my movement and adjusted his position a little bit lower, curving his bare feet under mine. I was completely enveloped by Van. I closed my eyes and allowed myself to relax, to let my feet rest on the tops of his.

I was barely breathing, taking shallow little breaths, my fingers distractedly playing with the softened, worn edge of the top sheet crumpled beneath my hip. I thought about what Izzie had said a couple of days ago: that no one smiled the way Van had smiled at me in the hallway unless they have feelings for you. I tried to concentrate on Van's rib cage moving in and out behind mine, seemingly unaffected, taking normal, long inhales. His lips had to be somewhere in my hair. Maybe this was the position we had slept in the other night. But that had happened accidentally.

I stared out the window I faced. The dark branches of the oak looked almost purple. With the lights off, my room was darker than the night sky.

Van shifted and lifted his head behind me, readjusting the position of his cheek on my hair. I pressed my feet down into his and he pressed up.

"What's your plan for prom? Are you going with John Michael?" he asked.

"No." I started to sit up but his arm stayed me and I settled back down. I felt his smile. I tensed, waiting for what he might say next.

There was a weighted silence. A pause.

I felt the surge, the overwhelming wave of attraction. Instinctively, I turned over to face Van. His lips met mine instantly.

Van rolled onto his back and pulled me on top of him, his mouth on mine, my hair brushing the sides of his face. Somewhere, in the back of my mind, I filed away the stunning fact that my first kiss was with Van.

His hands were in my hair and then traveled over my back. I propped myself up on my elbows for better access to Van's lips and he gently held my face in both hands, his fingertips on my cheekbones.

After long minutes, he swiftly turned us to our sides. There was a split-second pause, both of us breathing like we'd just run a race. When I reached for him, he held himself away.

"Give me a second," he rasped, tipping his head back and inhaling. Then, he lay there watching me as he calmed his breathing. I wanted to know what he was thinking. But he stayed silent, and it seemed like he was waiting for me to say something first. I loosened my fistful of his shirt and slipped my hand beneath it, gliding my fingers up the long, smooth planes of his chest, feeling the lean muscle. Van sucked in his breath and his hand high on my rib cage moved lower, curving around my backside. I spread my palm on his bare skin, over his heart. It pounded against my hand.

I let my fingertips trail down his chest and fall away. We stared at each other and his eyes were onyx. Van leaned forward and kissed my jawline quickly and naturally, like we did this all the time. "Are you cold?" he whispered.

"Um—" I started to speak but Van was already reaching for

the yellow flower-print duvet that had half slithered off the foot of the bed.

Any second, I expected the weight of the blanket over us so I could pull him back to me. We still had hours.

Instead, Van came to sit up more fully, his attention caught on the window.

CHAPTER THIRTY-ONE

A golden light suddenly bathed my room.

"What?" I sat up. Then I realized the weak, on-again, off-again yellow light of the neighbor's outdoor motion sensor had come to life.

Our shoulders hovered next to each other's before Van sprang off the bed in one lithe motion. Alone in the middle of the bed, I felt the absence of his warmth. Van took up his usual post, his body tucked against the chipped white window frame, off to one side where no one could see him. I was finding it hard to mentally shift gears after what had happened ten seconds before.

"Come here," Van whispered. I rolled over and walked three feet to stand next to him. Without looking at me, Van loosely wrapped an arm around my waist and then positioned me away from the window and closer to him. I allowed myself to rest my head on his shoulder. He tightened his arm around my waist.

Because we'd been watching for such a long time, it was hard to believe there was finally action next door. It was like staring at an empty horizon for so long that you doubt your eyes when the view changes. When I finally comprehended that this wasn't a drill, I broke away and took a giant step to the other side of the window, both of us attempting to hide our bodies in the dark and just barely turn our heads to see out the edge of the window.

Two people were shuffling in the alley below, their shoes making the softest, muffled crunching sounds in the pea gravel. One of them bumped into a trash can. They froze, as if waiting for someone to round the corner and catch them. They were carrying something low and working together, one person walking backward. They resumed their work.

When he tipped his face up into the light, I recognized the boy as a senior named Jack who sometimes hung out around Seba. And then Seba moved into the light. What was notable was how absolutely silent they were. If it hadn't been for the light, Van and I would still be lying in bed.

"What the hell," Van said one second before I saw for myself what they were carrying, now visible in the puddle of light. I covered my mouth with my hand. A boy's body dangled, stretched out between the two boys who carried him by the arms and legs. They began to back out of the open gate with the dead weight.

Wilson ran up, shirtless, a younger girl right behind him. We couldn't hear what they were saying but Wilson stopped their progress. They lowered the body to the gravel. Seba paced and threaded his fingers on the top of his head, elbows high in the air.

Both Van and I jumped when we heard the jarring buzz of Van's phone, vibrating on the glass-topped side table. I expected the group below to immediately look up at the noise. Van stretched long to retrieve the phone. He looked at the caller. "What?" he answered harshly. Then, Van walked out in front of the window, in full view.

Below, I watched as Wilson spoke into his phone while he

looked in the direction of Van's house across the street. I heard his voice clearly through the phone, an eerie sensation when we were peering right at him. "I need your help," Wilson said. He sounded extremely calm. "I'm across the street." Then, as if he sensed Van, Wilson looked up at my window.

Van took the stairs two at a time with me right on his heels. He fumbled with the back door's lock so I took over and flung the door open. With bare feet, we tore over the prickly oak leaves, down the alley between the houses. When we pushed opened the gate, the small group stood waiting for Van, taut and desperate.

Max's body was splayed out on the gravel. Van immediately kneeled and put his hand on Max's chest and then began to slap his cheeks. I knelt on Max's other side. His breath was shallow.

"He's freezing. Why is he so cold?" Van sat fully down on the ground and pulled Max into his lap. "Call 911." He looked directly at me.

I came to Van's side and was fishing his phone out of his pocket when Seba knocked it out of my hand.

"We can't," Wilson said. I saw then that his pupils were scary small. In them, you could see his mind whirling. "You need to take him in your car, Van. Please." I noticed Wilson's tattoo. And how skinny he was compared to only a few months ago, the outline of his ribs visible beneath seal-smooth skin. The girl with him couldn't have been more than fifteen and was obviously high on something, too.

"He's passed out and freezing cold," I said.

"He's fucked up. He's going to be fine. Just try to wake him up," Seba said.

"Wilson, tell Seba to give me back my phone," Van said, deadly.

All at once, everyone started talking fast and pointing fingers.

The girl quickly backed away and disappeared. The arguing was reaching a volume that would wake neighbors and Jack was desperately shushing Wilson, Seba, and Van.

"Let's turn him on his side." My voice sounded like it belonged to someone else. So high-pitched and scared.

"Give it to me," Van demanded, but he was looking at Wilson.

Wilson's eyes looked like he'd just put his finger in an electrical socket. Then he looked confused, pulled between two masters. His sustained eye contact with Van finally seemed to center him. Wilson turned to Seba. "Give it to him, man."

After a long pause, all eyes trained on him, Seba threw the phone at Van's chest. "Get everyone out. Dump everything. It's over," Seba said with disgust, like it was such a shame everyone had to go and ruin his good time. He and Jack left us, presumably to take care of business inside the house.

I picked up the phone by Van's hip.

"911, what's your emergency?"

I cleared my throat and went into the mode I called on when I needed to shut out fear and focus.

"Alcohol poisoning." At the operator's next question, I looked to Wilson. "Did he take anything?"

"Xanax." Wilson looked like a little boy. He scrubbed his arms anxiously.

Van kept slapping Max's cheeks. Max tried to turn his face away and he began mumbling protests but his eyes stayed closed. Still, it was a big relief.

After I gave the information, they told me to stay on the line. In silence, we waited, just the four of us, Max's head in Van's lap, Van's long fingers gently holding the sides of Max's face. I sat on the other side and counted inside my head, waiting for a siren, waiting out the scary-long pauses until Max's chest lifted. Max's breath was noticeably slow.

Finally, like he couldn't help himself, Van spoke, his voice dripping with accusation. "You were selling the shit we found inside the house, weren't you? And throwing parties?"

"They weren't parties. We were quiet. We kept the circle so tight. We just did things and let people use the rooms," Wilson said.

"Like some seedy motel?"

"It was only going to be a few times. Then Seba found the prescription pad."

I sat back on my heels, phone to my ear, and looked from Van to Wilson.

"What really happened that night?"

Wilson immediately knew what Van was referring to. "What are you talking about? You were passed out," Wilson said dismissively.

"No," Van said with such finality that I forgot about the phone and watched him closely. "I trust myself. I trust what I saw." His expression didn't change but there was a steadiness in his eyes I'd never seen before.

Wilson's body language transformed. His shoulders slumped and he looked ashamed, like the stronger version of himself had vanished in a cloud.

"You saw the hole in the wall," Wilson finally said.

"What's the fucking 'hole in the wall'?"

"It's the path. How people came in and out from the greenbelt. It's how this whole thing worked."

"Those are our woods. We know all the trails." Van sounded confused. And a little bit like his younger self.

"We didn't look hard enough. Seba found it."

"Who was that girl I called the police about? The one who screamed and then disappeared into the greenbelt?" I asked.

"A couple in a room had a fight that night," Wilson said.

Van looked at Wilson like he no longer recognized him. "You thought I was so fucked up, you could go across the street to run your business? Then tell me I imagined what I saw?" Van said. "You made me feel crazy."

"We wanted to protect you."

"From what?"

Wilson shook his head, like he wasn't ready to answer. "There was some other shit, man."

"What? Did I do something that night? To Caroline?" Van asked. "Just tell me!"

"What would you have done to her? You barely left the couch."

"Did you guys do something to her?"

"God, no!"

"But Caroline was there in this backyard. She knew about the trail?"

Wilson was quiet. Then, "She was using it, too."

"So, all of you lied to me. Just to do drugs without me?"

Wilson remained silent.

"Why didn't you tell me?" Van asked.

"We just started doing different things. You had your band."

"No, really, Wilson. Why? Both of you could barely look me in the eye."

Wilson rocked back and forth on his heels. Then, finally, he met Van's eyes. "I didn't want to stop and I didn't want you to see."

Wilson sat down with us, by Max's feet. "It was like once I made the first mistake, I couldn't get out of the hole. We just kept getting in deeper. I knew that when you were around."

The sirens became just barely audible. Dogs started barking. A light came on somewhere in the vicinity and the sky beyond the fenced yard became a shade brighter. The street was waking up.

Wilson swiped at his cheek with the crook of his arm and stared down at Max. Max stirred, then pulled his knees close to his chest. I didn't get why Max's head kept moving and then I realized Van's hands were shaking.

None of us spoke. Then Van suddenly kicked Wilson's foot to get his attention. "I've got you." Van's tone implied, *You know that, right?* I watched as Van held Wilson's eyes. "No matter what."

✳

The sirens were faint, and then louder and louder until they screamed down our cul-de-sac. Max's parents, Roz and Pete, were woken up and then everything was a blur of motion as the paramedics worked over Max and calmly asked questions.

When I was pushed out to the edges of the commotion, I backed farther into the dark recess of the overgrown yard. I felt the imposing presence of the greenbelt, suddenly alive to me. Then I saw that the sliding glass door was open, calling me, drawing me into the house.

There was a flurry of movement. Everyone was abandoning ship. The state of the house was night and day from the other times I'd been inside. It was trashed. The contents of a large bag of popcorn had spilled everywhere. Bits of toilet paper were stuck to the floor. Condoms were available on the table and there was a full bar, like they were running an establishment. I saw a forgotten stack of bills on the kitchen table.

My eyes came to rest on the picture frames. Slowly, I stepped forward to take one more look at all three. This time I saw it—it was the one of the little girl with Santa. Up close, it reflected the small amount of light from down the hall a bit differently than the frames next to it, because the glass wasn't as dirty. I dragged one finger along the top edge of each picture frame. A thick film of dust coated my finger from two. I checked the Santa photo last. It was completely clean. The boys had actually replaced it. They were either that thorough or it had become like a game to mess with Van's memory.

I counted six people leave the house. Of the three people I recognized, two were complete surprises. They streamed past me, exiting the back of the house, headed no doubt to the hole in the wall. I watched the outline of a girl's back and for the flash of an instant, I thought I saw her slip into the sheer green block that appeared black at night. I couldn't see much but I could tell she was gone. It was what Van had described that first night—it did look surreal, like something from a dream.

I heard flushing down the hall and followed the sound to the doorway of a red wallpapered bathroom with an ornate gold sink. The windowless, interior bathroom was the only fully lit room in the house. The countertop was covered with cut-up straws and there was a smell that reminded me of the taste of aspirin.

Seba was scraping pills off the counter and shoving them into his pockets. Then he lowered his head to do a line of something crushed up on the white-and-gold-speckled countertop. He snorted it and had such a look of pleasure on his face, I almost looked away. Seba slowly turned his head and gave me a look that was cockiness trying to mask fear, like he was a little boy who said the spanking didn't hurt. He knew his time was up and he'd lost the boys.

He threw up his hands in mock exasperation. "Can't anyone at this school handle their drugs?"

"Stay away from Max and Wilson," I said. Maybe it was three in the morning. Maybe I had lost my filter after no sleep for weeks, but I also meant it.

Seba laughed at me, reminding me of a spoiled young

nobleman in the red-and-faux-gold powder room. "Those two thought they were so cool, that they were all *Risky Business* with this place. They weren't even making real money." Seba put his face right up to mine to study me. Then, as if he'd come to his conclusion, "Do you know how boring you are? I don't get why those guys are so careful with you and so scared for you to find shit out. The only exciting thing about you was your father's picture in *Us Weekly* with a barely legal, pregnant Brooke Carter. I remember thinking that was so cool."

Jack appeared at the door. "Let's go. Now there's a fire truck."

Seemingly in no hurry, Seba said, "Van's going to get sick of you so fast. Whose idea do you think it was to break into this house in the first place? You don't party, you can't keep up with him like his much hotter girlfriend." He pushed past me.

I decided not to mention the dusting of white ringing his nostrils like powdered sugar.

The flashing lights brightened the front rooms behind me. I knew the house well enough to know I could probably slip out the back porch and into my own yard and avoid the crowd. The wood floor creaked and I used my hand as a guide against the greasy walls as I crept to the back of the house.

I caught sight of movement outside a bedroom window. I knew I needed to go but just for a second, from my usual distance, I looked out the window at Van and Wilson by Max's side, the three of them just beyond my grasp.

CHAPTER THIRTY-TWO

Van didn't text.

I hadn't bothered trying to sleep. Actually, when was the last time I'd even sincerely tried? Life had become too exciting for sleep.

Max.

I took up Van's post and stared down at the house. The house used to live large in my mind like a monster from a horror film. What had made it so terrorizing was not knowing exactly what was going on inside, only that *something* was. Now the house reminded me of a bad teenager who had been caught and chastised. The paint looked sad, the porch looked droopy. It was just a rich kids' playground. How they'd managed to stay so quiet and keep other people quiet, I'd never know. For a moment, I remembered the lonely little girl with the braids who sat by herself on that porch. Where the hell was she now? We all cared so much about Max, but that little girl had been practically invisible. I hadn't wanted to see her. She'd reminded me of helplessness, and of adults inside who left you to your own devices.

I moved to the street-facing window. The light of a fresh spring morning blossomed over the cul-de-sac. Everything looked mussed, as if neighbors had trampled on their grass to run out to the middle of the street, to gather, to watch.

The street reminded me of an aisle at Target selling postseason holiday goods. Too much of a good thing. Too many pretty colors. Too late of a night. The cul-de-sac looked hungover. Van's house was uncharacteristically quiet though all three cars were in the driveway.

Why hadn't he texted? Should I not have left when I did last night? Did Van think I was selfish, leaving him to deal on his own?

I placed my hands over my eyes and saw Max's slowed breathing all over again.

I heard a hum below and uncovered my eyes. Pete, Max's dad, swung his royal-blue Prius into their driveway and unhurriedly climbed out. From where I stood, I couldn't see more than his grizzled man-bun and pajama pants. If I was closer, I'd see his chipped, painted toenails and smell a whiff of pot. Like Max, he was skinny, but he walked in a kind of stagger as if he was tripping on pants that were too long. Max's parents had been multimillionaires before they were thirty and, as far as I could tell, devoted most of young retirement to rescuing cats.

Pete picked up the newspaper from the driveway, unfurled it, and began to read the front page. His relaxed body language told me his son had to be okay. A couple of cats came running from the shrubs at the sound of Pete's arrival and swirled about his ankles on the warming blacktop.

The swish of curtains caught my eye. Faces peered out to watch Pete. The fishbowl.

I sensed the strength of the community gathering like a tornado. Led by the retirees, certain neighbors would want to take charge and clean up the mess of the house that had corrupted kids beneath their noses. Emotional messes, well, each family would handle that differently. Wilson's moms would be mortified and wonder if they should move. Roz and Pete would take the opposite route and treat Max like he was their friend, maybe blame someone else. I doubted they would make him go to counseling. I had no idea what Lisa, not to mention Kevin, would do.

I checked my phone again. Nothing. I felt selfish even wondering whether Van was thinking about me and what happened between us.

His water glass from just hours ago sat on my nightstand. The tall glass was a favorite of my mother's; it was tinted a Caribbean blue and decorated with gold leaf, part of a set once bought from a fancy department store in Beverly Hills. Dust already skimmed the top.

CHAPTER THIRTY-THREE

I waited restlessly for Izzie and the others in front of the auditorium—our after-school meeting spot. Today, the school felt claustrophobic and clammy and polluted.

As far as I could tell, Wilson and Seba had been absent. My heart leapt when I thought I saw Van's car in the parking lot first thing in the morning. But when I looked closer, it was a completely different car. He wasn't in class and he wasn't in any of the usual places where I might see him from a distance.

How's Max? How are you? That was all I had texted at 4 A.M. It hadn't occurred to me that he wouldn't respond. Unless something was really wrong. I wanted to know how Van felt about the hole in the wall and about Max and Wilson lying to him, mainly because they hadn't wanted to disappoint him.

By midday, word had spread far and wide about last night: the secret party house, Max having his stomach pumped, and the naming of names of who had been there. I heard in math class that Max was home from the hospital. By lunch, everywhere I went, it felt like there was whispering. Kids seemed to look at me differently, speculatively.

I hadn't seen Izzie yet today because of her orthodontist appointment. She'd texted me a photo of a dog poster in the waiting room because she knew I loved puppies. The image of five golden retriever puppies tugging on a rain boot made me wish Izzie and I were ten instead of seventeen.

"What the . . ." I saw the teal-painted fingernails wrap around my sleeve just as I registered the voice, then Izzie's bewildered face.

"Hi," I said.

"What happened? I got to school and everyone is saying that Max overdosed. And you were there?" Her dark eyes were as large as I'd ever seen them.

"It was alcohol poisoning. Not an overdose. There was a lot of commotion next door."

"His head was in your lap?"

Wow. That fact was wrong but the level of detail surprised me. I scanned the hallway for Van again, automatically, the way I always did in this hallway at this time of day. He must have had his phone taken away. That was all I could come up with.

"Max's head wasn't in my lap. It was in Van's."

"Were you with all of them? Before that, I mean?" Izzie's expression showed her total confusion at the social reordering. I was supposed to be up in my room, separate from the boys because that was how it had been since she'd met me.

I felt a tap on my shoulder. "Can I talk to you for a second?" The voice near my left ear was hoarse and wrecked, like its owner had been up too late, partying too hard.

Caroline fixed me with a preoccupied gaze and I noted that she didn't acknowledge Izzie.

"Of course," I answered. I could just hear Izzie's thought-text that our conversation wasn't over. Next thing I knew, Caroline pulled me by the hand into an empty classroom. Heads turned in our wake.

The classroom's linoleum floors shined like they'd just been polished and my white tennis shoes slipped a bit on the waxy surface as I entered. I reminded myself that I hadn't done anything wrong. This was Caroline being worried about what I knew. It made sense—with her cool daring, I could see her experimenting with everything. Seba had no doubt loved that he'd had Max and Wilson keeping secrets from Van. But Seba must have especially loved that Caroline was lying to Van. She was the girl Seba really wanted but could never get.

Caroline plunked herself inelegantly into one of the desk chairs and slunk down low. Her phone fell out of her pocket and bounced on the shiny floor. "Dammit," she muttered. When she inspected it, I saw that the screen had shattered.

I studied her while she swiped her thumbs across the surface of her phone, testing to see if it still worked. For Caroline, she looked disheveled in a white T-shirt with very slight yellowing at the armpits. It didn't seem fitting for her to be wearing something with a flaw that other people could see. Something was off, and it put me even more on edge than I always was around her. Why *was* I always on edge around her? Because I wanted to impress her? Because I fell in love with her boyfriend while they were dating? Because I had a girl crush on her and wanted to absorb how to be perfect at everything?

I remained standing, not quite knowing what to do with my hands. How did she know a teacher wouldn't walk in and ask us to leave? All the rules I worried about, she never bothered with.

Satisfied, Caroline replaced her phone in her pocket. Then she surveyed me. I shifted nervously, crossing my arms loosely. Maybe this was going to be about me helping her keep the drug use and partying from Coach Mike, but it was mainly going to be about Van. It was a long time coming. I'd been surprised she hadn't said anything after she saw me with Van the night they broke up.

Caroline began chewing her nails and I noticed they were bitten to the quick. She was nervous. A memory of her face from the day of the meet, seconds before I hit my head, popped into my mind.

"You were with Van last night? That's what I heard."

She didn't say it meanly or possessively. Just conversationally, the tip of one nail between her teeth.

I was having trouble forming an answer—what would Van say if someone asked? I'd always assumed he'd want to hide it. I settled on, "The whole thing was right next door." She knew what I was talking about.

"I heard he was with you in your house when Wilson called."

"We're just neighbors."

Caroline nodded as if this made sense to her and she could live with that. "Have you spoken to him today?" she asked.

Caroline stopped chewing her nails and folded her hands tightly like a little girl in church. A parent's voice was obviously ingrained in her head: *Stop chewing your nails!* It struck me how little I'd heard about Caroline's family. I knew her parents had moved back to California in January and Caroline was finishing out the semester in Texas, living with family friends. It was one more fact about Caroline that made her seem like she was ten years older than me instead of one.

But right now, she looked more her age than I'd ever seen her. Messy, deliberately working to appear relaxed in her slumped position in a high school classroom, signs that read NO VAPING posted on the beige wall behind her.

I shook my head. "No, I haven't talked to him." He wasn't her boyfriend anymore, I reminded myself. Why had she brought me to this room? Did she want him back as soon as she'd heard a rumor about Van and me?

Once I gave this answer, Caroline relaxed for real. She unclasped her hands and draped her arms over the back of the chair, back in a power pose. I saw fresh red stains on her white shirt. Splinters of glass from her phone must have made her fingers bleed.

"I won't tell Mike. Don't worry," she said, shifting gears and sounding more controlled, more like herself. She stood, crossed to the overhead projector that sat on a cart next to me, and began to fidget with its settings for no apparent reason. I wanted to tell her to stop, that it might mess things up for the teacher who used it.

"There's nothing to tell Mike. There was commotion beneath my window. That's it," I said. She was suddenly making this about me.

"Yeah, but you don't want to be associated with any of that. I would get far away from those guys."

I half turned to leave the room, wanting to finish the uncomfortable conversation. I didn't like that I couldn't pin her down. Was she threatening me? Or trying to be helpful? In my past dealings with Caroline, I'd always believed she was looking out for me. I prided myself on reading people well. That came with being an outsider. Always observing. But this time, I wasn't so sure.

"Ingrid, I'm saying this as someone who has spent a lot of time with those boys. At least for the last couple of months. Don't let them get you off track," she said. Now she sounded authentically kind. "I've heard Mike tell you the same thing they used to tell me in gymnastics—that you're not a normal teenager. You're better. Anyway, Van said he's going to be under house arrest for a while, which makes it easy. He's hard to stay away from."

Wait. Caroline had spoken to him?

Caroline reached over and gave me a hug. I smelled her perfume, and her old white T-shirt was soft on my chin.

"Doesn't Mike say the same thing to you? That you're not a normal teenager?" I asked, pulling away first.

I heard real regret in her voice when she said, "I guess I became one. But that wasn't the plan. When I was a gymnast, I was going to be a national champion like you."

*

"What the hell was that?" Izzie asked when I rejoined her. I wasn't imagining it; people were staring at me as they walked by. I wore cutoffs and an oversize long-sleeve black T-shirt. My hair hung straight to the tops of my shoulder blades and now I self-consciously tucked one side behind my ear.

"She was making sure I was okay after last night."

"I heard you were the one who answered Van's phone late last night. That you were with him when they needed help with Max," Izzie said, sounding somewhere between confused and aggressive. It was like she could tell something was different about me today. For the hundredth time, I replayed the moment when my lips first touched Van's, followed by him firmly but gently pulling me on top of him. . . .

My brain was buzzing with Caroline's weird warning. And I felt like I should be in the know about Max. In my mind, I was one of them, and I hated that in the bright light of today, I clearly was not.

Colette and Preeti slowly approached us, as if they wanted to make sure Izzie and I weren't fighting. Colette started in. "You were there last night? At Seba's secret club?" When she used his first name, it was with a familiarity that was misplaced.

"Yep," I said clearly, maybe enunciating a little too much on the "p."

"Did you know they were renting rooms?" The way she said it—kind of impressed and in awe—made me sick.

"Wait. Back up. Tell us what happened! People are saying you and Van were together at your house before it happened?" Preeti asked. From her tone, it sounded like I had performed a miracle, like the parting of the Red Sea.

Everyone was waiting for my answer. If I said we had been together, it would make it sound like something it wasn't. But after last night, I wondered what *it* was, exactly.

"That's crazy," I said.

That seemed to make sense to the group. Colette nodded.

"Does anyone know more about Max?" I asked. At that point, I still thought I would hear from Van.

"Oh, I heard he's fine. Back home."

"I never want to have my stomach pumped. They stick a tube down and then don't they use charcoal or something?"

"Oh, gross. Not before lunch. Come on, let's get our table."

Life moved on. But Izzie was watching me closely. I knew she saw the red staining my cheeks.

CHAPTER THIRTY-FOUR

That was the first night that Van was a no-show.

CHAPTER THIRTY-FIVE

The humid night poured through my open window, softly blowing my curtains. It had been three days since I last remembered falling asleep for more than a brief nap. Slowly, I moved the curtains aside to glance across the street. Van's bedroom was black.

I adjusted the strap of my tank top and felt a strip of sweat where the skinny strap had been.

After Van didn't show for the first time in sixteen nights, I thought maybe it was something I'd done during the emergency. Maybe Van thought I'd overstepped?

Or what if he regretted what happened right before the phone call? I had been positive Van felt what I had. In my mind, Van couldn't have that kind of chemistry with anyone else. But now I was second-guessing everything.

Then I'd received one text from Van that read: *Max is back at home. He's fine.*

It felt curt to me and made me more paranoid. I'd decided not to text back.

Van hadn't been at school again. Caroline had said he was under "house arrest." But how would she know? Had they stayed friends and I'd had no clue? I became acutely aware that I only saw Van from 1 A.M. to 4 A.M. every night.

That conversation in the classroom with Caroline continued to bother me. I kept seeing the unsteady expression on her face when she first sat down in the classroom and confronted me. There was a moment of vulnerability that brought me back to the day I hit my head and I wanted to know why. And why it made me uneasy.

A text came in from Coach Mike: *Great news—it's official. Construction on the swim center will begin in June. Let's prove we've earned it. So see you on FRIDAY. I know you're not supposed to come on FRIDAY but you should come on FRIDAY. So I'll see you FRIDAY? Right?*

I almost smiled. He wanted to make me laugh with his high-pressure sales tactics. I replaced my phone at my side and continued to stare out onto the street. Alix had called earlier in the week and complained about Mike's intensity at practice lately. Alix wondered if he was trying to be worthy of a state-of-the-art facility. I wondered if he was feeling desperate to hold on to what he'd built.

Wilson's mom's Mercedes station wagon caught my eye as it passed below, then slowly turned into their driveway farther down the street. Their dark brown house had recently been renovated and now had a wide porch and craftsman-style touches rare in a neighborhood filled with ranch houses.

In the garage light, I saw that Mira wore all white—white linen pants, white ruffled blouse, and a circular straw purse with Gucci markings. Her straight black hair hung down her back almost to her waist. She looked more LA than Austin, which had been the case since her Indian restaurant had flourished into a restaurant group. Wilson's other mom, Leigh, was the CFO. What I always remembered about Mira was her habit of eating peaches and cream ice cream bars in satin pajamas in bed. She ate one a night, Wilson had told us as kids. She bought us Popsicles stored in the garage refrigerator so we wouldn't lay a finger on her stash. Once, when the boys were teasing me, Mira let me up on the bed to eat one beside her. The boys were so jealous and said it was because I was a girl.

Wilson appeared, exiting the car moments after Mira. I saw him trudge after his mother slowly, clearly in the dog house.

Mr. Kitchen was watering his grass late at night, close to Wilson's house, and had no qualms about openly watching them, like he wanted to convey that he had his eye on Wilson. You could just hear what Mr. Kitchen was thinking as he thumbed his white goatee: spoiled kid, self-obsessed parents, no common sense.

The question was how long the shaming would last and whether Wilson's parents would forgive him for his part in what happened with Max. Things would be bad enough even without parents ever knowing what had really been going on in the house. Mira was very loving but she and Leigh had always been exacting and tough on Wilson. Wilson's involvement in the partying had most likely blindsided them. As far as they were concerned, their kid had been on the straight-and-narrow, Ivy League bound. If his outfit of white button-down and black pants was any indication, I imagined Wilson's social life had been cut short and he was now working every evening and on the weekends at one of his mom's restaurants where she could watch him.

Wilson's garage door closed, putting an end to my brief sighting of one of the boys.

There was a loud bang as someone slammed the back door of the Moores' house and my focus shifted to across the street. One second later, Lisa stalked into sight, Kevin close on her heels.

"Lisa," Kevin called after her. The two walked onto the front lawn into the glow of the outdoor lighting scheme.

When she reached the row of olive trees, Lisa turned around and flung Kevin's hands off of her when he tried to slow her.

I couldn't hear their words but Kevin was speaking to her gently. "Just go!" Lisa shouted, not caring if the neighbors heard.

Maybe she knew about the affair now.

I saw the scuttle of curtains, and the twins' faces appeared next to each other in the large front window. One of them knocked on the glass. Lisa saw them and then swiftly turned around so they couldn't see her face.

Lisa swiped her eyes and held her face in her hands for a moment. Then she squared her shoulders and walked back to the house, returning to the twins, who were supposed to be in bed.

Kevin stayed behind. He shook his head slowly and then looked up into the night sky.

I remembered myself and realized I was spying. I was about to replace the curtain, when another set of headlights traveled into the cul-de-sac. It slowed to a stop at the curb in front of Van's house.

Caroline's BMW. Under the yellow glare of the streetlamp, I glimpsed Van in the front seat.

I heard my own sharp exhale.

For endless minutes, they sat in the dark car. I couldn't see what they were doing.

Look away, Ingrid.

But I couldn't.

Maybe they were just friends.

That was naive. They weren't just friends.

Van let himself out from the passenger side and stepped up onto his front lawn. I could only see his back as he lingered, waiting for Caroline.

A weird rational voice in my head said, *It's high school. Of course they would be on-again, off-again.* Followed by the darker thought: *She always gets what she wants.*

That was unfair. It was Van's choice, too.

It was okay, I told myself. There was no reason to feel shell-shocked. Or even disappointed. Van and I had never been a couple. We'd only hung out to pass the time. I didn't have a claim on him just because we'd kissed one time.

Caroline turned off the engine and exited the car like a polite date, ready to walk Van to his doorstep.

Kevin's bark jarred me. I'd forgotten he was standing in the shadows.

"Get your ass inside. Your mother is worried sick," Kevin said, loud enough for neighbors like me to hear.

From my slice of window, I saw Van saunter past Kevin, cocky. *Don't do it*, I thought.

Van walked close enough to Kevin to brush his shoulder when he passed by. Like the quick strike of a snake, Kevin grabbed Van's shirtfront. For such a heavy guy, the speed was unexpected. Van towered over Kevin but leaned back, startled by the move. Then, slowly, Van placed his hand on top of Kevin's and pried it off. Kevin watched Van let himself in through the garage.

Caroline had halted once she saw Kevin and for a second, she stood frozen, her slim frame and suntanned skin illuminated in the headlights. When Kevin set his sights on her, she remembered herself and swiftly crossed back to her car.

In my mind's eye, I saw Caroline's naked expression in the classroom again. This time it was accompanied by that metallic taste I'd had when I came out of EMDR. Then a sharp fragment of a different memory—my view of her as I climbed the ladder seconds before the accident. Why were the memories tied together? One had followed the other, flashing through my mind throughout the day, nagging me.

I remembered Alix's words. *Look at them.*

I let the curtain settle into place behind me. I became very methodical. It was better than feeling stupid.

I powered off my phone.

I gathered up everything that reminded me of Van. My favorite jeans I'd worn the night Van and I had biked to karaoke were still unwashed. Funny how I'd been reluctant to clean them and now I collected them so I could wash everything on hot. Twice.

Van had left a sweatshirt on the back of my desk chair a week ago. When he didn't collect it night after night, I folded it up and put it in my drawer before my mom asked any questions. I'd covered my favorite bathing suit with it—the one I'd been wearing when I had the accident—as if Van's sweatshirt could give my bathing suit healing energy. Now I ripped open the drawer, removed the navy-blue hoodie and, still unable to look at my bathing suit, slammed the drawer closed with my foot.

I dropped my face into Van's sweatshirt and breathed him in, letting the world go dark again.

I heard my mom's voice from years ago. *This is what we do: We don't look back.*

When I was too young to know better, I'd asked my mom how she got over my dad so quickly. She'd given me a look. Then after a rare introspective pause, she'd said it had helped having moved from Sweden at a young age. At first, she was so homesick she couldn't move, she couldn't speak to anyone new. Then she realized it was better if she stopped thinking about home altogether. What was the point if she wasn't going back? That was when she got a life.

It had made an impression and moving forward was something I'd mastered. I'd gotten sloppy with Van. He was the past.

That metallic, rising nausea was worsening.

I decided to take a shower. The pressure was intense and for a moment, I let the water drill my face.

The image of Caroline looking up at me from that desk slipped into my head again. Why? *What was it?* There was something about her expression that was bothering me. That naked expression reminded me of something else. It was like a floating fragment that hit against something else in my brain.

Then, suddenly, a piece of memory broke loose.

After all this time, I remembered my last dive. Like walking into a different world, I relived the entire sequence of events.

Van's hand was on Caroline's back and she looked around to see who was watching her with an insolent expression. Then Caroline walked back to the team. With no choice but to take my turn, I headed to the three-meter springboard. At the bottom of the ladder, I took one last look. That was always the point when I'd automatically glance to Coach Mike. Before a dive, I would look at him in the distance, looking at me, ready for me to go. Caroline was talking to Coach Mike but he was annoyed and walked a few feet away. All I could see was his back.

In my previous memory of that day, Coach Mike was watching my dive. Just like always. Arms folded in, ready to analyze my dive and give me his feedback. Because he never missed a moment. He and I were the perfect team.

Maybe the break in routine had been enough to unnerve me. Because, for the first time, instead of lightly skipping up to the top, adjusting the fulcrum, taking my place, seeing my dive and shutting everything else out like the incredible machine I trusted myself to be, I was aware of the many layers around me. The heavy chlorinated air, the splashes and voices echoing off the walls.

With no choice, I went ahead.

CHAPTER THIRTY-SIX

I'd fallen into a restless sleep just before it was time to wake up. When the alarm sounded, I was already exhausted and I couldn't imagine pulling myself out of bed, getting dressed, and completing the day of school ahead of me. Last night I'd noticed my fingers were puffy. I went online and read that my body was most likely having an inflammatory response due to lack of sleep. Insomnia was breaking down my health now.

When I finally rose from my bed, I turned my phone back on. I had one missed call from Van. No message. But that was fine. I didn't want to hear what he had to say yet. Not until I got some sleep. Until then, I was too afraid I might cry in front of him.

At lunchtime, the sea of kids rushed around me but my mind was on the cafeteria. If I could make it in there, I'd be safe. No more opportunities for chance encounters. Wilson, Seba, and Max were still absent. I knew Van was at school because I'd seen his car.

I may have let an expression of *Oh no* pass across my face

I could feel exactly what had happened now. I could rewind and actually feel in my body the mistake of leaning back a millisecond too early. Why this ability to see had disappeared for weeks, I didn't know. Why Caroline's face had been the trigger to remembering, I didn't know. But it was over. I understood what had gone wrong. At least physically.

I thrust open the large glass door, opaque with steam. I reached for the worn yellow towel Van had probably dried his hands on. The shower had been a few degrees too hot and, light-headed, I pushed out of the bathroom for the cooler air of my bedroom. I dropped the towel.

Had it mattered that much to me that Coach Mike wasn't paying attention? It was one time. Was I worried he was losing interest because of the little mistakes I'd started to make? That I was that easy to move on from?

After drying off, I wrapped the towel around me, sat on the edge of my bed, and texted Coach Mike: *I know you said Friday but can I meet with you before practice tomorrow?*

Coach Mike texted back immediately: *"Failure is only the opportunity to begin again more intelligently."*—Henry Ford.

when I saw that I'd just missed my chance to skirt out of the main hall in time. Van and some of his soccer friends were entering from another wing.

Van beelined for me as if he knew this was where he'd find me. He hefted his backpack to his other shoulder and plowed through the masses, a head taller than most. Like the exhausted zombie I was, I forgot to stop staring. I could never picture him in between sightings, driving myself just crazy enough to go back for another look. Today, Van wore a light blue T-shirt, jeans, and Vans. A voice in my head said, *How weird. We've kissed.* Seeing him now, Van represented everything to me: friendship, love, family. Nothing I could have like other, normal people.

"Hey," he said, coming right up to me. Why did it feel like all life stopped and everyone—teems of people—watched? Because they were watching. The two of us talking was a strange sight. Beautiful Van and quiet me who no one really knew.

"Can we talk?" Van tilted his head a bit to find my eyes.

I noticed now how my first impression was off. Van didn't look like himself. Something in his eyes had changed. He was dreading this conversation.

I drew a deep breath but it made that staggered sound, like I was about to cry. That couldn't happen. I trained my eyes on a point just over his shoulder. A poster for what else? Prom. Swirly red-painted cursive advertised the tickets, the day, the time. The poster depicted an old-fashioned couple dancing ballroom-style with a horse and carriage behind them.

Van put his hands on my shoulders and angled me to face him so I'd look into his eyes. Really? He thought we needed a breakup scene in the school hallway?

"Are you okay?" he asked.

I ignored that. "How's Max?"

"He's good. There's a lot of talk of wilderness rehab school in Utah for the three of us." Van half laughed.

It wasn't funny. "You didn't do anything."

Van shrugged. "My mom and Kevin will calm down. My mom's just scared right now. Can we go somewhere?"

The resounding bang of lockers reverberated in my ears. I'd dressed too warmly and a trail of sweat trickled from between my shoulder blades to my lower back. Van waited for me to answer. I saw the boys from the soccer team whisper to each other while they watched us. One of them laughed and shook his head.

If we continued the conversation, I worried Van would tell me he was sorry. We'd stand along a less populated corridor where he would rush through, get it over with, tell me that he and Caroline were giving it another chance and he couldn't see me at night anymore. He would think he was a good guy doing it in person instead of over the phone. He might even put a hand on my shoulder to make sure we were friends and things were cool between us.

I would save face by pretending I didn't know what he was talking about; we were just friends, after all. That night in my room wasn't a big deal. There was no need to be sorry.

I could avoid that if I made this easy for both of us. I looked Van straight in the eye and said, "Now that we know the truth about next door, let's get some rest. Maybe we can, now that it's over." I gently pulled from his grasp and started down the hall.

"But it's not over," I thought I heard Van say.

There was a touch of sadness in his voice that I didn't quite understand. I kept on walking.

✳

"What is going *on*?" Izzie asked as I settled at the lunch table.

"He was making sure I was okay after the other night."

"Van was holding your shoulders."

Molly and Preeti sat down to join us. "Wait. Back up. Am I crazy or was Van talking to you in the hallway?" Molly asked.

"It's nothing. He was telling me about Max."

Izzie extricated herself from the bench and walked out.

✳

"Izzie."

"You don't tell me anything. You never have."

We stood outside the library on a small square of grass. The metal poles supporting the ancient flat roof were painted maroon in keeping with the school colors.

I opened my mouth to speak. Then I closed it. I couldn't talk about it because then I would never stop. I loved Izzie so much but I didn't trust that she wouldn't mention a word to other people. It was mortifying.

Izzie turned up her palms and narrowed her eyes. "Seriously?" she said, incredulous. Then, as if it was a decision she'd been weighing for some time, she said, "If you say nothing, I can't be friends with you anymore."

"What? Izzie. Come on. They live next door. That's why I was there."

"Then why are you being weird?"

"I'm not!"

Sometimes you know when you've lost the ability to be a good liar.

I dreaded what was coming and it was worse than I expected.

Izzie's expression closed off, like she inserted a barrier between us. Then it started.

She took a step back and began shaking her head. "I thought I'd have more time with you this month. Finally. But I feel like I know you even less. You never, *ever* crack. My mom says it's because your mom and your coach are all about strength." Izzie raised her eyebrows and widened her eyes again. "I used to admire it and I've always felt like a mess compared to you but you know what? I'm happy I'm a weirdo and can cry. Because what you're doing—always trying to be perfect—seems awful.

"Now you're living this double life and I'm not important enough—or too nerdy—to be included. Exclusive parties and you have some relationship with Van going on. Do you think I'm stupid? I know you've been in love with him since at least freshman year. I've been waiting for you to admit it for three years. I see how you look at him from across the classroom. How you ignore him every time he walks by and even when he's right across the street. How you go into this weird Queen Elizabeth frozen walk whenever he's around, like you know he's there but you're pretending he's not. And I see those guys look at you. All three of them. And I have to say, you have lost your shit since Van started dating Caroline. Maybe you've lost it even more since they broke up."

I swallowed to stave off the gigantic, ominous lump climbing my throat. I literally couldn't speak. Izzie gave me her back and left me in the dust.

It was fitting that Caroline and two girlfriends walked by five minutes later. I was still rooted to the spot where Izzie had left me.

"Hi!" Caroline acknowledged me with a dazzling smile as she passed.

As I waved, I quickly brushed a tear away with the side of my hand and smiled at the girls like everything was just perfect. "Hey."

CHAPTER THIRTY-SEVEN

I slid the car into "my" parking spot at the swim center. Mike's hatchback was two spaces to my right. The aquatics center was located in a section of campus on a hill and the parking lot had a broad vista of the university's eclectic architecture. A couple playing Frisbee on the green below were straight out of a college catalog. Next to me, the dark gray aquatics center loomed large and had the look of a nuclear power plant.

If I wanted to speak with Mike before the team arrived for practice, I had to do it now. I'd rehearsed a bit on how to finally tell him.

I trusted him. He'd never let me down. He was Mike.

When I opened the car door, my legs began to shake uncontrollably, knees knocking together. Totally, completely irrational. Totally, completely not me.

"What? What is it?" I whispered out loud, helplessly angry. I remembered my last dive. I knew what had been going on next door. I shouldn't be scared anymore.

I shut the car door, pulled out swiftly, and breathed a sigh of utter relief when I blended into traffic.

✳

I drove miles and miles, to the outskirts of town. It had been years since I'd gone to the swimming hole with Izzie's family.

Back then, on a Sunday afternoon filled with canned soda and fire-ant bites, I'd shown off to Izzie's family with backflips on the lawn. There was a rope swing over the warm, black water in the shade of the towering trees on the cliff above. Except for crazy, drunk frat boys, no one took the rope swing off the cliff. Except for me. Izzie's mom kept fretting, "Are you sure your mom would be okay with this?"

I remembered now how Izzie's sister had barely scraped her knee that day. When Izzie's mom ran to get a Band-Aid from the first aid kit in the trunk, I couldn't believe it. I had been disdainful yet kind of jealous at the totally unapologetic show of weakness. When I'd had strep throat in fourth grade, Mike had called my mom to come get me. She was in nursing school and I begged him not to call her, knowing she'd be mad. He must not have believed me until my mother appeared at practice to collect me and didn't say a single word. Mike actually patted my shoulder before I reluctantly left his side. Sure enough, she'd stalked ten steps ahead of me to the car. I could still see her pointy-toed flats attacking the pavement.

"I'm not mad at you," she'd said half an hour later as she tucked me into bed, having fully transitioned to mom mode by then. "It's just terrible timing."

I accepted her apology because I knew she was in a tough position, pulled in different directions. My being sick had just been more than she could handle at that moment. For her sake,

I wanted to get better fast, and all night I had fitful, feverish dreams of going to school the next day, desperate to get out of my mom's hair. Instead, I went to the doctor and got antibiotics, my mom white-lipped as she pulled out her credit card and missed her test.

Today, the park was empty. I knew the water would be cold but I also knew it was deep enough after heavy rains this winter.

I sauntered over to the fraying rope swing and gave it a tug, giving it my full body weight for a moment. I thought about the news story: a dumb teenage girl died hitting her head on a rock at Indigo Creek. The old me would have done it.

Instead, I followed the path down to the water and waded in, fully dressed. I gently lay down in the water and floated on my back in the piercingly cold water and stared up at the branches above that made a lace umbrella.

Was it that I was afraid Mike would be mad at me? The way I was afraid of my mom sometimes getting mad at a show of weakness?

My dad, on the other hand—he had known all of my weaknesses. When I used to tell him I was afraid of the ghosts under my bed, he would lie down next to me until I fell back to sleep. I always trusted that he would be there when I cried out. So completely.

My teeth were chattering. I closed my eyes and let myself drift but the cold was becoming harder and harder to ignore.

CHAPTER THIRTY-EIGHT

When I entered the house, something wasn't right. The air was completely different—warm and still. Our house was like a bowl of soup. The air-conditioning had officially blown out. A hand-written note from my mother on the kitchen counter said she'd contact that repair company with the catchy jingle we always heard on the radio.

There had been texts from my mom over the past couple of days but I'd never gone this many days in a row without seeing her face-to-face. But it was perfect timing; by the time she came up for air at the end of the week, the Wilson-Max-Van story about the ambulance and the party at the house next door would be old news. A nosy neighbor or Lisa and Kevin wouldn't really think to stop her in the driveway to inform her. They would assume she already knew.

My freezing-cold swim had lowered my body temperature and even though I really should have taken a shower to rinse off the filthy pond water, I peeled off my sticky, damp shorts and T-shirt that smelled of algae and changed directly into another identical outfit. I put on a yellow diving T-shirt from a meet two years before in San Antonio. I detangled my hair with both hands as best I could and let it hang down my back to dry.

There was no choice but to open both windows in my bedroom. I sat down to do homework. After fifteen minutes, the air was too stifling. I pulled the curtain halfway to actually let the air in. Thankfully, it was cooling down with the sunset. The light outside was transforming the sky into a royal blue. It was a beautiful, breezy evening.

There was an essay to write. There was AP chemistry homework. The words and equations swam in front of me. As a distraction, I checked my grades online. My computer wheezed scarily, showing its age, while the rainbow wheel onscreen spun mercilessly.

When results popped up, at first, I wasn't sure if I was asleep and having a nightmare. But after I slapped my cheeks and shook my head, it became clear that what I saw was real and what was in my head was a lot less reliable. Missing assignments littered the grid. My grade from last week's chemistry exam was posted—C. The computer went dark after I'd been staring, unmoving, for too long. I snapped the screen down and lay down on my bed facedown. I grabbed the duvet at the foot of the bed and pulled it over my head.

How had I let this happen? I had lost my mind. I hadn't even been keeping track of what was passing me by. Spring of my junior year.

I had been absolutely confident that I'd been handling everything. Staying up all night. School during the day. What else had I missed?

I dug in my backpack for my phone where it was buried deep. The screen had fogged from the wet sweatshirt I'd put over it while I drove home in a sports bra. I saw there were no texts from Izzie, and my stomach clenched when I realized Coach Mike hadn't responded to my lame text about a forgotten doctor's appointment. There was one message from Van.

I need to talk to you. Call me, text me. Whenever.

I knew better than to call. This mess was why it was safer to get my thrills in diving. I'd been smarter as a ten-year-old when I'd poured everything into training instead of friends, my mom, people who were absent.

My phone buzzed. It was my mom, checking in. Under the covers, I kicked the phone all the way to the foot of the bed until it tumbled into the curve of the tucked sheet.

For hours, the phone proceeded to consistently buzz, punctuating my worry loop at regular intervals.

The mystery wasn't what was happening next door. Or why I couldn't sleep. It was why I was falling apart.

The rusted old gate in the side yard budged, scraping the pea gravel next door. At the noise, there was a sharp intake of breath. With my window open, it sounded like the person was in my room.

The duvet came off my head, releasing me into cooler air.

The sound again. Then a little, muffled, female sneeze.

If I'd had my window open for the past few weeks, Van and I would have caught the secret parties next door. I could hear everything.

I wandered over to the window, staying close to the wall, and peeked around the edge to see outside.

It was Caroline. I caught just the back of her—I knew that beautiful, shampoo-commercial blond hair anywhere—before she disappeared into the shadows of the backyard.

A wind had kicked up, the whine of it swirling around my

house. Bright yellow pollen would litter the cars parked in drive-
ways.

The clock said 1 A.M. It made sense. Van would be out in
a minute. He hadn't changed his nighttime activities, just the
players. Yet I moved to the other window to see if I was correct.

I was chewing my nail when Van appeared approximately
seven minutes later. He gripped the back of his neck with one
hand and paused on the sidewalk to stare at the abandoned
house. Then he dropped his arm to his side and jogged quickly
across the street.

Seeing them sneaking out together was almost pleasant in
that strange, bottom-of-the-barrel way when you know things
can only get better from there. Caroline was important enough
to Van that he was willing to risk getting caught. Everyone was
watching that house, ready to take it back from the jerk kids who
were rotten enough to corrupt the sweet cul-de-sac. This era was
going to be whispered about in the history of the block, like the
time there was the robbery at the convenience store. Or the lore
of how, back in the '90s, one of the neighbor's sons dropped acid
and fried his brain. Today he biked circles and circles around the
neighborhood and lived with his parents.

The wind howled louder and before my room was dusted
with a layer of dirt, I went to shut my windows. While I cranked
in slow, stubborn circles, I glanced across the street at Van's
house. The windows were black, quiet. Everyone asleep. Then,
before my eyes, every single light came on in the house, like a
row of falling dominoes.

Moving from right to left, the entire line of upstairs rooms
came alive. I saw a blur of people and the tail end of a robe swish
out of vision.

I froze when Kevin entered Van's room. Kevin stood shirtless, in his boxers, his large, hairy belly hanging over his waistband. But it wasn't funny. Somehow it was scary because he seemed to be looking directly back at me. I couldn't tell if we made eye contact.

Then downstairs. Kevin's figure appeared in the living room through the windows. Soon the entire house was ablaze.

Kevin would search the house next door first.

Torn, I knew Kevin still needed to get dressed before he took off to catch Van. I was closer to the empty house than Kevin. There was still time to warn Van.

But forget it. What did I care if Kevin caught Van? If Van's phone was taken away or he couldn't play with his band.

Because Van wasn't a bad person. He was one of the best people I knew. The best. The loss he'd suffered early had only made him more kind and more loyal. Not broken. His only fault was that he didn't want me.

✴

The moon was bright, which made it easier to see. When I stepped onto the neighbor's property, mulch squeezed between my toes as I sunk into a layer of topsoil. It had rained in the last few days and the house grounds were damp and loamy.

I wasn't afraid of the house anymore but that same metallic taste of fear filled my mouth. Why was I suddenly scared?

The backyard was made up of mostly overgrown lawn, almost knee-high in patches taken over by weeds, with wild shrubs bordering the looming greenbelt. I could distinguish individual trees closest to the house, but farther back, the blue-black melted together into one block of forest. I turned to trot up the wooden steps to the back door one last time, when an arm yanked me back.

A scream tore from my mouth but only one small note escaped before a hand slapped across my mouth and my head was pulled back hard against the shoulder of someone much taller and stronger. Pinning me.

My arms were free and I clawed at the hand across my mouth.

"It's me. It's me. Shhhh," Van's voice said next to my ear.

Van released his hand and I got out, "Kevin," before he shushed me. We heard the back-gate groan at the same time.

Without a word, Van grabbed my hand and led me in the direction of the greenbelt.

For a bit, I followed, picking my way behind him.

"Van," I started to say when he'd led me through the slimmest opening in the imposing green border—the hole in the wall. Wilson must have shown him. Battling branches that scratched my face and arms, we sidled through the crevice that remarkably led to the twisted trail we knew and had traveled for years. Earth crumbled away beneath our feet as we descended. Van was going in the wrong direction and I could barely see the back of his maroon soccer jersey in front of me. We could reenter onto the street just one block over and Kevin wouldn't find us there. I doubted Kevin knew that trick. But Van led me downhill toward the creek, where it was too dark and the terrain too wild. We didn't need to go so deep into the woods.

Van shushed me again. Then he stopped, holding a wispy branch high to let me pass. After I'd inched past him, he held perfectly still, listening. I saw an abandoned hammock strung between two trees close to the path, right next to us. The greenbelt was inhabited at night. People lived down here. I imagined an infrared camera showing the bodies that were no doubt right near us. We didn't know where they were and I didn't want to take anyone by surprise. I wanted to get back home, back to the light.

"Kevin woke up," I whispered. "I wanted to warn you. That's all."

"What did you see? From your window," Van whispered back. The trail was tight and he stood above me. I felt like the trees were compressing us, closing in. I slapped at tiny bugs that swarmed my hair.

I avoided his question, embarrassed that I'd been looking. A voyeur.

"It's important," Van said. There was urgency in his voice.

"Caroline."

"You saw her, too?" he asked.

"Yes. First her, then you. Do you need help finding her?"

"No. I think I know where she is. I can take you back."

We both saw the pinpoint of a phone flashlight up the hill, through the thick trees. No doubt following the light of Van's.

"Fucking Kevin," Van muttered. "Of course he'd figure it out."

Van pushed in front of me and grabbed my hand. I let him hold it even though it was awkward to be led and would have been easier to have both of my hands in case I fell. I was just scared enough that I wanted him to hold it. Van didn't let go, even after we connected to the well-worn, often-used path that led the masses to the creek when it was flowing. When I stepped into the moonlit clearing by the creek bed, I stopped.

"I got it from here. I know how to get home," I said. I dropped his hand. He could go meet his girlfriend.

Van just stood still, hesitating, like he wanted to tell me something.

"Hurry up. Kevin's going to catch you."

Van didn't say anything.

"What?" I finally said, exasperated.

"I don't know," he said.

"What do you mean, you don't know?" I asked, annoyed, confused.

"There's something I think I've known for a long time. For a few weeks, at least. It's part of what I was watching for—why I kept looking out your window. You know what? Go back. I'll take you," he said, changing his mind.

"What, Van? Why are you being so weird?"

"Caroline was also using the house," Van said.

"She was partying with the boys there, right?"

"No, she was doing her own thing. She had an agreement with them to share."

"Wait, what was she doing there?"

"She was meeting someone."

Oh. "You mean, 'meet' someone, like she was cheating on you? *Was* it Max? Or Seba?"

"No."

"Then who?"

"I have a feeling, but I need to know for sure."

"Who do you think?" I pressed.

Van remained inexplicably quiet.

"You think you'll see them together right now?" I finally asked.

"Yes."

"I'll go with you."

"Ingrid, I don't know," he said again. I was about to get even more exasperated by his hedging, when Kevin was making his way down the slope. Then Van said, "Because I don't know if you should see. But then I kind of think the only way you'll believe me is if you do."

Why did he care so much about me?

"I'll go with you. It's fine."

"Okay," he said after a pause.

I followed Van over the dry creek bed, the smooth gray stones bleached in the moonlight. Without the protection of the woods, the wind whipped straight down the tunnel of the creek, nearly knocking me over. Dry branches crackled with the gust.

My flip-flops weren't doing me any favors as I navigated sloppily over the rocks. I was almost to the other side, trailing in Van's footsteps, when the strap of my cheap shoe popped out and broke.

Van didn't notice so I kept going, testing whether I could stand walking with one bare foot. Just on the other side of the creek, a path led up to the street and the apartment complexes and a convenience store I knew well. It was the Minute Mart, where my dad used to take me and Van. Van started up the trail.

I ran up the hill and passed him, trying to shorten the amount of time I had to walk barefoot on the painful path. I wanted that smooth pavement in the parking lot just above.

When I reached the top, I saw the lit signage for the dry cleaner that glowed all night. My eyes adjusted to the fluorescent streetlamps and I saw a lone car in the parking lot. Then I saw a female figure emerge from the blinding glare. She pushed angrily at the chest of someone who lazily leaned against a familiar car. The man grabbed at her arm and yanked her to him and kissed her, as if to quell the tantrum.

Van was behind me. Then next to me. Then he moved in front of me, blocking my view. I wondered if I was seeing this at all.

"You asshole," I heard Van yell. Then Van was under the lights of the parking lot.

"No, no, no, no, no," Caroline's voice came out, high-pitched. I stepped closer.

Caroline stayed pressed up against the dark figure, like a deer in the headlights that had forgotten how to choose a direction and move.

I kept walking toward them so I could see better. When the

man saw me, there was a pause, then he immediately thrust Caroline away.

Look at them.

I met Mike's eyes.

He moved for the front of the car, rounding to the driver's seat like he was going to flee the scene. Caroline lunged after him and grabbed for his arm. Directly under the streetlamp, I saw the naked look on Caroline's face. I knew that look. I'd seen it years before.

I'd watched it play out on two people's faces now, first my mom's and now Caroline's. It was the realization that the floor had just fallen out from under you. It was a mirror of what was happening inside me.

It reminded me of a different expression I'd seen on Caroline's face, seconds before my last dive. Mike had ignored her and she'd looked at him like she wanted him to care. She wanted Mike to care that she'd brought around a boy to make him jealous. Annoyed, he'd walked away from her drama. That was why his back was turned on me when it was my turn to dive.

Look at them, Alix had said, in a tone of awe and scandal. She'd meant Mike and Caroline. The signs must have been there—obvious enough that the team was guessing—but I'd blocked it out. Maybe that was why I'd been messing up in the weeks before the accident. The knowledge had been getting under my skin.

When I saw their interaction seconds before the accident, I knew for sure—some secret part of me must have understood. But my mind wouldn't comprehend it; I hadn't wanted to believe it.

Now, in the scene in front of me, Van was shouting and Caroline was struggling to get Van's attention. But I couldn't hear words. Coach Mike kept trying to get in his car but Van had a vise grip on the front of his shirt. Mike's eyes were downcast. Suddenly he grabbed the hair on the back of Van's head, pulling it back hard, trying to hurt him so Van would let him go.

Two strong hands moved me aside. Kevin jogged ahead and inserted himself between Mike and Van, protecting Van and prying this man off his stepson.

Van said something to Kevin who then took a closer look at Mike. Mike took the opportunity to try to duck into his car. It was Kevin's turn to pull him up by his shirt and not let him go. In the beam of light, I saw spit fly from Kevin's mouth as he yelled at Mike.

Caroline looked like she was pleading. She kept talking and talking and talking.

That last dive, when I was up on the board on display, I knew before I knew.

Sound popped on again.

"First thing tomorrow, I'm reporting you. Fucking predator," Kevin shouted in Mike's face.

I heard Mike implore Kevin, "I ended it tonight. Please. I'll never coach again."

"I'm eighteen!" Over and over again, Caroline kept saying it.

I turned around and began to walk. Away from all of it. Away from all of them.

CHAPTER THIRTY-NINE

Mike and Caroline. Caroline pushing him. Mike subduing, then kissing her.

I lay on my bed, on my side. When the gentle tapping on the back door began, I ignored it. When the knocking began in earnest, I ignored it. Then there was pounding. I hadn't expected Van to remember where the key was hidden: under the stone toad at the foot of the back door, covered in algae and moss.

The mattress sagged under his weight.

"We took Caroline home."

I stayed on my side, facing away from him. I wanted him to stop talking.

"I have to give Kevin credit. He spoke with the family friends Caroline's living with and then he called her parents. They're reporting Mike to USA Diving tomorrow."

Van stood and flipped on the overhead light, a first.

"Holy shit. Your foot is bleeding all over the bed. Come on. Let's go to the bathroom."

"I'm fine," I said calmly.

"Jesus." Van got up and the overhead light from the bathroom blossomed on my closed eyelids. A second later, "Here."

I propped myself up on my elbow as Van wrapped my foot in a clean white towel. One of the good ones. Of course he wouldn't know about not ruining towels. He had a safe life of extras and plenty.

There was silence. "I'm sorry," he said.

I had to speak or he'd think something was wrong. "It's fine."

More silence. "It's not fine. Ingrid. He wasn't just your coach. He's been there since you were small."

"It doesn't matter," I said. I was the cornerstone of his entire program.

"It matters."

"I can do it on my own until I find a new coach. Can you turn off the light?" I was pretty sure I was dead inside but I had to get him out in case I cried. I tried to remind myself there was a high that came with not caring about anything. Total fucking freedom.

Van came around the bed and kneeled on the floor at my side, getting right up to my face. I couldn't turn over or move at all. If I held perfectly still, I could hold back what I'd seen; keep it so I was a distant observer. Every micro-detail was magnified in close-up: Van's long eyelashes, the chip in the lip of my nearby water glass, the dark window behind him. The one he'd been spying from for weeks. He finally got what he came for.

"Did you know?" he asked.

No. And yes. It made sense why I'd been a little bit off at practice for a month. It hadn't just been one day. It had been a nag that built. Because when you're an observer like me, you become attuned to subtleties in people's behavior. To changes. To body language. To shifts in attention. Especially after being the primary focus for so many years. I'd picked up on it. At least subconsciously.

When I didn't answer, Van asked the dreaded question: "Did he ever try . . . with you?" he slowly, awkwardly asked.

"No!"

"What about other divers?"

That hadn't occurred to me. "Not that I know of." I paused. "Did you know about them?"

Van sat back on his heels. "I told you about that night, how I saw Caroline in the backyard and she disappeared into the greenbelt. And then she lied about it and made me feel crazy just like Wilson and Max. What I couldn't get over was the image of her walking into the woods. It was so weird. She knew exactly where she was going."

Van sat cross-legged below me. "One night when we were dating, she wanted to walk home alone. My family and I drove by minutes later and I saw her getting into a gray car a few blocks from my house. Then that same car parked in front of your house this week when your coach came by."

Van ran his fingertips over the carpet, back and forth, nervously. "When Max came home from the hospital, he and Wilson confessed to me that they hadn't told me everything about the night I wandered over to the house. While I was supposedly passed out across the street, they went over to let people in. They surprised Caroline there. She was with some older guy they didn't recognize. What I saw was the aftermath—Max was freaking out on her, she saw them letting in people from the greenbelt. But my friends got over it apparently because they all made a pact not to say anything. Max and Wilson were doing their thing, she was clearly doing hers—all behind my back. When Caroline couldn't use the house, she'd use the path to sneak out of the neighborhood.

"Then, of course, when everything blew up, Caroline tried to keep me close so she'd know if they told on her. I'm sorry I was distant. I've been freaking out since I started suspecting who it was and how fucked that would be for you. But I didn't want to say anything until I knew it was true."

"But they wouldn't use the house next door to me," I stated. He was wrong. Caroline and Mike wouldn't do that—not right under my nose.

"I think they did. She knew about it because I took her there. She knew about the path to get there from Seba. Where else did they have to go? Where do any of us have to go besides our parents' houses or the back of a car? And that guy is arrogant enough to think he'd never get caught. That everyone loves him."

Everyone did love him. I'd loved him.

The image of Mike's very pregnant wife came to mind. It was like right when he got everything you'd think he wanted—a family, a facility built for him—he'd decided to blow it up. With a teenager. "So you needed my window. This whole time, you suspected."

"I wanted to know what was going on. With Max. With Wilson. But I also wanted to watch for her. At first it was because I wanted to catch her cheating on me. She was the first girl I was actually excited about since—"

Van quit talking and stared up at the ceiling as if that's where he'd find the words he was searching for. Then he continued, changing course. "But Caroline was totally on-again, off-again, like she couldn't make up her mind if she was interested, and then she'd ghost on me for long periods of time. . . ." Van trailed off. "Kevin's going to talk to your mom in the morning," he said, abruptly changing the subject again.

I had been passively listening, staying uninvolved for the most part but I became alert at that. "No, no, no. She doesn't need to know." I had an enormous instinct to protect my mom.

"What are you talking about? Your coach—who has practically raised you—was having an affair with your teammate. She needs to know."

"I don't want her to be disappointed again."

"Again?"

"Never mind."

"Ingrid, you just lost someone. Everyone is going to be worried about you."

"No, I'm fine. Honestly. I'll find another coach. I'll figure it out." He was not going to paint me as a victim. Poor Ingrid, who bad things kept happening to. Who couldn't catch a break with the people she trusted. It was like I was dirtied. At a certain point, this reflected on me.

I crossed my arms. "You could have just told me you were suspicious your girlfriend was cheating on you. You didn't have to keep me up for weeks to catch them together."

Van took a deep breath, like he was gearing up for something. "I told myself that was why I kept coming here, but really it was an excuse to be with you."

That got my attention.

Van was waiting for me to speak. After a long silence, Van said quietly, "I've been in love with you since I moved to this street."

A piece of my heart broke loose in my chest. A larger part of me couldn't deal with it.

"You were my best friend, my first crush, and you broke my heart when you quit talking to me. In eighth grade, I sat in my room writing you love letters I never sent. I've dated girls but no one was you. Then I met Caroline and I finally moved on. But it's like she brought us back together in a fucked-up way." Van waited for my response, watching me carefully. "Are you going to say something?"

My brain held out a giant stop sign. "It's too much right now," I heard myself say.

"Maybe I'm crazy," he said, "but I think you might feel the same way." Van gently touched my back.

"I'm a diver. I'm not a regular girl," I said. Coach Mike's words. Along with: *You are special.*

Van's hand fell away and he immediately jumped to his feet, as if deciding he didn't need to hear the rejection speech. At the bedroom door, he turned back. "Do you love it that much?"

"If I can't dive, I have nothing." I forced myself to meet his eyes.

"Your mom is nothing? I'm nothing?"

"My dad was a diver." The words just came out.

For a second, Van didn't speak. Then, "He's been gone for so long, he's just a memory. It's something I know all about."

I asked Van what I'd wanted to know for seven years. "What did he say to you that day he left? He said something just to you."

Van held the doorjamb with both hands. He looked back over his shoulder at me. "He told me to take care of you."

CHAPTER FORTY

After Van left, my brain was an electrical storm.

I hadn't slept at all in twenty-four hours. Maybe forty-eight. Maybe seventy-two.

I knew what my mother was going to think: *What an incredible waste of money.* To have my diving world implode junior year . . .

The diving community (and college coaches) would wonder: *What else was happening in that corrupt club?*

I knew what the other divers would think. I was always apart because I was at a more advanced level, the favorite. Coach Mike spent far more time with me than any other diver. It was like he and I were running a side business during practice and meets—priming me for the regional and then national competitions, talking about college diving programs, discussing an individualized workout. How many nights had I stayed behind by myself because Mike wanted to work with me?

You have a family. You have your mom, me, and Laura.

Mike patting my back, telling me it would be okay when I was so sick, my mom at the entrance, stone-faced.

First things first. Get the hell out of this house. This neighborhood.

＊

A small packed bag held everything I needed to stay out all day. My car made a toylike whining sound when I backed out of the driveway fast, into the dark predawn.

A hand banged down on my trunk. Hard. I nearly jumped to the roof.

Mr. Kitchen rode his bike around to my window, standing on the pedals and balancing shakily as he raged at me to watch where I was going, dying to school me. The old me would have apologized profusely. Now, I didn't roll down the window. Instead, I backed out slowly, leaving him spitting anger in my driveway.

I made my way out of the neighborhood onto twinkling city streets and looked at the clock. A second later, I forgot what time it was and checked again.

First stop: coffee. At a drive-through, I purchased two of their largest size available. No, I didn't want any food.

Outside the aquatics center, sleepy swimmers shuffled in. I blew on my coffee and eyed the drop-offs, the swimmers who carpooled together, all carrying their tiny duffels and backpacks.

I finished the massive coffee and felt the crazy caffeine rush and acid burn. I drank half of the next one, then flung open my car door.

It was easy to sneak in with the swimmers. I wore a bathing suit, shorts, flip-flops. No one questioned me when I walked over to the divers' dryland workout equipment. I was aware of the inspirational quote Coach Mike had pasted on the wall behind me. I refused to look at it but I could recite it from memory:

"To be as good as it can be, a team has to buy into what you as the coach are doing. They have to feel you're a part of them and they're a part of you."—Bobby Knight

I wondered how long it would take to forget it.

I hauled myself up onto the trampoline and gave it three practice bounces to get my sea legs back. Snap to stand. Jump to twist. Swivel seat.

Back drop. Back dive tuck. Then onto the somersaults. Over and over and over again. Some coaches would have said enough already. That I was being reckless, careless at this point. Mike would have said the more practice, the better.

My body took over in that strange way it always did when, deep down, I knew what I was doing. Yes, my muscles were weaker. Yes, my head was about to split. Yes, my acrobatics weren't neat. They were wild. But that wasn't the point. I'd been afraid to come even this far before. Acknowledging the truth about Coach Mike was a relief and now I was free to continue. The harder I worked, the sooner it would come back.

"Excuse me?"

I landed a somersault tuck. "What?" I sounded ready for a fight.

A kid, maybe fourteen or so, stood at the base of the trampoline. His water polo sweatshirt read *Yang*. I hated water polo players. They always hogged the pool. Had his coach sent him over to tell me to get out of here? No divers until after school?

"I don't really know anything about this equipment but it looks like you've popped a few springs." He pointed to the back edge of the trampoline.

I twisted to look. Shit.

"It's fine," I said. He shrugged and sauntered away as I swiped at the sweaty hair sticking to my face. Now the water polo coach had his eye on me. Assholes. I could practice my dive list in the pool if they weren't here.

I freed myself from the equipment and took to the stadium stairs. The last time I'd done stairs had been with Caroline. I buried the thought of her.

Keep it up, keep it up, keep it up.

The pounding. If I listened to the pounding, I wouldn't feel the pain.

Other sounds began to penetrate my concentration—a whistle blow, the crash of swim strokes.

I've been in love with you since I moved to this street.

The vomit caught me by surprise. I lunged to the closest trash can. Volumes of coffee came up. Who knew I could hold that much liquid?

The industrial wall clock read 7:00 A.M. It was time to get ready for school. I wiped my mouth with the back of my hand and made my way to the showers. In the locker room, I glimpsed a stranger's beet-red face in the mirror, realized it was me and averted my eyes, struck for a second by evidence that I existed.

✳

I spent the morning visiting my teachers, one by one, before the bell rang or for a few minutes after class. Some were excited to speak with me, glad I was taking responsibility for my missing grades. Two teachers weren't even really sure who I was. Five times, I explained my situation—my concussion—my confusion when I saw my grades. Each of them complied with my request and we went back through the grades online as I made a master list of assignments I needed to turn in and tests to retake.

A few acquaintances said hello. Preeti gave me a dirty look

in the hall, obviously sympathizing with Izzie about what a cold bitch I was. Otherwise, it was business as usual. Diving was something that took place far from school. A few days, at least, was the time it would take for word to spread about Mike and Caroline.

I looked at my phone one time during the school day. There was an email that practice was canceled. A few texts from teammates asking if I knew what was going on. If Mike's wife had gone into early labor. There was a message from the neurologist's office that I'd missed my follow-up. Nothing yet from my mom.

At lunch, I downed the rest of the cold, second large coffee while I drove to a drive-through for more. Somehow the vomit incident hadn't deterred me. The thought of food, however, made me nauseous.

This was called getting my shit together and it felt fantastic.

CHAPTER FORTY-ONE

After lunch, the latest injection of caffeine sang like a high note through my veins as I took my seat in Spanish.

Two of Van's soccer friends were in the class but, otherwise, I didn't know a soul, which would make it my easiest class of the day to navigate.

I crossed my ankles, slid lower in my chair, and tried to shake the feeling that the two soccer players were looking at me more than usual. I thought I heard some whispering and a brief cackle from one of them. I proceeded to work on a math take-home test while pretending to jot notes on Señora Lozano's lecture.

"Señorita Ingrid?"

Señora Lozano asked me a question to which I replied automatically in surprisingly rapid-fire Spanish. For a second, I had no idea whether what I'd said was even in the correct language. But it seemed to be, because she moved on. Who knew caffeine and three weeks without sleep had made me smarter? I was beginning to love living on adrenaline.

The insistent sensation of someone staring a hole in my back penetrated my focus. I glanced over my shoulder and one of the soccer players—Ethan—matched my stare with a curled lip. His friend guffawed. I shifted uncomfortably and fixed my eyes forward again. The classroom phone began to bleat.

"¿Hola?" Señora Lozano answered, removing one turquoise clip-on earring. Her eyes snapped to mine. "Yes, she's here. Okay. Sending her now." Señora Lozano placed the phone in its cradle and looked at me with dawning interest. "Ingrid, you're wanted at the counselor's office."

Everyone stared at me as I sat, unmoving.

"Honey, they said to gather your things for early release."

*

Mrs. White was around thirty-five, I guessed. Her hair was highlighted bright blond and she wore an eyelet-patterned, knee-length skirt and a neon-green tank top beneath a white blazer. She spoke fast. On her desk were scattered photos of toddler-age twin boys, she and her seven bridesmaids from her wedding, and one of a man—presumably her husband—wearing wrap-around sunglasses and holding up a tropical drink, his cheek pressed to hers.

I'd never met Mrs. White before. I assumed my huge high school must have multiple counselors. I pegged Mrs. White as the cool one. The one the students could talk to about their friends, their love lives, or other *sensitive* matters.

"Ingrid. Hi! I'm Christina White." She held out a manicured hand and gave mine a petite shake. "Take a seat."

I said nothing. Mrs. White glanced down at my incessant foot-tapping. I stopped and pressed my fingernails hard into my palm. Why couldn't I sit still? For a second, Mrs. White, surrounded by the sunlight pouring in through the window behind her, became a blur of green neon as if I'd looked directly at the sun. I refocused my eyes.

"Everything all right?"

"I'm good."

"A student from your diving team withdrew from the high school today. Some serious allegations are being made about your coach's conduct, as I'm sure you've heard by now."

Caroline was gone?

"We wanted to check in with you. Let you know there are resources here if you need someone to talk to. About anything."

Less than twelve hours and the high school counselor had heard the rumors. Those boys in Spanish class had obviously heard. It was truly amazing how fast word traveled. And, clearly, everyone was speculating about the nature of my relationship with Coach Mike.

You had to be kidding me.

"I can't help but notice a precipitous drop in your grades," Mrs. White prodded.

"I'm fine," I said quickly. "I had an injury—a concussion—so I missed some school. I have all my assignments. I'm back on track."

Mrs. White consulted her computer screen. "You live with your mom?"

I nodded. Yes, I lived with a single mother.

"Any siblings?"

"No. It's just the two of us."

"If there is anything that's hard to discuss with your mom, I want you to know you can always come here to talk."

"No. We're good. She works a night shift and sleeps in the day mostly." I was spinning and understood too late that I now sounded like one of those neglected kids who was perfect for a close family friend or Boy Scout leader—or coach—to prey on.

All kinds of alarm bells were going off in Mrs. White's eyes.

"I'm good. I promise."

"I'm here if you need me, Astrid."

"Ingrid."

Mrs. White brightened three shades of red. "Ingrid! I'm sorry."

After that, she consented to my hasty exit.

∗

The bell sounded as soon as I left Mrs. White's office. Twenty seconds later, the halls swarmed with students, trickling in from every available doorway.

I'd almost made a clean escape.

I was at the farthest possible point on campus from the parking lot and I impatiently made my way through the crowd, hoping no one would notice me.

I bumped into someone's arm, jostling his red backpack.

"Ingrid!" It was John Michael, my former would-be prom date. I waited for the familiar spark of worship in his eyes, the excuses I'd have to make to get away from him. I was taken aback when I saw something more like leeriness. Like I was slightly gross.

"Hi," I said, studying his reaction to me with a twisted kind of interest.

John Michael nodded his princely head and moved on quickly.

I looked around, unable to stop myself. Two senior girls watched me. I eyed them coolly. No one mattered, I repeated to myself, even as I cast my eyes downward.

When I entered the parking lot, I pretended to riffle through my backpack for keys to look busy. When I passed a silver jeep, I heard a male voice say something I couldn't hear and then, "Caroline." Laughter in response.

For the first time, I thought of how Van was feeling right now, how he was affected by the gossip. His girlfriend was the one who had cheated on him with a thirty-four-year-old.

I tucked myself into my hot car and relished the sound of the automatic locks sealing me inside, away from the unsettling hostility. The stench. My soiled T-shirt from the morning was balled up in the backseat, radiating the smell of coffee and bile. I started the car to get the air going. Nothing happened but a click.

I lifted my eyes and scanned front and side to side. The people closest had heard and were now waiting expectantly for my car to start.

I wiped at the sweat on my upper lip. *Please let this piece-of-trash car start and get me the hell out of this place. I will be perfect from now on.*

I went for it and turned the key. For a second it wheezed and there was hope the engine would turn over, the car whining louder and louder and straining. Now many eyes were on my car and the futile noises it was making.

I stopped. Instinctively, I looked to where I knew the boys would be. They weren't in their usual spot anymore. I was ashamed of myself for even checking. What was I going to do? Go ask Van for a ride?

A knock on my window startled me so badly, I heard my own audible gasp. A boy with black horn-rimmed glasses and thick, glossy hair that fell over one eye waited patiently for me to roll down my window. Without power, that wasn't something that was going to happen. I opened the car door a crack and the boy stepped back.

"Do you need any help?" he asked.

The kindness of strangers.

I didn't need any of that today.

"No, thanks. I'm good."

I exited the car and breezed past the boy as if this had been part of my master plan for the day.

*

I woke with a start. At first, I didn't know where I was and I couldn't place the older woman with gray hair and oily pink eyelids looming above me. I noticed the stacks of imposing bookshelves. The librarian was shaking my shoulder gently.

"It's five p.m. I'm going home, hon."

"Oh, I'm so sorry," I said, sitting up in the stiff-backed chair.

"Don't be. You kids need all the sleep you can get."

With trepidation, I checked my phone. There were more texts from teammates. I didn't read them. There was a voice mail from Caroline. I ignored it.

I had one message from my mom: *Went in early again. Thought I'd see you before I left. Can you bring in the trash cans?*

Did she still not know?

I took off for home on foot, ditching my car and listing a tad as I hauled both my heavy backpack and swim duffel, the latter strapped across my chest.

CHAPTER FORTY-TWO

More coffee. I couldn't believe I'd ever been upset about not sleeping at night. I needed the extra hours. First, I'd catch up on schoolwork. There was so much to get done. But after that, I could cram in more schoolwork, more workouts. I felt a little smug, like I could lap everyone with my achievements.

I made a list, broken down by the half hour. No more naps at the library. If I calculated correctly, I could finish all of my assignments over the next two days. I also plotted out time for three workouts per day.

With a knot in my stomach and increasingly swollen hands, I sent a polite email to the competitor USA Diving club in town. I needed a coach soon because their college connections were necessary. I was scared that despite my record, they would say no, that they wouldn't want the stink of scandal in their club. But if I could fix this before my mom found out . . . if I could fix all of it, everything would go back to how it was before the accident.

I was running on schedule. When math was complete, there

was the essay for English to begin. I wondered if Van had turned it in. My eyes flicked to the window but I didn't get up from my desk.

I started an outline for the essay but I suddenly couldn't form a reasonable argument. Whenever I tried to think deeply, I wasn't clear-headed. I kept hitting a wall and spinning my wheels, unable to hold a thought for more than a few seconds.

My attention was all over the place as I clicked through windows on my computer, not really doing anything but totally unable to tear myself away from the screen. I was scanning my email when I felt the prick of an idea. I went into my drive to the diving team's shared folder. At the top of the listed documents was the slideshow from the awards dinner that Mike had posted.

I enlarged the slideshow to full screen and hit play. I knew what I wanted to see. Immediately, I hit pause on the first photo. It was grainy at first and then corrected into crystal clear focus.

For the second time, I was looking at Mike with the high school team he'd once coached. And there it was. *She* was. It had just barely caught my awareness that night. Like a half-formed thought, I hadn't even known what I'd wanted to go back and see. Then the urgent feeling had dissipated when my thoughts moved on to how grand Mike and I looked together in the photos that followed.

There was Laura, Mike's wife. In the back row. Her black beauty mark was visible even though her hair was much darker, wet, and slicked back.

This was a high school team.

I'd never really asked how they'd met. I knew Laura was younger than Mike. I knew they had Florida in common and the diving world was a small one. Not for one second had it ever occurred to me that he had been her coach.

CHAPTER FORTY-THREE

Erase Mike from memory. Focus, Ingrid.

Coffee.

I trotted downstairs and when I arrived in the blindingly bright kitchen, I briefly forgot why I was there.

It was 4:30 A.M. Time for my run to school. If all went well, I'd call the tow truck and get a jump before anyone saw me, and I'd still make it to the aquatics center to enter with the swimmers at 5:45 A.M.

I began to jog out of the cul-de-sac, past Van's lit window, when I realized something had been different about the entry of the house. I circled back and put the key in the lock but the door opened wide as soon as I touched it. I'd forgotten to lock up.

Someone had slipped a note beneath the door.

I unfolded the yellow legal paper, torn jaggedly from a pad, ready to read the words "*Slut*" or "*Whore.*"

Ingrid,
I heard your car battery died. Text me if you want a jump.
—Wilson

That was unexpected. And embarrassing. Though I had to admit it was nice.

I crumpled up the paper, rechecked the time, and was about to start my run in the dark.

I could take care of myself.

"Ingrid!"

I whipped around. "Wilson." He'd scared me to death. He must have just slid the note beneath my door and was walking back to his house when he saw me exit.

Wilson stepped over the untrimmed hedge and walked into the light of the doorstep. He looked freshly showered.

"Hi," I said tentatively. I really didn't want any contact with another human being, but we had shared that terrifying night and I hadn't spoken to him since we were bent over Max four days ago.

Wilson lifted his chin in the direction of the note in my hand, then tucked a damp lock of jet-black hair behind his ear. "Do you need a jump?"

"No, I'm fine. It's all fine."

Wilson still didn't walk away and we stood together, the rattle of cicadas in stereo around us.

"How are you?" I finally asked. I kept my tone even so I wouldn't offend him. He didn't need me feeling sorry for him. I knew what that felt like.

Wilson wiped his nose quickly with his sleeve. "So-so. I think I convinced my moms I don't need a scared-straight wilderness school." He laughed but it didn't reach his eyes.

"What about Max?" I asked. "Where is he? I haven't seen him anywhere."

"At home. 'Resting.' He's fine now. Completely fine. You know Max."

"Are you?"

"Yeah." Wilson shuffled the leaves around at his feet, then met my eyes. "I just showered because I woke up and everything was soaking wet. Isn't that crazy? I didn't understand why I kept sweating. Then Van said, 'You're going through withdrawal, stupid.' Fuck, I didn't even know I was addicted."

"It's scary how fast it happens." As if I had any idea.

"I didn't think it would happen to me. I'm not that person. It was a weekend thing." Wilson blew into the air, maybe mistakenly thinking he would see a cloud of his own breath. But it was spring now.

"I'm sorry about your coach," Wilson said suddenly. "I didn't know who he was when I saw him at the house."

At the mention of Caroline and Mike, I immediately wanted to get away yet I couldn't help but say, "At the very least, you couldn't tell your best friend his girlfriend was cheating on him?"

Wilson winced. "I was so shocked to see him standing there that night, I didn't know what to do. Max and I felt like shit. When we invited you and Van to the house, that wasn't one of our times to use it—we were weekends when Mary Seitzman was gone and Van was usually with the band. We wanted to surprise Caroline that night so Van would find out on his own. Seba was so pissed. In his own messed-up way, he'd do anything for Caroline."

I was about to make my excuses and start running when Wilson flared his nose in disgust—at Mike, at Caroline, at himself, I wasn't sure.

"But I should have done something. For her. The thing about the drugs? What was almost worse than doing them was what I did because of them. I didn't tell anyone about Caroline and this old dude because I was having fun and I didn't want it to end. That night, when we accidentally came face-to-face in the house? The thing was, Caroline was wasted. Just a kid drunk off her ass. When your coach looked at us, he seemed completely sober. He took off sprinting like an Olympic athlete. Or a guy with a lot to lose."

"I gotta go, Wilson." My voice cracked. No more. It kept getting more appalling. How many ways could your hero fall?

I put a hand on Wilson's shoulder, squeezed, then wordlessly left him on my porch and began running into the dark.

✳

Mid-workout, there was the first tingle in the back of my throat. I ignored it as I practiced from the springboard into the foam pit, dragging myself up and out, again and again.

By the end of the workout, I was hot and my throat was scratchy. Nothing that couldn't be overcome by a trip to the convenience store.

My car was a lone soldier in the school parking lot when I'd come to her rescue earlier. By some miracle, the car had started when I gave it one last try. Now, I lucked out again when I returned to it after my workout. For thirty seconds, I allowed myself to rest my head on my arms, draped across the steering wheel.

Pain is weakness leaving the body.

I hated that phrase. Both Mike and Caroline had used it, I realized in hindsight. I wondered who had said it to the other first. Coach Mike had trained me to keep moving, to ignore pain. Now I was going to use his advice and erase him. Wherever he was, he hadn't even reached out to make excuses or to apologize.

Before school started, I made a quick trip to the convenience store. I stocked up on ibuprofen, a coffee, and splurged on orange-flavored vitamin C powder to add to my water bottle. Twenty minutes, I told myself, and I'd feel like a new person.

※

"Are you okay?" Izzie deigned to ask me later that day in English. She had willfully ignored me since her tirade. I lifted my head from the cool desk to answer her. Van was talking with a friend across the room before class started. Back to how things had been. He was a stranger again. He felt me look at him and we met eyes. He looked away first and continued his conversation.

"Yeah, I'm good," I answered Izzie, straightening my posture. My answer seemed to annoy her. Her usually friendly, excited eyes flattened and she didn't say another word.

Popping three more ibuprofen before class had seemed like a good idea at the time. On the one hand, I quit sweating, but my stomach wasn't happy. I knew I should leave in case I threw up all over the floor. In one motion, I rose and hooked my backpack over my shoulder. More eyes on me as I slipped out mid-class.

In the gloriously cold bathroom, riddled with graffiti on the beige stall doors and on the mirror above the trough sink, I texted my mom. Just to touch base. Kevin must have reached her. Or another diving parent, most of whom were crazy-involved. Surely my mom had heard by now. I gazed unseeing in the mirror and wondered when I'd spoken to my mom last. I couldn't recall.

I waited a few minutes for her reply. She was always home at this hour, though she could be asleep. I replaced my phone in my backpack when two girls burst into the bathroom—all loud, mischievous, freshman glee.

"Your shirt's on inside out," one of them said in greeting after looking me up and down, purple vaping pen in hand.

In response, I held my white T-shirt away from my body to

check it out. Sure enough, the threads around the V-neck were on display. "Oh," I said lamely.

The two girls had stopped talking to watch me, obviously waiting on me to leave so they could get to it. Just to piss them off, I took my time splashing cold water on my face, then slowly patting it dry with stiff, brown paper towel. Then I kicked the door open with my foot and made my exit.

I was doing better. The nausea had passed. It was perfect—I'd leave school early and try starting the car when no one was around to witness my humiliation if it died again. At home, I'd take advantage of the ibuprofen and go on a run. If I timed the run just so, I could arrive back home right before my mom needed to leave for her shift and there wouldn't be enough time to get into things too deeply. Then I'd finish up the list of assignments. If I could just keep pushing, stay on my schedule, everything would be okay. I did my best work when I pressured myself hard.

On the one hand, I knew I was being insane, driving myself like this. On the other, it didn't matter. Because if I didn't keep up with my plan, I would dissolve into nothing.

When I arrived home, I knew I had missed my mom by minutes since the garage light was still on. I texted again, giving her a little more information this time, informing her I was home and going on a run. I didn't let her know I was sick because what was the point? There wasn't anything she could do besides be concerned. Or annoyed.

Hours later, after an oddly exhilarating five-mile run around Lady Bird Lake, some science homework, and the completion of my essay, I wasn't able to stay ahead of the fever. I lay down on my bed and shivered, soaking my sheets through. The ibuprofen was downstairs and it felt like I'd have to crawl through the Sahara Desert to claim it. I wasn't willing. I kept my phone by my side and waited for the chirp that said I had a text from my mom.

CHAPTER FORTY-FOUR

My dream was an endless torture loop.

I stared at stains in my carpet, the green-and-gold-leaf spine of *Anne of Green Gables* on the bookshelf, the babyish elephant art on the walls, taking in their detail for the first time in years from my sweaty mess of tangled sheets. I knew I was sick, I knew I was in my room. Coach Mike was entering in and out of my half-conscious state.

I was on the springboard. About to do the dive again. The reverse two and a half on the three-meter. Coach Mike was below, watching.

I'd remember I was in my room, not at the swim center, not about to dive, then, a second later, I was about to dive again. But I wouldn't. I couldn't move.

Mike was lecturing me, "You have a block. You are allowing a psychological obstacle to subvert you."

"Why did you do it?" I asked him. He looked like my dad from the recent photo Izzie had forwarded: tattoos, shaved head, black jacket hooked with a thumb over his shoulder. He looked around distractedly and then removed his sunglasses. His eyes were the same as mine and he appeared like he had ten years ago, younger than he must look now. But, while he might seem like my father, I knew he was really Coach Mike.

"It had nothing to do with you," Mike said to me. I could see in his eyes that he believed that.

All of the noise in my head, the warning bells telling me something was off, undermining my trust in him, the team's trust in a beloved adult. My trust in what he'd told me about myself: that I was strong, powerful, special. Mike had informed how I saw myself in this world.

The fact that he had not only looked at one of his divers that way but acted on it was a betrayal of all of us.

"How am I going to do this without you?" I asked him. I wasn't sure if I meant diving or life. Both.

Mike scoffed and looked over at the parents filling the stands. "You're going to have to."

My alarm went off, far too loud, scaring me out of limbo. Thank god. Thank god I wasn't really there on the diving board, frozen. With Mike.

Slowly, I sat up and put my face in my hands. Clammy.

My limbs were weak and when I first stood, I was dizzy, using the wall to get to the bathroom just like I had in those first days post-concussion. Shampooing my hair, getting clean, brushing my teeth all helped. Slowly, carefully, I got dressed. This was going to pass.

I made my way downstairs to the kitchen, almost kissed the bottle of ibuprofen that sat innocently where I'd left it on the clean, smooth countertop, and realized in total horror that we'd run out of coffee. I checked the freezer. Nothing. Not even the frostbitten bag of Swedish coffee from two Christmases ago, stuffed in the way back. I'd polished that off sometime over the past few days.

On the way to the garage, I rested on the leather bench in the hallway to gather my strength. Then I spent so much time just sitting there, weakly, that I was going to be too late to sneak in with the swimmers if I didn't get up.

This was ridiculous. Once I had coffee in me, I'd feel better. But I was running out of time to make a stop. I used that as my carrot and stumbled my way to the car in the garage. I started the engine and knowing I was short on time, I backed out fast.

Then all was ear-splitting sound. Sounds I'd never heard before. The sound of my car crashing into the garage door and the scraping of metal on metal.

Like a criminal on the run who'd finally been caught, all I kept thinking was: *It's over.*

⁕

Mr. Kitchen was the first to arrive on the scene. From my vantage point next to the mangled garage door, my car poking half out, I zeroed in on him with shocked tunnel vision as he sprinted to me on his bike from the end of the cul-de-sac. I stood by my car helplessly, nowhere to hide.

A small crowd formed, the bolder neighbors coming onto the property. I watched mutely as Mr. Kitchen, hands on his bicycle shorts, feathers puffed up, inspected the damage to my car and to the garage, leaning this way and that, speaking to the neighbors but not to me. Kevin and Lisa arrived, the adults I knew best on the cul-de-sac.

"We got this, Larry," said Kevin. They stood face-to-face, two self-appointed neighborhood watchmen. For the first time, I felt gratitude for Kevin.

There was a bit of a stare-down. "I'll call Elsa," Mr. Kitchen announced, referring to my mom.

"No need," Kevin said. "We'll take care of it, man." After a pause, Mr. Kitchen huffed off on his bike.

"Come with me, honey. You can sit on my daybed until your mother comes," Mrs. Connor said, a widow who lived in the pink house next door to Max.

"I've got her, Dolores." Lisa came to my side and put her arm around my shoulders, resting her head against mine.

"Oh, sweet girl," she said to me.

Her words of endearment caused the tears. I gave a great gulping gasp that came from deep within, containing so much fear. And loneliness.

Kevin came to my other side and gave me an awkward pat. With the Moores flanking me, I looked like I had parents, and the neighbors who came out to inspect the noise began to disperse.

"Come on," Lisa said. "Let's go to our house and just sit."

*

Van was at soccer practice so it was only me, Kevin, and Lisa and one of the twins who lay sprawled out on the den sofa in a pair of pj's with trains on them. Stella scratched in her crate behind where Kevin, Lisa, and I sat at the kitchen table. I held my glass of cold water tightly.

"How are you doing?" Lisa asked.

"Fine." I'd stopped crying but now my voice cracked. Lisa's face fell and she reached over again and gave me a squeeze and kissed the top of my head. I could playact for just a bit and enjoy the comfort; pretend this was a way of life.

"I left a message for your mom," Kevin said, crossing his arms, "but I haven't heard back."

"She's been working a lot lately," I said. It was past 8:00 A.M. She would arrive home any minute.

"Caroline's parents sent me an update. They flew in and made sure the coach was suspended immediately. Now there's going to be an inquiry." Kevin waited for some response from me, so I nodded. Then he seemed to look at me more closely and said, "Do you want me to tell your mom?"

I wasn't sure how he knew I hadn't told my mom yet.

"That's okay. I'll do it today."

Lisa stood to get more coffee, tugging down her white ruffled tennis skirt. With horror I realized she was missing her tennis game. When I started to apologize, she interrupted and looked at me like I was crazy. "Ingrid, we love you. You saved my son when we moved onto this block. Of course we're staying right here until your mom comes home."

"Van's a really good person," I said to Lisa. It was also for Kevin's benefit. Though I noticed Lisa wouldn't look at Kevin, I saw that he was trying.

"That's really nice to hear." I could tell Lisa meant it, that it was a relief. Kevin left it alone and didn't make a snarky comment but he did leave the table and wander to the kitchen sink, looking out the window, onto the street.

"Elsa is home," Kevin reported from his post. He faced me, resting his bulk against the sink. "Want me to go with you? She doesn't look too happy."

For a second, I saw what had drawn Lisa to Kevin: his confidence, his protector attitude, and for a second, I actually wanted to lean on him, of all people.

"No. But thank you." I had been taught to be self-reliant. It would be strange to stop now.

✳

"Mom." I approached her back slowly, crossing from the Moores' side of the world back to mine. My mom stood by her car, staring at the hole in the garage and the wreckage. She wore pink scrubs and dangled a travel coffee mug from one thumb. A thick strand of blond hair was loose from her bun.

It felt like a year since I'd seen her. I anticipated her face when she turned around. This person I loved so much. I realized the thing I dreaded most—more than anything in this world—was that look of stress. I had planned a life around trying to make it better.

But when she turned around, my mom only asked, "What happened?" Her voice contained some wonder and amazement, like she'd pulled up to the wrong house. She searched my face and whatever she saw made her guide me to the front door. "Let's go inside."

When I peered behind me, I saw Lisa, the twins, and Kevin, all watching from the kitchen window.

CHAPTER FORTY-FIVE

When I finally told my mom about Mike, the first thing she said was, "Thank you for telling me. I know this is really hard." My mom was doing her best to remain calm but I'd never seen her so upset.

So she could change my sheets, she directed me to her bed. An hour later, my mom put down her cell phone somewhere in the bed covers, having finally listened to the twelve messages from unknown numbers that had rolled in over the course of the past two days.

"What happened? What did the messages say?" I asked.

"There's a parent meeting tomorrow night with the powers that be. Everyone has a lot of questions about how this could have happened and who knew." She hesitated for a moment and then looked beside herself when she asked me, "Did you know?"

"I tried to pretend I didn't."

My mom covered her face with her hands for a second. When she looked at me again, there was so much self-recrimination in her eyes. "You know you can tell me anything. I will always be there for you. You don't have to carry everything on your own."

"It's not your fault. I'm almost an adult."

"No, you're not an adult. Not yet. It's my job to protect you. Mike created a relationship with you that, in hindsight, was not okay. I thought it was—he was Mike. But you shouldn't have been at his house, socializing without other teammates. He shouldn't have been at family occasions. He was your teacher. I'll take the blame for not creating a better boundary. But now I'm here." My mom stared quietly at the carpet for a long moment, thinking.

"What happens to the team?" I sounded hoarse.

"The diving program needs to tell us how they're going to handle this."

"I mean, competition-wise. Is the team going to fall apart?"

"No, we're going to fight to keep it together. We don't want to let Mike hurt you kids. Coach Ericka is going to step up and coach your age division and an assistant is going to cover the younger kids until someone new is hired. It sounds like practice will resume in two days. And that's perfect, Ingrid. When you kick this virus, you can go back. You'll be done with your month of rest."

She collected her phone, grabbed the blanket at the foot of her bed, and spread it over me. I was shivering hard, the fever spiking again. My mom was about to walk out the bedroom door, on to what she was best at: tasks.

"Mom?"

She turned. "I'm going to grab your sheets for the wash. Then I'm going to call a garage-door repair place. We'll deal with your car next."

"I'm sorry. Let me deal with it."

"Um, no, you won't. You need to rest."

"You're not mad?"

"I mean, I'm not happy, but I'm more worried about you."

"I'll be okay."

My mom came back over and sat down at the bedside again. "This is going to be a thing you're going to have to carry and I hate that, but this is not about you. This was never about you." Then, in a softer voice, "I want to make sure you know it is not a big deal that you were close to Mike. I know he was like a father to you and I understand your need for that close relationship given that your father is . . ."

To make her feel better, I said, "No, I have a father."

She touched my hair. "No, honey. Not really."

I was so taken aback, I turned my face to the wall so she wouldn't see the immediate effect her words had.

"He went away and he missed so much. Even if you win twenty Olympic gold medals, he can never come back and raise you."

My chest was tight and I couldn't breathe except for small, short inhales through my noise. Finally, I managed, "What's wrong with me?"

"What?" My mom sounded like she hadn't heard my question.

"What's wrong with me?" The question came out between hyperventilating breaths. "Why doesn't he want to see me?" I was exploding and I was trying to stuff it back down as hard and as fast as I could but I was losing control.

"Oh, honey. Oh, honey." My mom's entire face changed to pure sadness and she put her head down next to mine on the pillow. "Nothing is wrong with you in the least."

"I remember holding on to him, trying to get him to stay, and he looked at me with disgust." I couldn't stop gasping.

My mom's expression was appalled, like she'd had no idea this was what I'd been thinking. We were face-to-face, just inches between us. Her eyes had lightened with unshed tears to an electric light blue. "It wasn't you."

"Why does it feel like it?"

"That's the fucked-up thing about shame. He made you feel ashamed when, at that moment, he just didn't want to feel how much he loved you and what he was giving up. It was all about him. But his actions affected you." My mom pushed her hand into my back, as if to let me know she had me and to steady herself, to remind us both that we were fine. She was gathering herself and I expected her to return to what she needed to get done. It was more of a conversation than we'd ever had about what had happened.

Then she paused. "I know it's confusing when someone you love behaves in a way you can't fathom, but they are not you. The only person you can ever understand is yourself. You're your own constant."

I wanted to be strong like my mom. "I'm going to put my head down, be quiet, plow through. I never want to think about Mike again."

"No. No," she said, surprising me.

"You seemed like you never thought about him again—Dad." It was like when I'd thrown up the other day; I'd had no idea it was coming and I kept spewing.

"Honey, I'm human. For years, I've wondered what he was thinking and how he could have abandoned you."

No one had ever said it out loud. I was an abandoned child.

"Ingrid?"

"What?" I refocused my eyes on hers.

"Raising you has been the best part of my life. I'm glad I got to be the one to do it."

I'd tried to make it easy. I'd tried to have perfect grades, be a perfect athlete, get college paid for so she didn't have to go back to my dad to ask for money. I had to tell her now. Keeping the secret had finally become the greater evil. It would be a relief.

"Mom, I haven't slept—not really—since the accident. I stay up all night and it never leaves the back of my mind that I'm scared to dive now. I don't know if it's Mike, or that I've realized how dangerous it is. It's like I woke up and realized how badly I can get hurt. And now I've been gone so long, I'm not sure I can force myself to go back. I could stand on that diving board and freeze."

My mom sat up against the headboard.

"What happens if I never dive again?" I wiped at the sweat that broke down the sides of my face. I stared at the pale blank wall, a shaft of sunlight making a picture frame behind her. That was the thing about my mom; she turned all the blank whiteness of this house into a mellow gold.

I knew she would talk me down, form a plan, tell me why I was feeling this way. Part of me wanted her to give me direction and part of me knew I would die inside when she did because, this time, I didn't think I could deliver.

"Ingrid, I am fine if you never, ever dive again. You need to follow what you love."

I paused, reluctant to point out reality. "What about the full scholarship? I don't want to ask Dad for money."

"We'll figure it out. Your happiness is what's most important."

I felt such incredible relief.

She reached out and smoothed my damp hair. "I had no idea any of this was going on."

"I thought I would figure it out on my own." Well, not quite on my own. I'd had Van.

"I need to apologize to you. I messed up. I always told myself I was there for you. That I could make it all work. I think a lot of the time, I just don't have much left over."

"You've been a really good mom." Looking at her now, I knew I'd been chasing the dream of my father, the one who left, but she was the one who'd been here all along.

Now I could see my mom's profound relief. "We've been on a journey together, haven't we?" she said. I knew what she meant. I could also see that we were almost near the end of it. But not yet.

Outside, birds sang, interrupted by the sound of a garbage truck heaving over a nearby speed bump. I had a taste of what my mom's mornings in the house by herself felt like. She still loomed above me, as if she hadn't decided whether to say what was on her mind.

"What? Did you want to say something?"

"My goal has always been to make you independent so when bad things happen—like your dad, now Mike, god forbid anything happening to me while you're still young—you'd be resilient. That's not totally realistic. Bad stuff has happened to us, to you. It's not weakness that it hurts. I want you to be excited about life and know that, even after what you've seen firsthand, being open is worth it. For instance, look, I have you," she said gently. She cleared her throat and I realized she was choking up.

"Sometimes it feels powerful to shut off. But I've realized that isn't life. It's sort of half of one. And I don't want that for you."

CHAPTER FORTY-SIX

Harp music marked the end of my first full night of sleep. I heard cursing and then a phone drop to the floor. Finally, the chords stopped and my mother rose from her side of the bed. I dropped back into the sleep of the dead.

CHAPTER FORTY-SEVEN

Are you okay? I haven't seen you around.

Hi. I got really sick. I'm finally better though. How are you?

With what? I'm sorry I've been an asshole.

No, I'm sorry I've been an asshole. This past month was really weird. I'm a mess. That's why I don't tell you things.

Who isn't? And you know I will always love you anyway. Can you come over?

Why Izzie would always love me, and why she was so loyal to me, I had no idea. But for once, I decided to trust it.

I was about to agree to her invitation, already looking forward to one of my favorite escapes in the world after days in bed. That was how our lopsided relationship worked: Izzie shared everything and I shared as little as possible.

I typed, *Want to come here?*

CHAPTER FORTY-EIGHT

I tried to keep my first day of diving practice as undramatic as possible. I told my mom I didn't want her to come.

The labyrinthine corridor took me through hallway after hallway while blood pounded in my ears. I felt like a little kid dragging my feet. I didn't want to be here. I noticed the paint job, the picture frames on walls, the stripe that ran the entire length of the tunnel like a version of the yellow brick road. All with the awareness that this could be the last time.

And then the claustrophobic tunnel opened onto the vast, bright swim deck and I thought I would die of a heart attack. It was so big and so frightening and there was still time to turn around, all of the swimmers obscuring me from the divers who were stick figures clear across three pools.

If I didn't face it now, it would only get worse. In my heart, I knew if I didn't walk over to my team today, I would never do it again. Wearing my favorite bathing suit, pulled from the back of the drawer where, ashamed, I'd stashed it more than a month ago, I walked toward my team, wondering what kind of team even still remained.

"Ingrid!"

I was quickly surrounded, pulled into hugs by divers in their team suits.

"Why did you call the other club? You wanted to leave us?"

I was startled that they'd seemed to miss me and thought of me as part of their community. "No. I just didn't know that we'd be taken care of. As a group, I mean."

"We were trying to find a coach for all of us."

"Ingrid, we're so happy to see you." Our new coach gave me the last hug, her black bob grazing my cheek. "I know the team has a lot of healing to do and I know I'm not Mike. But I am here to help however you think is best. I don't want to mess with what you have going on. We'll just start. Okay? Let's get going." She was nervous and I was about to pass out. Just like that, it was time to dive. I'd expected a one-on-one off to the side with the coach to give her my litany of excuses and the setting of low to zero expectations. But there wasn't time and no one was listening. It seemed to be my turn.

Outside of myself, I realized in one moment, I would be up on that board. In front of everyone. I had no idea what was going to happen.

The glance-around for Mike would be a habit for a long time. He was gone now and never coming back. And no matter what I achieved in this sport, I understood that my dad was gone and never coming back. Most likely, I wouldn't know if he was proud of me or if he even thought about me. There was no fighting it or outrunning it; it was just sad.

I wasn't sure what any of it meant—to have people you trusted devastate you—and what to do with my memories of the good times. The past month, sensing what was coming, that question had completely displaced me and, in the end, I couldn't mount a new effort to shut it out.

When I walked to the end of the springboard, instead of possessing my machinelike mentality from a month before, I was scared. That bold little girl was long gone. I was diving from a different part of myself.

The smattering of voices and echoes, the glassy, undulating water below. Closing my eyes, I heard my own breathing and stretched out that last second. I knew if I dove, I could possibly get hurt, I could disappoint myself, my life could change course from where it had been headed.

But it would be much worse to turn around and be eaten alive in that particular way that happens when you stayed on the sidelines. I knew, because that was where I had been living the rest of my life when I wasn't up here. Van showing up at diving with Caroline that day had pushed me and I couldn't keep lying that I didn't want things.

In a terror-filled moment, many, many eyes on me, some probably craving my failure, I went for it, self-preservation screaming in my ears. Immediately, my angle was off, I was leaning back too far, so I saved myself by hipping out. The dive was a mess.

I crashed into the water below, hitting it hard. I plunged fast beneath the surface, then gradually slowed and began to rise. I looked above to the light, awash with relief at facing my gigantic red wall of fear. I was back in my favorite moment, by myself, the stream of bubbles shooting up around me. Now I could feel every bit of how terrified I was. About everything. I didn't know anything anymore. But I also felt like my real self. I'd been gone for a while.

For a long time, it had seemed like I was winning. But the fearless me had been on eggshells, the most scared person I knew.

CHAPTER FORTY-NINE

I listened to Caroline's message, her voice still beautiful and lilting from wherever she was—San Diego? It didn't seem fair.

"Hey, Ingrid. It's me. I wanted to say I'm sorry. Believe me, I didn't mean for you to lose your coach. I didn't mean for Mike to lose his job. To have to move in with his parents. I'm sure you hate me. It was just—I was ready, you know? I was so ready. To get out of there, to not be in high school, to be an adult. I wasn't ready for other people to get hurt, though."

Caroline's voice lowered, confessional. *"My mom keeps saying I didn't have a choice. I want you to know that's not true. It didn't even start at dive practice. I ran into Mike at the convenience store a couple of months ago when I was out on a run. Maybe it's messed up that he bought me alcohol."* Caroline laughed darkly. *"Ha, don't tell my mom that! But you know me. I don't do anything I don't want to do."*

She coughed a little bit and then came back to the phone. *"About a month ago, when we were partying at that house, you came up in conversation. Van said he's always been in love with you. I was so pissed I wouldn't talk to him for days and I didn't tell him why. Granted, he was wasted but . . . Whether you know this already or not, he wants to be with you. I'm sorry if I got in the way of that, too.*

"I'm sorry. I know we won't talk again most likely but I really, really liked you and I looked up to you. I still do. Bye."

I placed my phone down on my desk and held one last thought of Caroline. She would always be another person I wouldn't be able to place. I'd never know quite how I felt about her. If I closed my eyes, I could still feel what it was like to be close to her, that extra pop of excitement to be near her confidence as she walked with her head held high, owning the world. Then I remembered that night when we'd caught her with Coach Mike and seeing her as a scared little girl.

Caroline said it had started at the convenience store. I could almost picture how the whole thing happened, the bell chiming as Caroline flings open the door, oblivious, or conscientiously oblivious, to the stares as the sweaty beauty with the damp ponytail walks into the small Minute Mart, smelling of cocoa butter and sunscreen. Mike is at the register, buying himself a six-pack. He sees Caroline first and watches as her face lights with recognition just before she lets out a singsong, "Hey, Coach Mikey!"

For some reason, she looks different to him, out of context, dressed in a sports bra instead of the swimsuit he sees her in every day.

They chitchat. For far longer than usual. Maybe they stand out in front of the store for a while, lingering, both growing excited as it morphs into an interaction with a new flavor. During that conversation, Mike begins entertaining the thought. It's the way Caroline looks at him, making him feel alive and so important.

When Coach Mike, six-pack dangling from two fingers, asks Caroline if she wants a ride, testing her, calling her bluff, does her smile falter? Just for one second.

∗

Later that afternoon, my mom strolled into my bedroom. "Hi! Are you going over?"

She walked directly to the window overlooking the house next door so she could take a peek. I joined her. The house was bright and clean, having been power-washed that morning. Yesterday, a fleet of landscapers came and trimmed, then hauled away debris. One day was all it had taken for a makeover. Apparently, for the past week, agents had been preparing the house for today's estate sale. How had that dingy house next door ever seemed so scary, like it was a person, watching me?

"I don't think so. You?"

"No. It's probably all junk." My mom glanced over at me. "You look one hundred percent better. You're so beautiful."

"Ha!" I shook off the compliment.

"You're always beautiful, but now you look healthy."

"Honestly, I never thought I would sleep again." It was strange to have no ailments: no weighed-down eyelids, sore throat, sore neck, fast and electric brain I couldn't trust. I hadn't felt better immediately after sleeping. At first, it had just made me slow and more exhausted, like I was walking in sand. But immediately, nothing was as scary and close to the surface. I wasn't as emotional; I had an attention span again. "That was torture," I said.

I wanted to know if Van was sleeping, if he'd had some kind of shift or closure or whatever it was he needed to pass through. As usual, from the moment I woke up to the moment I fell asleep and probably even in my dreams, I couldn't stop thinking about him. Why had I ever thought that was going to change? Now it would only be worse.

My mom stooped to collect dirty clothes from my floor. I tried to intervene and scoop them up before she had to. "Ingrid, stop. It's okay."

"Thanks, Mom." She looked sad, like she'd trained me too well, that I was always concerned she'd be frustrated with me. When she straightened, something caught her eye out the street-facing window and she wandered over. A huge smile broke out over her face. "Look at them. Those boys," she said affectionately.

There was a catch in my stomach as I joined her. Below, Van, Max, and Wilson were gathered together for pictures. They were dressed up for prom—all three of them in dark suits and so handsome. I wasn't used to Van looking this way. It was almost hard to look at him because he took my breath away.

All three sets of parents had agreed to let the boys go tonight. They were on the Moores' lawn, snapping photos as Kevin ordered the boys to move from the shadows. The boys didn't look or act cocky like they would have in a photo like this a year ago, even three months ago. They had lost a little boyishness. For the first time in a long time, there was a lightness in the air. I realized what was different—everyone seemed to be looking each other in the eye.

My mom laughed to herself and tilted her head. Through her silky hair, I caught a glimmer of her favorite silver earrings, the ones she wore back when she could still carry me. I would watch them dangle and sway as she walked. And laughed.

"What's so funny?" I asked.

"I was just about to tell you to go over there and thank Van. But you got it, I'm not making you do anything."

"Thank him for what?"

"For stopping by your diving practice. I can't believe how

sweet that was. I told Lisa today was your first day back and how nervous you were."

"Mom!"'

"Sorry! Anyway, I ran into her in the driveway and she said Van told her you did great. You two may not interact very much, but he is a loyal friend. It's like perfect bookends that he was there when you got hurt and there to see you return. Almost like he felt responsible."

"Wait a minute. He went to my practice?" My voice seemed to go up three octaves.

I saw my mom try not to smile. "You wouldn't even let me go!" She reset her eyes on the boys, considering them. "I think the three of them will be okay. They have their families. They have each other, at least for one more year."

"I think those three will be close forever."

My mom consulted the pink clock by my bed. "I hate to do it but I've got to get going. I have the next two days off, though. Let's get out of here tomorrow and do something together." I loved her for not asking me what I was doing tonight and making me feel self-conscious that I hadn't been asked to prom.

I placed my head on her shoulder for just one second, allowing myself to depend on her. "I love you, Mom."

"I love you so much. Congratulations on today. That couldn't have been easy." She pressed her lips to my forehead and then I heard her gentle tread on the stairs.

From behind my pane of glass, I watched as the boys broke apart after the photo session. Van laughed at something Wilson said. Then, I wasn't sure if I imagined it, but I thought Van raised his eyes to my window. I held my breath.

Kevin came over to Van's side and clapped him on the back as if wanting to take some credit for the smart, considerate adult Van was clearly becoming. It was shining from Van tonight.

Maybe Kevin did deserve a little credit. He'd made life stable for Van and in turn Van was protective of the people he loved.

Kevin followed Van to the driver's side of the car and, a whole head shorter, leaned in close to Van as if to impart wisdom or warnings: *Don't drink and drive; use a condom; keep an eye on your cup.* Van nodded his bent head as in, *Yeah, yeah,* but when he looked up he was smiling good-naturedly. Then the boys piled into the car and drove away into the evening. Probably to go pick up their dates—pretty girls in pretty dresses.

I wiped my sweaty palms on my gray sweats. Outside, the early evening yelled promise and spring and I craved something I couldn't put my finger on. Excitement, maybe. The thought of a beginning, of starting fresh. A whole night ahead.

If I settled in with Netflix, the night would pass like any night. But I didn't want to be cooped up. I wanted to celebrate. I wanted to be young, like the boys.

I went out to the street to lose myself in the hustle and bustle of the neighbors still in front of the house next door. I trailed onto the sidewalk.

Estate sale agents were coming in and out of the house, carrying boxes of items that hadn't sold.

"Ingrid! How are you?" I was greeted by nosy Mrs. Kitchen. But I didn't mind. I was glad to see her, to not be alone. I stood with a crowd of women from the cul-de-sac and they accepted me in, like I belonged. They discussed their finds from the estate sale. One of them had scored a small flat-screen TV. Mrs. Seitzman felt awful for buying the wedding silver for only one hundred dollars.

Mary Seitzman danced up to our small group. "What happened to the family, Mom? Did you ever hear?"

Mrs. Seitzman opened her mouth to speak just as a smartly dressed estate sale agent passed by and interjected, "They're in

San Francisco. For an experimental cancer treatment for the husband. It's very sad."

"They didn't want their stuff?" Mary said it more as an exclamation.

"It's just stuff, honey. They have each other," her mom said.

"They told me they wanted a fresh start. That being together was the most important thing," the agent said, and gave Mary an apologetic smile.

I'd been so anxious about the little girl, but it was okay, she was loved.

Mary plucked a doll from a nearby box. "They didn't want the toys? Look at all of these toys. Boxes and boxes of them." When she removed the doll, Mary revealed piles of the little girl's artwork and photographs.

That had been all I wanted when I was a child and my dad left. To get out of here. To start over. Away from these people and this cul-de-sac and their prying eyes.

An agent wheeled a child's bike down the driveway toward a truck bed filled to the brim with black trash bags. He lifted it up, the bike Van had once given me, and roughly heaved it on top of the other garbage.

"Wait!" I wanted to cry out and jog after him and grab hold of my childhood that was rushing away from me. But, glued in place, I watched the truck pull out and drive off, the rusted handlebars of the bike jostling up and down. Then the truck turned the corner, out of sight.

My phone buzzed and I flipped it over, my heart immediately pounding when I saw the message from Coach Mike.

I'm so sorry.

You've got it from here.

"I hope she gets through it okay. She has a lot ahead of her," Mary said.

"Who?" I asked.

Mary considered me. "This little girl." She held out the photo in her hand for me to see. It was a school photo of the daughter, a fake beach background with cattails and sand dunes behind her, her two front teeth missing. In the picture, she was beaming. "I hope she remembers how happy she was once," Mary said.

I suddenly really liked Mary.

Soon the sky was pinkening and the cars were pulling away from the once-abandoned house, now clean and empty and almost ready to put on the market. I wandered down the driveway, reluctant to return home. At the mailbox, I kicked away a tangle of overgrown plants from the curb with my flip-flop. Writing in the concrete caught my eye. *Sarah* was written in the cement where it had once been wet. I smiled to myself. The little girl had made her mark after all. She had lived here.

I still lived here. And even long after my mom moved away, I'd always think of this cul-de-sac as my home.

✳

Gradually, I watched the sky grow darker and the Moore house lights grow brighter. The neighbors left the estate sale and the agents closed the last trunk and drove away. I lingered outside, wanting something so badly.

I saw Lisa and Kevin in their kitchen window. Kevin said something that made Lisa laugh. From down the street came sounds of a kid practicing their clarinet. Mr. Kitchen worked on his bike in the driveway. Wilson's mom Mira drove down the street and gave me a wave. I knew what she was thinking: *Why isn't Ingrid at prom?*

I wanted to be with the boys. It was the craziest thought but I wanted to be where they were. I wanted Van more than anything and for the first time, I didn't fight the feeling.

I'd held it in for years. I'd longed for him from across the street no matter how hard I'd tried to stop. And now I couldn't go back to not having his friendship. Not just Van's, all three of the boys'.

The adrenaline kicked in. Then the daring feeling. It would be much safer to wait until morning or tomorrow afternoon when he woke up. I could just talk to him then.

I ran upstairs to change.

✳

I wore the same black dress I'd worn to the awards dinner, which was embarrassing, but otherwise it would have been jeans. I'd put my hair up like my mom's and I'd tried to put on eye makeup the way I'd seen her do it. In the end, it didn't look like me, and I shook out my hair and wiped away the eye shadow.

I was tempted to leave my car in the fire lane so I could dash to it like Cinderella if everything went wrong.

I opened the car door, feeling like I was going into free fall, amazed I wasn't dying when I took the red carpeted steps into the rented park pavilion. Twinkling white lights lit the entrance. I inhaled and heaved open the heavy wood door that led into a foyer.

I hesitated there, where the music was muted but surely blasting just behind a set of double doors where prom was taking place. What the hell was I doing?

"Ingrid! Oh my god!" I was picked up from behind by Izzie.

I turned to face her, still wrapped in her arms. Then I gave her a huge hug. For the first time in the history of our friendship, Izzie was the one to let go first.

"Come join us!" Izzie seemed to sparkle from within.

"Thanks for being my best friend, Izzie," I said.

She looked a little taken aback and then very pleased. "Thanks for being mine."

"Have you seen Van, by any chance?"

Izzie tried to read my expression and was about to ask a million questions but seemed to stop herself. Then she simply said, "He's here. By himself."

Izzie yanked open one of the doors and led me into an overly warm, dim room. It took my eyes a second to adjust. Dancing bodies were plastered onto the dance floor and more tiny lights gave off sparkles in the large room. There was something timeless about it. My heart picked up the beat of the bass. I knew where Van was before I looked.

To my right, I saw Wilson standing above Max and Van who sat together at a table, looking like the cool kids. Wilson felt my stare and glanced up. I froze, expecting a blank look from him, but instead he gave me a welcoming smile. He bent down and whispered to Van. That one second before Van looked up was equivalent to the moment my feet left the board earlier in the day.

We met eyes. Van didn't smile but he didn't look away. He was going to make me come to him.

"Go!" Izzie gave me a gentle push.

The three boys watched me as I picked my way around people and chairs to join them.

"You're here!" Wilson put his arm around me. I kissed his cheek and thought I felt Van bristle. Max stood up and fully encircled me in a hug. We hadn't really spoken in years but time collapsed. I'd been there that terrible night and we'd known each other since we were small.

When Max released me, I looked to Van. He didn't stand up.

The boys didn't recede. They stood waiting to see what I would do next. Then, of course, the music stopped.

"Hey," I said to Van.

"Hey," he said. He wasn't going to give me anything. No meeting me halfway.

I was about to ask him if we could talk outside but then the music cranked up and it was impossible to hear. I stood over him like an idiot.

Adrenaline washed down my body.

I placed my hand on Van's cheek, then I bent low and gently touched my lips to his.

There was a gasp from the next table.

I heard Van's sharp intake of breath but he didn't respond to the kiss.

Dying, I straightened and didn't wait around for what was going to happen or not happen next. People were staring and whispering. Wilson and Max said nothing. I didn't know where Izzie was but surely she'd witnessed the whole thing.

I turned and walked, trying to hold my head high. I heard a "What the hell, man?" from behind me. "You can't eat, you can't sleep because of her."

I made it through the heavy doors, which required a lot of muscle to open, and it was hard to look dignified. I expected the immediate recriminations, berating myself about what a bad idea that had been.

Instead I was kind of worn out. And relieved that I had done it. Van knew where I stood. For once, when it came to him, I'd been honest.

I almost had to laugh. I imagined Izzie's texts asking me what was I thinking? How absolutely out of character that was; the athletic girl who actively avoided any unwanted attention had walked into prom and kissed the hottest guy in the junior class.

I heard the wash of music strengthen and then fade again as the doors opened, then closed.

"Don't go." Van's voice was raspy.

He put a hand on my shoulder and spun me around. "What did that mean?" he asked.

"I love you," I said.

"Are you sure?"

"I've always been sure. I was just scared." I reached out for his hand and our fingers intertwined like that day in eighth grade.

Van rested his forehead against mine. "It got to a point where I didn't think I could spend one more night with you and not touch you. Then, that last night before Max, lying in your bed . . ." Unable to wait anymore, I silenced him with a kiss. Immediately, it escalated in intensity.

Then Van tensed and stepped back but he still didn't drop my hand. "I'm nervous. I don't want to lose you as a friend. I'm scared it will happen again. . . ." He trailed off.

"Don't be," I said. My voice held a challenge, egging him on, just like I had when we were seven years old and I was the daring one.

There was a long pause before Van met my eyes again. This time, Van stepped forward and threaded both hands in my hair, bringing his lips down to mine. This beautiful person I'd stared at for years—in class, in the halls, from my bedroom.

Vaguely, I heard the doors open once more, the loud voices and music pouring out.

"Finally." It sounded like Max. Or Wilson. It could have been either, or both.

"Finally," Van whispered.

The doors closed and we deepened the kiss.

ACKNOWLEDGMENTS

I have many people to thank for their help with this book.

My thoughtful, smart, insightful editor, Sarah Barley, and the dream team at Flatiron Books.

My agent, Kerry Sparks, for her enthusiasm, support, and for championing this story. I am so grateful for your partnership. Thank you, also, to Dominic Yarabe and the folks at Levine Greenberg Rostan.

May Cobb, for your endless support. That is an understatement. Amanda Eyre Ward and Peternelle van Arsdale, for early reads and amazing editorial guidance.

Kathryn Findlen, for fielding my diving-related questions and introducing me to Jonathan Wilcox who answered so many technical questions. Any mistakes are my own.

Elizabeth Burns Kramer, for her expertise and willingness to talk about Ingrid's psyche over and over again. Thank you for being an incredible friend.

Megan Frederick, Meghal Mehta, Andre Beskrowni, Vivian Raksakulthai, Mina Kumar, Leila Sales, Leigh Sebastian, Crispa Aeschbach Jachmann, and Tara Goedjen, for either answering medical questions, plot questions, lending an ear, or all of the above.

My mom and dad, Kathleen and David Weisenberg, for so much love and childcare. And always Kjersti, Rick, and Jack Mc-Cormick.

My husband, Jeff Gothard, for seeing me through this book and lending sharp editorial skills and great story instinct along the way. And my girls, Astrid and Margot, who are growing up so fast. Thanks for being you and making me laugh.

ABOUT THE AUTHOR

Marit Weisenberg received her BA in English from Bowdoin College and her master's degree from the UCLA School of Theater, Film and Television. Marit has worked in film and television development at Warner Bros., Universal, and Disney. She lives in Austin, Texas, with her husband and two daughters. Her previous titles include *Select* and *Select Few*.